MARRIED TO A PIRATE

ROMANCING THE SEAS
BOOK 1

ATHENA ROSE

BURTON & BURCHELL

COPYRIGHT

A NOTE FROM THE AUTHOR

This fantasy romance is set in a fictional/alternate 18th Century England. Names and places may differ from actual historical figures and it is not designed to be factually accurate. Mythological characters from across the world are interwoven in this tale, and their names, personalities and backstory may differ from actual mythology.

Trigger Warnings:

This dark fantasy romance novel alludes to sexual violence, suicide and domineering/possessive attitudes.

This book is written in U.S. English

CHARACTER ART

Georgette and Captain Stone

1

GEORGETTE

Georgette Harrington looked out at the rolling seas. She inhaled the salty breeze as it washed over her, whipping her curls back. Though the skies were clear, she did not fancy the look of the ominous green tinge creeping across the horizon.

She felt restless. And as a flock of seagulls honked overhead, she knew she wasn't the only living soul sensing the unsettling change in the wind.

Something untoward was coming to Port Harbor. She rubbed the goosebumps on her arms in a vain attempt to soothe them. It did nothing to slow her quickened heart rate.

Prince Edward's blue eyes moved to her slender hands and a tight crease formed between his tidy brows.

"Are you well, my lady?" he asked, his voice full of concern. "Perhaps we should return to the palace."

Georgette dropped her hands. The hairs on the back of her bare neck were up now, but she forced a refined smile. "There is no need, Your Majesty, I am but a little excited about the ball, is all."

She glanced at Rose, the maiden walking three paces behind them. She had drawn the short straw to be their chaperone.

Georgette knew that there were numerous duties her maids would prefer over the tedium of walking three paces behind herself and the Prince. She wondered what it must be like for Rose and the other girls, having to pretend to not hear their every word even as they listened for orders and kept a hawk's eye on the Prince's body language.

As though her thoughts had triggered a reaction, Rose uttered a short, sharp gasp. Georgette realized why a second later, when the Prince's royal jacket was suddenly being draped around her shoulders. His body heat flooded her with a comforting warmth that competed with the heat flooding her cheeks. The Prince had just taken off his royal garments for her sake.

Their eyes met, and he held her gaze for a long moment. "You are trembling," he said finally. Georgette's heartbeat slowed, and she simply stared, lost in the depth of his ocean blue eyes. She soon recovered herself.

"Your Royal Highness," she demurred, lowering her eyes. "You are too kind."

"I must enquire as to when you will call me Edward, my lady. On our wedding night, perhaps?" Prince Edward asked, his lips lifting into a smile. Georgette bit against a grin as she heard Rose's breathing quicken. If the Prince were to carry on talking on this matter, she feared her maid would faint.

Georgette stepped back a little to ease the tension rising between them. The inside of the Prince's jacket was filled with his scent. As she moved, his perfume wafted up and enveloped her. She took a deep breath. "I shall call you by name the day you address me by mine."

Prince Edward took her hands by the fingertips and gave her a wanting look. "Miss Georgette, then."

He stood too close to be proper, but he seemed to have forgotten his manners in the moment.

His face hovered mere inches away from hers. Georgette was able to admire every angle of it. There was much to admire. Georgette considered him handsome, to be sure. He sported clean-shaven cheeks and jaws, with smooth, dark hair tied back with a piece of ribbon. Everything about his appearance was meticulously clean.

Even his teeth were unusually straight, probably not daring to be out of line.

She thought him a fine man indeed. Prince Edward; captain of the Royal British Navy and heir to the throne.

To be matched with a prince was in Georgette's destiny long before she had reached adulthood. Her father, Lord Harrington, was a good friend of the King, and though Prince Edward was almost a decade her senior, it had been decided that Georgette would marry the Prince when she came of age.

Georgette never questioned it. Having no mother nor siblings, she wanted to please her father and make him proud. The man had endured enough heartache to last a thousand lifetimes, and Georgette was not interested in causing any further pain.

She was raised by the Governess, who taught her all the manners and customs of being a lady in 18th century England.

She took music lessons and became quite skilled at the piano. On more than one occasion, the Governess had referred to her needlework as "impressive."

She could even tolerate sitting with her ankles crossed in a tight corset for six hours straight without having to be excused; a most important skill for royal life.

Georgette was ready to be a princess of England. She

only hoped that she could do her duty to bear the Prince a healthy son.

That, and ignore the substantial pull of the sea.

They'd lost her mother to the sea when Georgette was just a baby. She'd reluctantly left Georgette behind, and died in a storm on the sea while sailing to France. Since then, her father had forbidden Georgette from ever going near the water. Still, she often found herself gazing upon the ocean from her balcony, daydreaming about a life away from the pressures and responsibilities placed upon her. She'd often see sailboats and all manner of ships come and go from the port, and long for the freedom to sail away into the great blue horizon.

Prince Edward and Georgette began their courtship on her twenty-first birthday.

All her years of preparation were finally coming to good use, but the Prince seemed set on throwing it all away out here on the palace grounds. He had her hands in a grip as strong as a vice, and she could hear his breaths coming out in short pants. One hot breath tickled her cheek and his smile faded. It was the first time in six months Georgette had seen his regal mask slip.

He dipped his head and shut his eyes as if to offer a prayer. "Georgette," he whispered. "I cannot wait to marry you."

Hearing her name uttered with such longing sent Georgette's head into a spin. For a moment, she thought he might kiss her. His lips, mere inches away a few moments ago, were suddenly a breath away from hers. They breathed each other's air for what felt like an eternity.

A squeak and a cough shattered the stillness. The Prince jolted back and dropped her hands as though they were hot coals. Rose had cleared her throat.

"You must only wait three days more... Edward," Georgette said, pouring all the tenderness she felt into the syllables of his name. Prince Edward's eyes flashed, and he turned to beam at her. But a far-off wave crashed and Georgette couldn't resist glancing at the sea again. The tide had crept in, and she watched the water toss and beat on itself with a little more zeal than usual. She looked back at Prince Edward.

"Pray tell, Edward. Do I please you?"

Prince Edward looked deeply into her eyes, another slight line forming between his brows as though the question had caused offense.

"Yes, Georgette. You are the most beautiful maiden I have ever laid eyes on."

Georgette forced a smile. Many people had remarked on her rare beauty over the years. She had sun-kissed blonde hair that sparkled in the sunshine like a headdress of millions of miniature diamonds, and her lips were naturally plump—as red as strawberries. But surely, he could see more than that.

"Thank you," she said, pretending to blush to hide her slight annoyance. "Is there anything else about me that pleases you?"

Prince Edward inclined his head. It reminded Georgette of a confused cocker spaniel for a moment. "I do not believe I understand."

Georgette swallowed. "How is it that after all these years, you still do not know me, Edward?" she asked, unable to hide the sharpness in her voice. She folded her hands and watched the Prince's brain at work. He scratched the back of his neck and stared at the ground as if he might find there a piece of parchment with script on what to say next.

"I assure you, I have been counting the days to the night I get to know you."

Now Georgette blushed for real. "That's not what I…" She couldn't finish the sentence. Her throat had gone dry.

"Ma'am, Lord Harrington's carriage has arrived."

Georgette jumped at the sound of her maid's voice and followed Rose's line of sight. The palace gardens were set on a hill, giving a perfect view of what lay beyond the stone wall encircling the palace. Rose was right. It was still a small object in the distance, but Georgette recognized her father's carriage by the family crest etched into the frame over one of the doors.

She removed the Prince's heavy jacket and gave it back to him. He bowed his head.

"I look forward to seeing you again, Miss Georgette," he said, folding his jacket over his arm.

As he escorted her back to the palace, Georgette couldn't help but notice that his eyes lingered on her. Her irritation faded.

"You will not have to wait long," she said, glancing at him with a shy smile. "The engagement ball is this evening." She found it difficult to remain annoyed at the Prince when he looked at her like that.

"*Our* engagement ball," he corrected, and his words made Georgette's heart flutter.

Their engagement ball. The long-awaited event. Every esteemed friend and acquaintance of the royal family would be in attendance. It would be their first public appearance as a couple, and Georgette had spent many late nights practicing her steps for their dance. The Prince must have misinterpreted her anxiety for concern, because he gave her an earnest look.

"Do not worry yourself, my dear," he said, as she

stepped through the palace doors ahead of him. "We have a lifetime to get to know each other."

ON THE WAY HOME, GEORGETTE STARED OUT THE little window of the carriage, listening to the babble of talk from the city folk walking the streets. A woman reprimanded a child for getting mud on his nice clothes. A man stood on the corner shouting out Bible references, calling all to repentance. Then the carriage passed a group of men chuckling darkly about something. Georgette could not quite make out their words, but she guessed it might have been about the preacher, because they were all looking at him.

The sounds merged into a toneless drone as she became lost in thought.

The Prince was sweet, but she couldn't ignore her reservations.

It was well known that his mother, the Queen, had fallen out of favor with the King. When that happened, he sent her to the Tower of London, never to be seen again. Soon after, the King announced her dead, and married a new Queen.

Georgette worried. If Prince Edward were to become

King and fall out of love with Georgette, would she meet the same fate?

Georgette tugged on the top of her tight bodice and touched her neck, as though checking she was still in one piece. Her fingertips grazed a string of pearls.

It marveled her that her father and the King were so close. She couldn't imagine her sweet, benevolent father condoning such actions. He worshipped her mother when she was alive and devoted much of his time to Georgette. They played chess by the fire many a night.

He told her several stories of his travels as a mere sailorman.

A sudden jolt forced Georgette out of her thoughts. Before she could process what was happening, the carriage tipped sideways and crashed to the ground. Georgette collided with the side of the carriage headfirst, and the world went black.

She woke in a commotion of screams and shouts. An acrid, burning smell clung to the back of her throat. She coughed and struggled to sit up. Disoriented, she looked up at the sound of squealing hinges and blinked at the sunlight streaming in through the open door.

"Take my hand."

Tanned, callous fingers with golden rings on every digit reached down toward her. Georgette's first instinct was to bat the hand away, but she held restraint and frowned up at the light instead.

"Take my hand or stay in there and burn."

Georgette scowled deeper at the harsh tone of the man's gruff voice and looked around her. The smell of smoke grew stronger and swirling clouds of black seeped in through the slits of the carriage's woodwork.

"This is your last chance," the gruff voice warned. Georgette shakily got to her feet, swayed at the thumping pain in her temple, and reached up for her savior's hand.

As soon as she gripped his wrist, another hand reached down and grabbed her forearm.

After some grunting above her head, her feet left the ground and Georgette's upper body emerged through the open door. Now standing next to the man who had pulled her out, Georgette studied his appearance.

He wore a long leather coat with fine gold buttons running along the seam. A soft, white, ruffled shirt hung open at the chest, giving Georgette an eyeful of the man's defined and sweat-drenched muscles.

She fought the urge to recoil. She had never seen a man like him before. Two dark eyes met hers, framed with thick black brows, wild dark hair, and a shaggy beard.

The man wrapped his arms around her waist to carry her safely away from the burning carriage, and suddenly, she was cradled so close to his body that her ear pressed up against his bare chest and she could hear the steady thump-thump of his heartbeat.

"Hold on to me," he said, his voice rumbling against Georgette's ear. She gripped the collar of his soft leather coat, but the man growled with dissatisfaction, took her hands, and placed them around his neck.

"Now wrap your legs around my waist," he ordered.

Georgette gasped as she wondered at the audacity of this stranger.

When she didn't obey his command, the man lifted her skirts roughly and grabbed a leg. Georgette squeaked. He huffed with impatience.

"In case you haven't noticed, the carriage is on fire. If you don't do as I say, we're both going to be engulfed in flames."

As though on cue, Georgette began to feel the heat from below. She glanced down, and red flames licked the bottom of her feet. Her heartbeat went wild. Sensing her alarm, the man pinned her thigh to his waist. She wrapped the other leg around him without hesitation.

"Good girl," he growled into her neck, and his voice sent a shiver through her body. She tried to ignore it as she focused on clinging onto him while he climbed down.

Georgette had never been this close to a man before. She wasn't sure if it was the fire or the intimacy causing her to break into a sweat. This was certainly no gentleman, but her body didn't care.

His wavy, shoulder-length hair smelled of the salty sea. Despite the horrid circumstances, she had never felt more safe in all her life.

When they reached the ground, dark smoke encircled them. Georgette stepped back to look at the man again. There was something familiar about his eyes. They stared back, dark and intense. A wild, wiry beard consumed a good portion of his face. She wondered what kind of man was underneath it.

He broke eye contact to secure his sleeve, and Georgette followed his movements. Just before he could hide it, she caught sight of the black P burned into his skin.

She gasped and locked eyes with him again. "You're a pirate," she whispered.

Oddly, he grimaced at the word. Had she caused offense? She opened her mouth to thank him, but found herself whipped into in the arms of Prince Edward instead, who had wrapped her up in a tight hug.

"When I saw the smoke, and then your carriage on its side, my heart stopped. Thank the heavens you are alive." He held her tight. Georgette frowned into his jacket. The scent of his clean clothes and warm spice did not make her feel anything but numb.

When he pulled back to search her eyes, Georgette forced a brave smile.

"I'm quite well. Please do not be alarmed. I'm just a little shocked, is all."

Prince Edward squeezed her hands and nodded, then he barked orders to the guards standing by to put out the fire.

Georgette stood frozen on the spot as more people came into view, staring at her like they were looking at a ghost. She was not concerned by the attention, she was scanning the faces, searching...

"How on God's green Earth did you get out?"

She whipped round to see her father, in his finest clothes, striding toward her. He put his arms around her and she relaxed into his warm embrace. "There was a man," she mumbled into his chest. Then she pulled back to look again.

But her efforts were fruitless. The man—the *pirate*—who had saved her was gone.

"We shall delay the ball, and I insist on escorting you back to the palace. I'll call for the doctor..." Prince Edward stopped at the sight of Georgette furiously shaking her head.

"No. I am unharmed, and I do not intend to delay our wedding a moment longer," she said. She had her concerns about joining the royal family, but there was simply nothing more torturous than staying in an anxious limbo for longer than necessary. She would find ways to keep the Prince happy.

Prince Edward's face lit up, but he forced a serious look a second later and nodded. "At least allow me to take you home in my carriage."

BACK IN HER FATHER'S MANOR, GEORGETTE SAT IN A TIN bath and stared at her knees while her maids poured warm water over her.

It made no difference what the temperature was. She had lost all feeling to a cold numbness since she caught sight of the dark P on the stranger's hand. For all she knew, they were pouring buckets of ice over her body.

"You've had quite the scare, Miss Harrington," one of the maids commented needlessly. "You're still trembling."

Georgette hugged her knees and bit her lip, willing her limbs to still. It was fruitless. Another shiver wracked her.

"Yes. I dread to think what might have happened if that pirate hadn't saved me."

A bucket dropped to the stone floor with a clang. One of the maids bent quickly to retrieve it, babbling a string of apologies. "Ma'am," another began fearfully. "Did you say, pirate?"

The word pirate was not often uttered in the Harrington household. Or indeed, many homes at Port Harbor. The small town was well-known to be far safer than London. So safe, in fact, that the royal family tended to spend most of their time there, instead of in the city. There had not been a pirate attack for more than two years, and the superstitious residents liked to keep it that way by refusing to name them. It was as though the mere utterance of the word *pirate* would summon them from the far reaches of the sea, to pillage and plunder their town.

"Yes," Georgette responded calmly. She rubbed a bar of soap over her body. "He was exceedingly ill-mannered. But if it weren't for him, I would surely be dead."

The maids whispered to each other, and one of them began to wash Georgette's long hair, so she sat back and shut her eyes while her brain replayed the events.

She could still feel his body heat between her thighs, and his hot breath on her neck. Then she remembered his words as he carried her down.

Good girl.

Her insides flopped like a fish out of water. She squirmed.

"Ma'am. Are you feeling well? You are flushed."

Georgette's eyes snapped open and she looked at the concerned maids staring down at her. Then she forced a smile to suppress the strange and new sensations flooding her body.

"Yes," she whispered. "In fact, I do believe I've never felt more alive."

2

CAPTAIN STONE

Captain Stone marched through the streets of Port Harbor with an eerie sense of foreboding hovering over him like a cloud. His mind weighed heavily with the burdens that lay on his shoulders. Of all the Greek gods, it was Atlas he related to the most. It was as though the entire world was on his back, and it was his burden alone to carry.

He would be a lesser man to let it show. Any sign of weakness could result in a mutiny. His crew were as loyal as tom cats in an alley full of felines in heat. If anyone sensed so much as a whiff of his worry, he may very well be stabbed in his sleep.

But if he didn't deliver their requests soon, no amount of strength would hold off the hideous fate that awaited him.

He shrugged his jacket more closely around him and dragged his thumb around the pads of his fingers. His heart thumped erratically, pumping adrenaline through his body.

He followed the Harrington carriage for several miles before he picked the mouse out of his jacket and dropped it in the horses' path.

Everything had gone according to plan.

The horses were spooked, and the driver lost control. Then the carriage rocked on its two wheels before it crashed on its side.

He had not foreseen one of the lanterns smashing, or the fire spreading greedily over the wood. A few seconds later, the carriage was smoking. If the occupant was dead, all his planning would have been for naught.

He climbed up, wrenched open the door and peered inside. He did not find Lord Harrington. A maiden cowered inside instead; a delicate creature in a pale pink gown with soft blonde curls framing her face and neck.

He reasoned she must have been the daughter Lord Harrington was always talking about.

When he pulled the timid woman out of the carriage, he set eyes upon hers and something stirred inside of him. He was not entirely certain what the feeling was, but it had been pleasant, and he had not felt that kind of pleasure in a long time.

Nonetheless, discovering her gave him an idea. She could be the key to solving all of his problems. How fitting that she was related to the man who owed him so many debts!

Captain Stone winked a thank you at the skies for bringing him this fortuitous stroke of luck. Perhaps the tide was finally changing and things would improve.

He could only hope.

He walked up to the heavy oak doors of Harrington Manor and rapped his knuckles on the thick wood.

The manor was the only stately home in Port Harbor that did not belong to the royals. The massive structure would be worth a pretty penny, for sure.

An old footman opened the door. His droopy eyes inspected Captain Stone for a moment, then his upper lip curled. The old man made to swing the door shut, but Captain Stone placed his boot in the way.

"Now, now," he said. "Don't be rude. Should you turn away an old friend of Lord Harrington?"

The footman stared at him with unbridled resentment, and Captain Stone grinned back. There was a ruckus somewhere deeper in the manor, then the scurrying of feet on polished stone floors.

The old man looked behind him, turned to flash an impious smile at Captain Stone, then stepped aside to allow Lord Harrington to come into view. The aristocrat turned ashen gray upon seeing Captain Stone. "Hello, old friend," he said, his voice wavering. He cleared his throat. "What brings me the pleasure of—"

"Let's cut the pleasantries, shall we?" Captain Stone said curtly. He brushed past and marched into the hall, tossing his hat to the coat stand. "I've never been a fan of sycophantic gestures." He glanced up at the sweeping staircase, wondering if the girl was upstairs and if she'd heard his voice.

If she had, did she recognize it?

Her sweet floral scent still lingered on his jacket.

Lord Harrington followed the pirate's line of sight and pinched his wispy brows together, as though reading Captain Stone's mind. Then he adjusted his fine jacket and gestured to the door across the hall. "Come, let me pour you a drink."

It was not the Captain's first time in Lord Harrington's study. The dimly lit room with its looming bookshelves of dark wood and cloying smell of old books was just the same as it had been the last time he'd visited. Oil lamps flickered as they entered the room. Captain Stone chose to recline in the soft leather armchair by the small iron fireplace, while Lord Harrington moved to the mahogany desk and poured them two glasses of whiskey.

"If this is about the money I owe…"

"This is exactly about the money you owe," Captain

Stone cut in, giving the man a sharp look. "I'm not a bank. Nor am I a charitable man."

Lord Harrington downed his drink. "If I could just have a little more time... My daughter's dowry is all I have left and—"

"Ah yes," Captain Stone murmured with a glint in his eye that Lord Harrington did not like. "I hear she is engaged to marry Prince Edward," the Captain continued. The pirate took a swig of his drink and the hard liquor burned his throat as it went down.

Lord Harrington's back stiffened and his thick, black mustache twitched. "You heard right. As you can imagine, things are incredibly busy. Tonight is the engagement ball, in fact, so I really must insist that we have this conversation another time..." he rambled, averting his eyes and gesturing to the door. Captain Stone did not move an inch from the chair. He surveyed the anxious man with a mixture of pity and amusement.

"Five thousand pounds," the pirate growled. "Now, are you going to repay your debts or do I need to recover what is owed with more... forceful measures?"

Lord Harringon bristled. "I cannot pay you at present. But, sir, if you will give me more time—"

"Judgement day waits for no man," Captain Stone intoned coldly. "Nor does it care for his frivolous concerns of dowries and royal balls. Today is your judgement day, Lord Harrington. Now, I shall ask you one last time..."

Lord Harrington blustered. "I will not ruin my daughter's—"

"Then how about a wager?" Captain Stone cut in, eyeing Lord Harrington like a lion stalking his prey. The man was cornered with nowhere to turn, but the sound of a wager sent his brows flying.

"One round of cards. If you win, I'll consider the debt settled and walk away. You'll never see me again."

Lord Harrington's silver brow cocked up. "And if I lose?"

Captain Stone looked around the dark study. "I'll take the deeds to your home to repay your debts and... I'll have your daughter."

The aristocrat choked and pulled out an embroidered handkerchief from his pocket to cough into. "Out of the question. My daughter is off the table."

Captain Stone pulled out a deck of cards from his jacket and slammed it on the table. "You can choose the game. Think about your options carefully, my old friend."

He watched with great delight as his debtor's inky black eyes darted from left to right. The cogs in Lord Harrington's mind spun.

"If you do nothing, I shall take everything you have.

Your daughter's dowry, your house... You'll have nothing. Then see how the royal family feels about being associated with a man of ruin."

Captain Stone took another swig of his drink with a smirk. "You'll lose your title. Your reputation will be in tatters. Who will your precious daughter marry then? You will ruin your life and hers, too. Tell me, can you ensure her safety without so much as a half-penny to your name?"

The color drained from Lord Harrington's face as he listened to Captain Stone's gravelly voice. Both men knew that there was no argument.

"What do you want with my daughter, anyway? She is but twenty-one years of age. You must be, at least, fifteen years her senior."

"My business is my own." Captain Stone set his drink down and drummed his fingers on the worn deck of cards in a wave. "But I'll be more than equipped to tend to her needs."

Lord Harrington's face soured. "She is engaged to Prince Edward and—"

"—He will have no interest in the girl." Captain Stone interrupted, the tone of his voice sharpening. "Mark my words. When the royal family discovers that their esteemed friend, Lord Harrington, spends late evenings in the pub, gambling away everything he owns, they will disassociate from you faster than you can say *bankruptcy*."

Lord Harrington's brow began to sweat under the swirls of his gray wig and the man sank to his knees. "Please. Don't do this. I can pay you next month. I have bonds in—"

Captain Stone leaned forward, grabbed the foolish man's shirt in one swift motion. "How dare you spit lies in my face?" he growled. "You think me a fool? Now, what say you? Will you roll over and let me take what is mine? Or will you play a game of cards and win back your life? The way I see it, you've got one shot. I suggest you take it."

"But you're asking me to barter my daughter," Lord Harrington said, his voice raspy. Captain Stone kept eye contact but let the man go.

"If you do nothing, your daughter is destined, at best, to be no more than an old maid for a rich governess. If you take a chance, she will either marry the Prince, or come away with me. Either prospect is far better than the former. So, what do you say?"

Seeing that there was no other option, Lord Harrington grabbed the deck of cards with shaking hands.

Captain Stone smirked and reclined in the leather

chair while he watched Lord Harrington shuffle the cards. "Good man. Now, what are we playing?"

Lord Harrington's thin lips opened and closed at rapid speed. He mumbled something inaudible, but then locked eyes with Captain Stone. "If you win, you will marry my daughter."

Captain Stone leaned forward and cocked his head to the side, wondering if he'd heard the old man correctly. "I don't believe you are in a position to negotiate."

Lord Harrington's eyes flashed. For the first time, Captain Stone sensed the man possessed a backbone. He respected that.

"You will make an honest woman out of her. You think I don't know what activities the likes of you get up to across those seas?"

Captain Stone crossed his arms, amused. The man was not wrong.

"Go on."

Heartened, Lord Harrington dealt the cards. "And you will protect her with your life. Even from yourself."

Captain Stone lifted a speculative brow. "Meaning?"

"You will see that she comes to no harm. By anyone. Not even you."

Lord Harrington and Captain Stone stared at each other in silence for several long moments. Then Captain

Stone blinked. He considered the old man's offer with a deep hum.

"Very well. If I win, I shall marry your daughter and protect her with my life."

The two men shook on it.

In that moment, Captain Stone could see in Lord Harrington's eyes that he expected to lose. He did not consider the old lord to be a visionary man, or someone in touch with the fates, but something in his instincts had told him that Lady Luck was not on his side that night.

He was right. The game of choice was poker, and it was a futile attempt at his freedom. The man's left nostril twitched—an obvious tell. It took precisely three and a half minutes for Captain Stone to produce a royal flush and declare himself the victor.

He got to his feet and stuffed the cards back into his jacket while Lord Harrington held his face in his hands. But just as Captain Stone started for the door to claim his prize, Lord Harrington grabbed his arm to stop him.

"Not like this. Please, I beg of you." He scurried to his desk, pulled out a rolled piece of parchment, and handed it over. "The deeds. For the debt that is owed. But please, allow me to keep my daughter for one more night. She is expected at the palace, after all!"

Captain Stone frowned. "You will have her attend the

royal ball, knowing that she will be married to me in the morning?"

Lord Harrington's pale face reddened across the brow. "I am sick. What has become of me?" He yanked at the collar of his shirt and paced the room. "How am I to tell her?"

Captain Stone secured the property deeds in his jacket. "Tell her what? That her father just gambled away her dowry, or sold her to a pirate?"

Lord Harrington's face lost color entirely and his eyes rolled back. The next moment, his body went limp, and he landed on the floor with a thump.

Captain Stone had no time to spare. He stepped over the old man's body and left the study. He didn't turn back once. "Thank you," he said to the footman who had promptly opened the front door upon seeing him. He looked out at the starry night sky and glanced back at the staircase. An old woman, presumably the governess, was standing near the very top. "A fine evening, is it not?"

The lady did not respond, but the whites of her eyes grew big as she watched Captain Stone pick up his feather hat from the coat stand and secure it. Then he marched out of the manor.

3

PRINCE EDWARD

Prince Edward stood in front of the wall-length mirror in his room, surrounded by men handing him various items of clothing in turn. His heartbeat had not stopped thumping in his ear since he found Georgette in the wreckage of her father's carriage.

He reasoned it would not be long before he could make sure she was always within his sights, but it did nothing to calm his nerves.

Marrying Georgette could not come a day too soon. He did not like the idea that she was alone now, possibly hurt, at Harrington Manor.

His bedroom door groaned open, and the attendants around him stiffened. Prince Edward kept his eyes fixed on his reflection, but he knew exactly who had just entered his bedroom.

His attendants were giving curt bows now, and he felt the air to his right shift as the person approached. He turned and met the discerning stare of his father, King George.

The man had an undeniable presence about him, one that could drop the temperature of a room by a few degrees. Prince Edward turned back to the mirror and his father stepped into frame behind him; eyes cold and back rigid.

In many ways, the man reminded Prince Edward of his older brother, the lost prince.

He shook the thought away as soon as it came. Since his brother was lost at sea, it had become unbearable to think about him. His step-mother expressly forbade anyone from bringing him up in conversation.

Still, finding his brother had been the sole reason why Prince Edward willingly took on the role of commandeering the British Royal Navy. For many years, sailing the seas in search of his brother was all he wanted to do.

It was unthinkable to believe he was dead. Prince Mannington was five years his senior, stronger than any man Edward knew, and fearless.

He couldn't be claimed by the sea.

But no one had seen nor heard of him in years.

Many theories of what became of him swept the palace in whispers. Some thought the belly of the sea must have swallowed him up in a terrible storm. Others swore he'd been captured by pirates and tortured until he was driven insane and finally slaughtered.

One wild theory came from one of the Queen's maids, who thought he was living in Africa under the guise of a humble sailor in a bid to run away from his royal responsibilities.

But Prince Edward knew his brother valued honor and had a sense of duty. He could never choose to lead a secret life, leaving his family to go through such turmoil.

A cough ripped him out of his thoughts, and he looked at his father expectantly. When the elder royal did not speak, Prince Edward raised a brow. "May I enquire what has compelled you to come to my room? I am certain it is not to check on my attire."

The King cleared his throat again, and began a stately pacing of the room with his hands held behind his back. "I've been told there was an incident today involving Miss Georgette Harrington. Is she well?"

Prince Edward shrugged on his fine jacket and secured the loops with care, while one of his aids dusted it off with a lint roller.

"Yes," he affirmed.

"Is she able to dance?"

Prince Edward knew his father's enquiries were not out of concern for Georgette's wellbeing but rather to confirm whether the young woman might embarrass the royal family in front of their many esteemed guests.

The thought tugged his mouth into a frown. "She is," he said, keeping his voice curt. The King stopped pacing and his azure eyes flashed. A heavy silence hung in the air. The royal aides stood back, waiting for further instruction.

Prompted by a single nod from the King, the room cleared, leaving Prince Edward and the King alone.

King George beamed at his son and placed a thin hand on his shoulder. The weight of it was like an anvil —still, nothing compared to the sense of responsibility on his shoulders.

"Good. Then I expect the wedding to go ahead as planned," he said with a small smile. He released Prince Edward's shoulder and turned to face the window. A line of carriages trailed all the way down the crooked street outside the palace gates.

Prince Edward fastened his tie and tugged on the hem of his jacket. "Indeed, everything is in hand. I expect Miss Harrington will be quite accommodating."

"Good, good," the King muttered, fiddling with his pocket watch. "You understand that once you are married, there will be more royal duties on your roster."

Prince Edward stiffened, but he gave a quick nod. When he did not speak, King George turned to give him a shrewd look. "You will not be able to go off gallivanting across the seas on your foolish missions under the guise of working with the Royal Navy."

Prince Edward refused to blink under the hard stare of his father. The King was no fool. He knew the real reason why Prince Edward took on every mission. He had probably known it from the moment the Prince expressed a wish to join the Navy.

His many attempts to trace his brother had proven futile so far, and he had imagined that marriage would hinder his plans to continue the search. Clearly, his parents had designs of their own.

"I thought I could hear my two favorite people talking in here."

Prince Edward and King George turned as Queen Catherine walked in. She kissed her son on the cheek and straightened his tie. "Are you quite sure about this, my dear? I am sure we can use this carriage incident as a reason to postpone or even cancel—"

"Why would I wish for that, mother?" Prince Edward cut in. He did not like the look his parents exchanged.

"Well, she did grow up without a good female role model in her life. That governess her father entrusted her to is as cold as ice and as dull as a plain slice of bread," the Queen said. Prince Edward frowned.

"What is the reason for this? The marriage has been arranged since Georgette was but a child," he said, affronted.

There were many things he was unsure of in life— what became of his brother, what kind of King he would be, and if he would ever make his father proud. But of one thing he was certain; uncovering all mysteries with Lady Harrington by his side.

"Nothing pleases me more than the thought of having Miss Harrington as my wife," he said in a firm voice.

And just like that, the conversation was over. His parents linked arms as they headed for the door.

"Very well, my son," the King said drily. "We are expected in the ballroom, our guests are waiting."

4

GEORGETTE

Georgette hissed when the hot curling iron touched her scalp. The maid released her tight curl from the iron and jumped back, her eyes like saucers.

"My sincere apologies, miss," she said, looking at the iron like it was a murder weapon. Georgette patted the scalded area and inspected it in the mirror. "No harm done, Lucile. Look… The red mark is already beginning to fade."

The maid nodded, but her hands were still trembling. Georgette thought it lucky that was the last strand of hair to be curled. She was not keen on the idea of having a hot iron near her skin again. By the sight of the maid's shaky hands, the next burn might have been her face.

That would have been a true disaster, a few hours before the royal ball. She turned back to the maid.

"You look quite shaken. Go and make yourself a cup of tea. There's nothing more you need to do here," she said, careful to keep her voice soft. Still, the maid looked at her like she had shouted.

"Yes, miss. I'm sorry, miss." She bobbed. Then she wrapped the curling iron in a cloth and carried it out of the room. The burning smell lingered.

Georgette turned back to the mirror and frowned. The smell of burning took her mind back to the accident in the carriage. Smoke had encircled her, stifling her nose and drying her throat. She would have soon lost the ability to breathe at all if that pirate hadn't come to rescue. She would have choked to death if the flames hadn't engulfed her first.

She shook the terrible thought out of her mind and pressed her eyes shut in a vain attempt to erase the memory forever. It was most inappropriate to think about pirates or being burned alive on the night of her engagement. Tonight, all eyes would be on her and Edward. She didn't want to make a fool of herself or get the steps wrong during their waltz.

She tugged on the low neckline of her maroon gown and took light breaths, thanks to the corset restricting her movements.

With a final glance at the tight curls pinned up and framing her face, she proceeded to practice her dance one last time.

She was so focused on what she was doing that she did not hear the light knock, nor the squeal of the hinges as her bedroom door opened wide.

She heard a floorboard creak and a cough. Flushed, she dropped her arms and stopped dancing with her imaginary prince.

Then her eyes landed on her father, and she grinned sheepishly.

"Please, do not stop on my account," he said, resting a hand over his heart.

He wore his best clothes. The silver jacket with elaborate gold embroidery along the seam, and big, shiny buttons down the front. The brass buckles on his shoes glinted in the light, and she observed, in slight amusement, that he had even oiled his mustache. To top it all off, he had a thin film of perspiration across his forehead. He was nervous. Of course. Only she and her father could know how much tonight meant to both of them.

It took him a few moments of silence to jump into life. He must have realized he was staring, because his cheeks grew pink and he coughed again.

"Have I ever told you how much you remind me of your mother?"

He walked over and sat in the seat by her mahogany dressing table. Georgette clasped her hands. The all-too familiar pang of heartache throbbed in her chest at the mention of her mother.

"Yes, father, though I never tire of hearing it."

Looking like her mother made Georgette feel close to her. Sometimes, to cure a pensive mood, she would look in the mirror for comfort and pretend her reflection was her mother smiling back at her.

It rarely took away the sadness.

She had never even met her, but the grief ebbed and flowed as unceasingly as the tide. Growing up motherless gave Georgette a deep sense of longing, never to be satisfied. She had her father, who had always been very present and very kind. Then there was his sister—her aunt, the Governess—who had taught her everything she needed to learn from a woman.

But it was the warmth that she imagined she missed —the tenderness and unconditional love that she had so often imagined her mother would offer.

Lord Harrington seemed to follow her thoughts, because he hummed as though in agreement.

"I have something for you."

Georgette snapped out of her reverie and watched as her father pulled out a gold locket from his pocket. "I was waiting to give this to you on your wedding day. It appears as though tonight is a more appropriate time."

He dropped the locket in Georgette's outstretched hands and she lifted it up by the dainty chain. It was a perfect oval that glowed in the firelight. "These markings, what language are they? I am quite unfamiliar with them," she remarked, inspecting the piece of jewelry. The delicate squiggles were fashioned in a way that seemed to be writing, although she could not make out words.

She looked up at her father, who was now looking at the floor, his bushy brows knit together. He sighed and lifted his gaze to meet hers.

"It belonged to your mother. Open it up."

Georgette's chest pinched. She dug a fingernail into the grove and opened the locket. It split open with ease, revealing two tiny painted portraits. One of her father, looking youthful with a sleek mop of brown hair tied back. Georgette smiled to see that even then he sported a fine mustache.

The second portrait was of her mother. She'd had porcelain skin and soft blonde curls cascading over her shoulders. Her eyes were a brilliant blue. Her father was right. It was almost as though she was looking at a picture of herself.

She closed the locket and held it to her heart, tears

flooding her eyes. "I shall treasure it for all of my life. Thank you, father."

She fiddled with the clasp and stuck her tongue between her teeth in concentration. Her father chuckled, and his soft hands sandwiched hers. "Allow me," he said, his voice like a low rumble.

He placed the locket on Georgette's neck and fastened the clasp while she watched in the mirror. The pendant sank low into her bosom, and was soon out of sight. When her father looked, he frowned. "I suppose your mother was taller than you are now. I can get it resized if you wish."

Georgette touched his arm with a shake of her head. "No. I like it this way. It's too special to have just anybody see it. Now, I can wear it all the time and keep it close to my heart... Where it belongs."

Lord Harrington's eyes grew misty and he wrapped Georgette up in a hug that lasted far longer than usual. "My sweet Georgette. How I do love you." He pulled back to look at her again, and this time, two tears rolled freely down his cheeks. The sight took Georgette aback. It was customary to have a stiff upper lip in England; a custom her father had always observed. Until now.

"I want you to remember this night. Remember what I tell you. There is nothing I would do unless it were for your benefit or happiness. Your safety and wellbeing mean everything to me."

Georgette nodded, though she was not sure she understood, and her father squeezed the tops of her arms.

Then he released her, sniffed, and lit up in a beaming smile.

"Well, then. I do believe we have a ball to attend. Shall we?"

He offered his arm, and Georgette grinned as she took it. "We shall."

It was agreed that Georgette would arrive at the engagement ball accompanied by her father, but fashionably late. As she had already been spoken for, she had never attended one before.

Waiting for the footman to announce their arrival, Georgette's heartbeat quickened. It thrummed against her ribcage like the feet of a wild horse. The sound of string music flooded the air, mingled with the polite chatter of the esteemed guests.

Georgette gripped her father's arm like it was a lifeline. If she let go, she may very well be lost in the sea of faces that had now turned in her direction.

She grew sick. A buildup of saliva filled her mouth, and she swallowed hard.

"Announcing Lord Harrington and his only daughter, Miss Georgette Harrington."

The well-dressed ladies whispered to each other, their eyes flashing as they evaluated Georgette. The gentlemen appraised her in an entirely different manner, although it was equally, if not more, unsettling.

As her father guided her forward, she noticed a woman not-so-subtly reproaching the man next to her. The woman hissed as they walked past, "For heaven's sake, close your mouth and stop ogling!"

Georgette forced back a smile and turned her attention to the three thrones seated at the far end of the ballroom.

They had been set up just for the ball, and her future in-laws sat rigid, looking expressionless as she approached them.

She locked eyes with Prince Edward, who sat on his father's right-hand side. He grinned, unabashed, and his eyes twinkled. *I adore you*, his gaze seemed to say. All of Georgette's worries faded.

She reached the King and was most relieved to curtsy and greet the royal family with nothing going amiss.

Then Prince Edward rose from his seat and Lord Harrington handed her to him.

She glanced back, and for a moment, she thought her father's face had twisted into a look of sheer devastation. But almost as soon as she'd seen it, it was gone, so she wondered if she had imagined it.

Prince Edward rested a heavy hand on the middle of Georgette's shoulder blades, and his touch warmed her even through the layers of fabric and corset. She posed her hand at his shoulder, almost hovering rather than resting. Then they clasped their free hands in the perfect pose to begin the Waltz.

Her father stepped back, and soon all the guests had edged to the walls of the hall to allow the Prince and Georgette to have their dance.

This was a highly anticipated moment for the people. This was where they would see their future princess and scrutinize everything about her.

She imagined the ladies remarking how thin her arms were. Indeed, as they danced the waltz by a row of young women, she thought she heard one of them say, "How is she to produce an heir when she is clearly malnourished?"

Another woman muttered, "That blonde hair must be a wig. It's far too bright and thick to be real. She looks like a pony."

Just then, the Prince's hand gave her a gentle squeeze.

"You are doing a wonderful job. Don't look at them. Look at me," he whispered.

Georgette met his concerned gaze and gave him a sheepish smile. "How do you do that?" she whispered back. He lifted an inquisitive brow, and she went on to explain her thoughts. "Stay so calm and sweet? While everyone is looking, judging…"

The Prince's lips curved upward, and he leaned in to whisper in her ear. "I imagine all of these people are desperate to empty their bowels, and there is but one chamber pot."

Georgette pulled back to give him a look of repulsion, but remembered she was being watched and corrected herself. "How vulgar!" she said through her fake smile. "How can your mind think of such things and what has made you so bold to speak about them to a lady?"

The Prince squeezed her hand again and his smile faded as his gaze hardened.

"I almost lost you today," he murmured. "I don't know what I would do without you, Georgette. If something were to happen—"

"But it didn't," Georgette interrupted. "Nevertheless, I must insist—even after we are married—I do not want to hear another word about chamber pots. Not from you."

They shared a light laugh, and for several beautiful minutes, they were lost in the transcendent music, dancing like two doves in the spring.

Then the song ended and there was a round of applause. Georgette could still feel the heat of everyone's stares, but this time, she didn't look back. She kept her gaze locked on the Prince's and it took a second for her to realize his eyes were growing bigger.

That's when the thought hit.

Is he going to kiss me? In front of everyone?

Just as his lips touched her cheek, a ruckus broke out.

In a flash, Prince Edward swung Georgette round to shield her with his body. She saw his hand move to the hilt of his sword.

The air rang with shouts and the ear-splitting clatter of armor hitting the stone floor. Guests scattered.

Bewildered, Georgette peered over the Prince's shoulder. A mob of men in dark sailor clothes flooded into the ballroom, like oil spewing out of a pierced barrel.

"Guards!" the King roared. Georgette screeched at the crash of swords. The guards fired their bayonets and filled the ballroom with gun smoke.

The Prince squeezed Georgette's waist as he withdrew his knife. "You have to go," he said over his shoulder to her, his jaw bulging.

The ballroom had become a bloodbath. Bodies

littered the polished mosaic floors, and thick pools of blood collected, staining the floors crimson. Most of the guests had vacated the room now. All that remained were a few palace guards, still firing at the intruders, and a growing number of the filthy men charging into the ballroom. There seemed no end to them.

"I'm not leaving you here to die," Georgette said to the Prince. A guard slumped by her feet and fell lifeless with a smack. She stooped to unsheathe his knife. Prince Edward withdrew his sword and stuck it in the torso of the man who had killed the guard.

Then he turned back to Georgette, "Please, go," he begged, his voice softening as he cupped her face with one hand. "I promise I will come for you."

Georgette sucked in a breath as the chaos around her blurred in her peripheral vision. All she could see were two shining blue eyes. Deep as the ocean and pleading.

"I will do as you wish. But you must promise me that you will not die."

The Prince smirked, then he stole a kiss. His soft lips caressed hers for the briefest moment, then he tore himself from her. "Now, go!" he shouted. Trembling, Georgette clutched the guard's knife and hurried for the back door.

She tried to block out the ugly sounds of grown men shrieking in agony, of bones crunching and swords clanging, and lifted her heavy skirts to step over fallen men. For the first time in her young life, she had cause to wonder why a woman needed so many skirts in the first place. But just as she reached the doors, a hand grabbed her waist and she shrieked.

"Where do you think you're going, pretty lady?"

The foul stench of the man's breath floated over her like a black cloud. Without thinking, she stuck the tip of the blade into the hand on her waist and dug it in.

The knife sank into flesh like the hand was nothing more than a chunk of beef. The man let out a succession of yelps, like a wounded animal. Georgette didn't look directly at who dared to grab her. She elbowed him in the gut and yanked him off her, leading to another howling cry and the thump of his body hitting the floor. Without one look back, she yanked the door open and hurried out into the hall.

The halls echoed with the menacing sounds of men tearing through the palace and Georgette's heart rate sped up as she hurried forward, wanting to put as much space between her and the ballroom as possible.

She reached the entrance hall to find that it, too, was flooded with men. No. Not men, she thought, looking at their rough apparel. They wore sailor clothes blackened by smoke. Many displayed thick tattoos that snaked up their arms like sleeves, and she knew. They were pirates.

She stifled a gasp with her fist and turned on her heels, hoping that none of them had seen her.

Rapid footsteps behind her told her that hope was in vain. Luckily, she had spent much of her life at the palace, and the Prince had shown her every nook and cranny, including the secret passageways. She held her breath, running as fast as her legs would carry her toward the oil paintings.

Her eyes scanned the pictures, looking for the right one. Then she saw it. The portrait of the Queen's late mother. Georgette's fingernails ran along the groove of the frame and something clicked. The picture came away from the wall like a door. The men were hot on her trail, but she had just enough time to bundle herself through the opening, shut the secret door behind her, and bolt it shut.

She backed into the darkness, both hands trembling as she held them over her mouth. Then she waited and strained her ears. She did not have to wait long before heavy footsteps approached and several thuds followed. She knew the men were trying to open the portrait door, but it would be in vain.

When she was a young girl, Prince Edward told her all the secrets of the palace. How the King ordered for several secret passages to be secured by an iron door disguised as a painting. The iron bolt would hold. She was sure of it.

Still, her heart raced and her mouth filled with saliva. She gulped and shut her eyes to steady her nerves. There was a moment of silence, then a tremendous bang. She jumped, nearly out of her skin, in the darkness. It sounded as though a crate of dynamite had been set off. The door remained intact, but smoke began to seep in through the edges, burning her nostrils with each inhale.

Knowing she couldn't stay there any longer, Georgette turned on her heels and hurried further into the dark passage, feeling the stone walls as she went.

For a moment, she worried there might be more pirates waiting for her on the other side, but she remembered this passage well. It led to the lost Prince's bedroom, which had been sealed-shut for years. There was no way the pirates could have gotten in.

Suddenly, another teeth-shattering bang flooded the air, followed by a deafening clang. Georgette quickened her pace at the rising voices. Perhaps the pirates did indeed have dynamite. For now, they were certainly in the passage with her. If she didn't move quickly, they would reach her in mere moments.

Finally, her hands found the back of a door. She pushed it open and hurried into the light.

Then, without thinking, she slammed the picture

back against the wall and slid the concealed lock into place.

Panting, Georgette wiped the sweat from her upper lip and staggered back until she pressed up against a bed. But when she sat, there was a grunt, and a pair of strong hands gripped her waist.

Georgette's breath caught in her throat and she would have screamed had she not been so taken aback. A familiar salty scent washed over her senses and she looked down at the rough hands at her waist. A gold ring on every finger.

Flooded with *déjà vu*, Georgette swiveled to look at the man she'd sat on.

Her eyes met a pair of dark ones, then registered his newly trimmed dark beard, his thick brows, and a mop of sleek, wavy, brown hair. Georgette tried to rise, but the pirate's hands only tightened around her waist.

"Stay," he commanded.

Georgette stiffened, hardly able to breathe, but mustered the courage to keep her expression hard— determined to show this pirate no fear. "You're the man who saved me from the carriage fire," she said with a confidence she did not feel. To her relief, the man nodded.

"And you are Lord Harrington's only daughter, if I

am not mistaken," he replied, his hands flexing at her waist.

Georgette frowned. "How do you know my father?"

The pirate's lips curved up into a smirk and his eyes twinkled at her as though he were eyeing a prize. "He sold you to me."

Georgette wrestled to break free from his clutches. He finally let go and she staggered to her feet. "Who are you? How *dare* you utter such lies!"

Too outraged to see the severity of the situation, Georgette scowled at the pirate sitting on the bed.

The sudden onset of bangs behind the picture made her jump, and the pirate rose to his feet. He advanced on her, marching her across the room, and Georgette stumbled away until her back hit the stone wall. The pirate towered over her, took a lock of her golden hair in his hand, and searched every inch of her face with his eyes. "My name is Captain Mannington Stone, and I have come for you."

"Why?" Georgette whispered, all-too aware of the mere inches between his mouth and hers. "What could you possibly want with me?"

Something flashed in the pirate's eyes, but Georgette could not read his expression. Was it fear? Irritation? His smile returned just as a deafening bang shot through the wall, vibrating Georgette's back.

The picture dropped to the floor and a stream of pirates flooded the room. Captain Stone raised a hand, and they stopped in their tracks.

Georgette looked at him again, holding her breath. Then he leaned in to whisper in her ear.

"Do as I say, and you will be unharmed. They can't touch you."

"And how can you be so sure?" Georgette said, thinking about how many times she had almost been snatched already.

Captain Stone pulled back to give her a fierce look, then he caged her against the wall between his arms. "Because you belong to me now."

5

CAPTAIN STONE

The air was heavy with smoke and screams as Captain Stone ordered his men to stop the attack and leave the palace grounds.

His ship had been taken and guarded by the Royal Navy, but as the entire navy was at the palace, it was now free for the taking.

It did not take long for his men to prepare her for sail. In the meantime, he kept his attention on the young woman. Her dainty hands were tied behind her back, and though she wrestled to get them free, her efforts came to no fruition.

He clutched her arm, urging her to walk, and she stumbled as they crossed the threshold of his quarters.

"Mr. Collins," he barked to his first mate. He jerked his head to the door, prompting him to walk in. Georgette looked at the two men. Her eyes were misty, but there was a sharpness to her expression. If Captain Stone didn't know any better, he would have guessed she was furious rather than afraid. His mouth curved into a smirk at her spirit. Even though she was in a helpless situation —onboard a pirate's ship with more than thirty men— she was not one to roll over and walk as a lamb to the slaughter. The feisty look in her eyes told him she would fight him every step of the way.

Captain Stone had no plans to fight her. He knew exactly how to ensure the damsel would do as he said.

He looked at his first mate standing by the door. The man wore a blank expression.

"Mr. Collins, you are here to be a witness."

"To what?" the lady asked, a sharpness in the tone of her voice.

Captain Stone took off his hat and placed it on his desk. "To our marriage."

The woman sucked in a breath with a hiss and lurched back. "I am engaged to the honorable Prince Edward," she began. Captain Stone raised a palm, and she stopped.

He marched across the room, towered over the woman, and gave her a steely look, his nose hovering an inch from hers.

"Do you value your life, girl?" he asked.

She met his stare with a defiant look. "I would rather die a slow death than marry a pirate," she spat.

Captain Stone frowned for a second. Then he tilted his head as an idea sprang to his mind. "And what of your father?" he asked.

"Would you rather *he* die a slow and painful death?"

Her blue eyes flashed and grew wider. Her pretty mouth formed the perfect 'o'. "You wouldn't," she whispered.

Captain Stone lifted his brows. "Wouldn't I?"

He shared a grin with his first mate. "You think I haven't killed before?" He pulled out his sword and held up the blood-stained blade to the light. For the first time, the woman's face paled, and she looked truly terrified.

"As I said. You belong to *me* now." He stepped closer to growl in her ear. "If you want your father to come to no harm, and for my crew to keep their filthy hands off you, then you will do as I say. Marry me."

He pulled back to see the woman's face contorted into a disgusted scowl.

"Forgive me, sir, but *that* is your proposal?" she said, giving him more sass than she ought, considering the situation.

Captain Stone smiled to himself. The ship creaked as it lurched forward. His crew had managed to set sail, but he knew that it wouldn't be long before the Royal Navy would be behind them.

"We have no time for this," he said, his temper rising. "Tell me, Lady Harrington, what is your birth name?"

The maiden's chest heaved as she stared at the wooden floor of the ship, her nostrils flaring with anger.

"There is no priest! It's not a wedding without a—"

"In case you haven't noticed, my lady, I am a captain," Captain Stone interrupted. The faint sounds of cannons flooded the air. He knew those cannons.

The Navy was already on the approach. Before long, he would be needed on deck.

"The name, miss!" he urged. "Or shall I send my men to your father's estate?"

"No," she snapped. Finally, she lifted her gaze to look at him. "Georgette."

Pretty name, Captain Stone thought. He thought it a pity, though, that she was not the obedient type. She would be a difficult mare to break.

"Georgette Harrington, do you take me to be your lawfully wedded husband?" Captain Stone said, puffing out his chest.

Georgette scowled at him, but mumbled, "I do."

"Splendid," Captain Stone said, his mood brightening. "I, Captain Mannington Stone, take you, Georgette Harrington, to be my lawfully wedded wife." He waved a hand. "Blah blah blah. I now pronounce us husband and wife. Now I may kiss the bride."

Georgette's scowl deepened but she didn't stop him when he leaned forward to kiss her.

They were like butter left in a cold cellar—stiff. Not that it unsettled Captain Stone. He knew that she would warm to him... Eventually. When that moment came, she would melt under his touch and let him taste the sweetest parts of her.

The ship rocked and men shouted, snapping Captain Stone out of his marital bliss.

"My apologies, my lady," he said, picking up his hat again and nodding to his first mate. "Duty calls. Our wedding night shall have to wait."

He marched to the door and turned to Mr. Collins. "Guard the door and keep her safe."

"Yes, Captain."

Heartened, Captain Stone scaled the ladder to stand at the helm and looked out at the fleet of ships in pursuit of their ship.

"Bring me more sails," he barked. "All hands to the cannons at the starboard side. Let's send these scumbags to Davy Jones' locker where they belong."

The crew roared back and set into action, while Captain Stone dipped his head low and stared at the approaching ships with a wicked grin. He pictured the

Prince onboard one of them, worrying for Georgette. Hoping to get her back. Then he wiped his lips with his fingers, tasting her as he dragged his tongue across them.

His body flooded with satisfaction at the knowledge that, no matter what the Prince did now, Georgette was no longer his for the taking.

His precious fiancée had married a pirate.

6

PRINCE EDWARD

Prince Edward wiped blood from his mouth as he stepped over the fallen bodies littering the ballroom and headed for the doors.

He found Lord Harrington cowering behind the large oak tree in the garden. His face was ashen-gray, and he wrung his hands.

"The pirates have taken Georgette," he said, his eyes misty in the lamplight. He looked up at the starry skies and seemed to utter a silent prayer.

"I will gather my men and make haste to bring her back to safety," Prince Edward promised, nodding to the old man. "Will you join me?" he asked.

Lord Harrington's mustache twitched, and to Prince Edward's surprise, he shook his head quickly. "I should think it best I stay here and make preparations for her return."

Prince Edward frowned, but he was not in a position to stay and talk, so he nodded and set off at a run, holding his bloodied sword at his side. He followed to the chaotic shouts down the streets of Port Harbor.

He was winded when he reached the docks, and dismayed to see the Duchess sailing off into the distance.

Cursing, he turned to the last of his men who had followed the pirates to the docks. "Set the Victory for sail! Do *not* lose that ship!" he barked. His men scurried about to carry out his orders.

A few moments later, he was on board the Victory, his mind working overtime.

He was sure one of the pirates had possessed a sense of familiarity about him. The strong physique, and a confidence that held presence in the room.

When Prince Edward saw him come marching out of the lost prince's bedroom with Georgette in his arms, he nearly passed out with shock.

In fact, for a splinter of a second, the man looked just like his lost older brother. But the uncouth manner in which the man handled Georgette quickly dispelled that thought from Prince Edward's mind. His brother was a gentleman. He would have never treated a woman with such disrespect.

The Victory sailed through the waters at a fantastic speed, and soon enough, they had gained on the Duchess. Prince Edward could make out the dirty faces of the pirates onboard the ship.

"Load the cannons," he shouted to his men.

He watched the pirates scramble in anticipation of attack. He could see no sign of Georgette.

"Anchor at Starboard. Fire!"

Prince Edward gripped the edge of the ship until the whites of his knuckles were on show.

His future wife was on that ship. Even though he wanted the cannons to tear the Duchess to pieces and send her to the bottom of the ocean, he did not wish to harm Georgette.

He prayed to any of the gods he knew of that she would not be caught in the crossfire. "Hold on, Georgette. I'm coming for you," he muttered into the wind.

7

GEORGETTE

The deafening blows came in sets of four, followed by a succession of gunshots. Georgette's heart raced until her ribs hurt. She sat in the Captain's quarters, frozen on the spot where Captain Stone had kissed her.

Her mind reeled over the sequence of events. From the moment her carriage tipped, everything spiraled into chaos.

She wondered if she'd hit her head in the accident, and all of this was happening in a dream. Perhaps she was in bed with the Prince by her side, praying for her swift recovery.

Georgette shut her eyes and pinched herself. Tears welled in her eyes.

But it was not the pinch that caused her tears. It was

the stark realization that her thoughts were nothing but the foolish hopes of a captured damsel.

This was real. She had been kidnapped by a pirate and forced to marry him.

The Royal Navy was in pursuit.

She needed to get away.

Perhaps, if she could jump into the water, the Navy would see her.

There were several flaws in that plan. First, she'd have to get out of the Captain's quarters because the two windows were sealed shut and far too small besides, for an adult to fit through. Even if she was able to pick the lock, there was the first mate to contend with.

Then there was the matter that Georgette had not been taught to swim. Her father simply forbade her from being anywhere near the water and put the fear of God into her about its dangers.

If the water didn't drag her down and choke her to death, the sharks would certainly kill her.

Then there were the tales.

She had heard stories of creatures more deadly and menacing than whales and sharks.

As beautiful as goddesses, but as ferocious as she-bears.

Sirens.

With shimmering tails as strong as an ox, and claw-like nails able to rip flesh from bone as easily as plucking the petals from a daisy.

Georgette trembled even though she did not entirely believe them to be real.

But if she didn't do something, she would be subjected to a life on the seas—the very place she vowed to her father she'd never go.

Held captive to a pirate, no less.

Her thighs clenched as she thought about her situation. She had just married a pirate. He may very well survive his fight with the Royal Navy, the same way he survived a storming of the palace. He would return hungry and frustrated, and no amount of food would satisfy that kind of appetite.

The way he looked at her after their kiss replayed in her mind's eye, sending a shiver down her spine. She clutched the arms of the chair and her heart began to beat wildly for the umpteenth time that day. She had never shared a bed with a man. She wouldn't even know what to do. The only preparation she had received from the Governess about her wedding night were instructions to lay back and let the Prince do all the work. "He'll know what to do," the Governess had said.

She thought of the rough pirate. The way his fingers sank into her thigh as he pulled her leg around his waist had sent a current through her body. It was a feeling she couldn't understand.

She wondered what else he could do with those hands, and for the first time, a flurry of excitement filled her midriff, like she had swallowed a jar of butterflies.

She shook herself. Thinking of such things was foolish. The Navy would catch up to the ship and destroy the pirate crew.

Before long, she would be in the arms of the Prince, her savior, and then she would never have to worry about pirates again.

An earth-shattering bang ripped through the belly of the ship. It began to groan, leaning to one side. A cannon ball must have smashed its way in. Georgette groaned in deep terror. If the ship was taking in water, it would soon sink, and then what?

She refused to remain waiting like a sitting duck. She needed to take her fate into her own hands.

She scanned the small room, it was sparse. Nothing but a small, lumpy bed in the corner. A desk littered with parchment papers. Two moth eaten chairs.

To the far side of the room sat a wooden trunk. She searched the drawers of the desk and found an iron letter opener.

The ship lurched awkwardly to the left and almost knocked Georgette off her feet. She scrambled to the trunk, her hands trembling as she slid the letter opener into the groove.

No amount of grunting and prizing would open the trunk. She slammed a fist on the trunk in frustration but cowered at the sight of a face suddenly pressed up to the glass doors. "What are you doing in there, wench? Keep it down!" The first mate's shout was muffled by the door, but it sent Georgette's heart racing all the same.

She returned to the task at hand and pressed her tongue between her teeth as she forced the letter opener deeper into the crack. The wood splintered, and just as she thought the lock was beginning to break, she slipped and scraped her fingers across the splintered wood. She hissed at the sting, her ears ringing so loud she could no longer hear the ruckus outside.

Neither did she hear the triumphant victory shouts. It was only when the door squealed open that she jumped, stuffed the letter opener into her bodice and rose to a stand. Captain Stone marched in with his eyes on the chair he'd left her sitting on. Seeing it empty, his brows lifted and his eyes darted around before they came to Georgette.

"The Navy has fallen behind," he announced. Then he nodded to Mr. Collins, his first mate, who was standing in the doorway. Georgette gulped as she watched the man nod back, then promptly close the door.

The Captain took off his hat and set it on the desk. He turned around, and for the first time, Georgette got a good look at him.

His eyes were the deepest, darkest shade of blue, framed with thick black lashes, dark, bushy brows and a short, scruffy beard.

His tanned skin was creased at the eyes and between his brows. His long, dark hair was wavy and wiry, sitting on his shoulders.

The man was mature, but not yet old enough to have more than a few streaks of gray hairs. He smiled at her abruptly, and one of his teeth sparkled like a diamond.

Georgette's heart sank at the news. "The Navy has fallen behind?" she repeated, clutching her hand and trying to ignore the throbbing in her finger.

Captain Stone pulled off his heavy jacket and tossed it to the chair, then tugged on the ties of his shirt until it fell open and loose. Georgette tried to look away, but not before she got an eyeful of his oily, tattooed chest.

In spite of herself, her heart fluttered.

The man reeked of dominance and confidence. On a purely biological level, Georgette was drawn to him.

But he was a pirate. Her enemy. A man to fear. Not to feel attraction toward. She felt a repulsion toward herself and these insensible feelings that she could not control.

The corner of his mouth lifted, his sparkly tooth on show once more as he took a few steps toward her. His body heat washed over Georgette.

"Where are we going?" she asked, trying to think of a way to divert his attention. His eyes dipped to her cleavage. She took shallow breaths, praying he could not see the letter opener hidden between her breasts.

He met her eyes again. "The ship has taken heavy damage. We'll need to stop at the Spanish port."

Georgette cocked her head to the side, picking up in the tone of his voice that Spain was not their true destination.

"And then?" she asked.

Captain Stone took another step closer. His chest was hardly an inch away from hers now. He raised a hand and grazed his fingers up her arm, leaving a burning trail in its wake.

"So inquisitive," he growled low. His voice vibrated against her cheek as he leaned in unbearably close and lifted her hair away from her neck. "So... Enchantingly beautiful," he added, pulling back to look her in the eye again.

Georgette stiffened, still clutching her hand like it was a life preserver.

"You're afraid of me," he said, watching Georgette. He dipped his head and gave her a firm look. "There are many people who should fear me, but you are not one of them."

Georgette held her breath and frowned. Then she shook her head, her courage rising. "You enslaved me!"

Captain Stone stepped back and lifted his palms. "Nay, my lady. I liberated you. There will be more liberating to come, if you behave." His eyes dipped to her mouth at the last part of his smug statement and his right brow cocked. Georgette felt a rush of heat in her core.

She didn't entirely know the meaning behind his words, but they set off a chain reaction of confusing sensations nonetheless.

Captain Stone bit his lip in a way that did something funny to her stomach. Then he looked at her hands. "What have you done?"

Georgette jumped. The sudden concern in his voice took her aback, but she held out her hand, hoping to keep the distraction going.

"No need to be alarmed. It is just a splinter."

Captain Stone frowned deeply, took her hands and tugged on them, pulling her forward so as to step into the light. "It has gone very deep," he remarked, keeping his focus on Georgette's finger. "If we don't take that out and clean it fast, you'll get an infection."

Before Georgette could respond, the Captain pulled her roughly and pushed her down on the chair. Then he knelt, one of his knees slotted firmly between her legs.

Georgette tried to focus on her breathing as Captain Stone inspected her finger. Then he looked up at her. "I'll be as gentle as I can, but I can't promise that it won't hurt."

Georgette nodded, having no idea what Captain Stone was going to do.

He lifted her finger to his mouth and kept his eyes on her while he sucked on it.

Then he nipped the skin where the splinter had gone in and Georgette yelped in shock. His grasp on her hand tightened, and he didn't pull back, but sucked on her finger with more concentration.

Finally, he dragged his teeth across her fingertip and spat into a handkerchief. Georgette leaned in to the see the slither of wood on it, then met the Captain's deep blues.

He licked his bottom lip, pulled it inward, and gave her a satisfied smirk. "Better?" he asked.

Georgette's arms tingled, and her finger was numb, but she nodded.

Then she watched, bewildered, as Captain Stone rummaged through the drawers of his desk and brought out a flask.

He popped the stopper, placed a cloth over the neck, and tipped the bottle upside down.

Then he settled again between Georgette's legs and dabbed her finger with the damp cloth. She sucked a deep breath in through her teeth at the sting, but Captain Stone continued undeterred.

When he was done, he took a swig from the flask and offered it to her. Georgette shook her head, unable to form the words to speak.

She wasn't sure what she was feeling. Her mind was too overwhelmed.

The Royal Navy was not able to rescue her. Her new husband was a pirate. His knee was hovering dangerously close to her most intimate parts. The way he had sucked on her finger made her dizzy.

She wasn't sure whether she wanted to open her legs and see what other things the pirate had in mind, or whether to use them and run for the door.

"Now, my lady, I have already told you," Captain Stone said, setting the flask on his desk and rising to a stand. "You have no need to fear me."

He swaggered across the room and everything in Georgette's body cooled. "Are you not planning to… to…" she swallowed, nervous. Then she grabbed the flask and took a greedy gulp to steal some courage.

The liquid burned a savage path down her throat, but warmed her insides in a good way.

Captain Stone chuckled in a low, rumbling hum. "Nay, my lady. I will not take your innocence."

"You will not?" Georgette asked, struggling to hide the disappointment in her tone. She could not understand why she was not relieved at the revelation. "Why force me into marriage, then? What plans could you possibly have for me?"

Captain Stone pulled off his shirt and gave Georgette more than an eyeful of his broad chest. With the lamplight dancing across his muscled torso, it took all of Georgette's resolve not to stare.

His muscles rippled as he pulled his hair into a ponytail and tied it back. Then he smirked.

"Make no mistake, I will be taking it." His eyes dipped to her mouth again. "But not until you get down on those pale, pretty knees and beg."

Georgette sat back and frowned. "I'm sorry to disappoint you, but that day will surely not come."

Captain Stone cocked his head to the side. "I have elaborate plans for you, Georgette. Soon enough, you will be screaming my name."

Georgette tugged on the neckline of her gown and swallowed again. "How can you possibly be so bold? What makes you think such things?"

Captain Stone laughed darkly and returned to her feet. His hands hovered over her arms and set the hairs on end. "Because even now, you're thinking about it. I can see it in your eyes."

Georgette forced her eyes shut, furious at their betrayal. They may as well have divulged her deepest secrets.

"Now, you have a choice," he whispered, his mouth dangerously close to her neck as he whispered into her ear. "Would you like to sleep here, with me? Or alone in a cell?"

Georgette opened her eyes and gave him a hard look. In spite of whatever fantasies were brewing in the dark corners of her mind, she was still the daughter of a governor. She had more sense than to lay in bed with a pirate. Married or not.

Most of all, she would not give her captor the satisfaction of being right. "I would rather rot in a filthy cell for the rest of my life than share a bed with you," she said through a sneer.

Captain Stone pulled back to read her eyes and Georgette tried to look back with repulsion. It must have worked, because a flash of hurt crossed the pirate's face. But then he gave her a grin and inclined his head.

"As you wish."

8

CAPTAIN STONE

Captain Stone lay in his bed, staring at the planks of wood above his head. Slithers of morning light poured through the cracks and shadows moved across him, signs that the night crew were swapping shifts with the morning crew.

Seagulls honked in the sky and the sea swayed the ship like a mother rocking her baby in a bassinet.

All was calm, the Royal Navy was long gone (for no one could outrun The Duchess), and his mission was a success.

The Duchess was his once more, and his new wife lay safe in the cells below deck.

In spite of these facts, Captain Stone could not quash the feeling that all was not well.

Perhaps it was that there remained a great deal of

worries on his mind. Some far greater than getting his old ship back or stealing the Prince's betrothed.

No. There was much work to be done to ease his troubled heart. Admittedly, he would have been far less concerned with his arms around a woman's warm body. Georgette's bare flesh pressed up to his would have surely given him some peace.

But it would have to wait. Georgette's spirit was like a wild horse, and he knew it would take a firm hand and a great deal of patience for her to break.

He rubbed the smooth stone on his gold ring absentmindedly. It had become habit. He stared at the swirls of green and silver on the stone and sighed. Ever since he got the blasted ring, he had experienced nothing but stress and headache.

He sat up and pulled on his boots with a grunt. Lying in bed offered him no rest. Being left to his thoughts was a form of torture, so he got dressed and marched out of his quarters, ready to face another day at sea.

"Morning, gents," he shouted as he climbed to the helm of the ship.

Mr. Collins stood back from the wheel and saluted. "Morning, Captain."

He relaxed when Captain Stone gave him a stern nod. "Report?"

Mr. Collins knitted his thick brows together and

looked ahead. "All quiet since dawn, sir. I think it's safe to assume the Navy has turned back."

"Never wise to assume, Mr. Collins," Captain Stone said, taking his spyglass and looking at the quiet horizon. "The wind is on our side, however. Conditions are good."

Mr. Collins nodded with gumption. "Yes, sir. We'll get to the port in about three more days if the seas stay true."

Captain Stone hummed in thought. "Let's make it two. I want you to get eight of our strongest men to take up the oars."

Mr. Collins looked at Captain Stone like he was mad for a moment, but the expression faded into a fixed smile as he nodded. He didn't need to say it, Captain Stone knew that Mr. Collins was concerned about the crew. They had spent much of the night fighting both on land and at sea. Many of them must be fatigued.

"What is the status of the crew?" the Captain asked.

Mr. Collins coughed and cast his eyes downward. "Fourteen unaccounted for, sir. Fell behind, I reckon. Three dead from the blast." He patted the wooden rail of the ship. "We've patched her up the best we can, but we'll need to fix her up good and proper once we reach the Spanish port.

"And what of my wife?" Captain Stone asked, giving Mr. Collins a hard look. His first mate rolled his lips inward until they formed a thin line in between his bushy beard.

"Quiet as a mouse, sir. We've offered the provisions you requested, but she rejected all of them."

Captain Stone smiled to himself. "Of course she did."

He looked through the spyglass again, hovering his gaze over the straight horizon. So clear and free. It was as if they were sailing to the edge of the world. The crisp, salty breeze whipped his hair back and invigorated his senses.

But Mr. Collins coughed again, dragging him out of his reverie. He took the spyglass away from his eyes to give his first mate a discerning stare.

"Don't be shy, Mr. Collins. Is there something on your mind?"

Mr. Collins stroked his oily mane of dark hair and grumbled something inaudible. But then he met Captain Stone's eyes and sighed. "There have been whispers among the crew."

"Whispers?" Captain Stone repeated.

"Aye, sir. They are questioning why we have the lady on board, and what you mean to do with her."

Captain Stone slammed his spyglass on the beam with a smack and the surrounding men jumped. "Is that so?" he barked, his voice carrying in the air. He looked out at the men on the deck. They had all stopped what they were doing and were now squinting up at him, shielding their eyes from the sun.

Captain Stone rolled his shoulders back. "Tell me, which one of you, ungrateful fools, are questioning my decisions?"

No one came forward.

"The lady is *Mrs.* Stone to you. And if one of you so much as touches a hair on her head, I'll cut you from belly to brain and toss you overboard for the sharks. Do I make myself clear?"

The crew muttered their responses, nodded with more gusto, and went about their chores. Captain Stone glared at Mr. Collins, who shrank away under his watch. "And you? What have you got to say on the matter?"

The man opened and closed his mouth soundlessly, eyeing Captain Stone's hand hovering over the hilt of his sword.

"Good," Captain Stone said. "Let there be no more questions on the matter. The lady belongs to me, and I may do with her whatever I please. It is nobody's business."

Mr. Collins adjusted his jacket and set his face to look serious. "Yes, Captain."

Satisfied, Captain Stone picked up the spyglass and

handed it to him. "Get those men to the oars and keep your eyes on that horizon. I want to waste no time."

He picked up a thick slice of bread and wrapped it in a cloth. Then he tucked it under his arm and grabbed a flask on his way down.

The crewmates avoided his gaze as he climbed down to the lower deck, but some muttered, "Morning, Captain."

The men were afraid of him. Which was good, Captain Stone thought. The very second those lawless men got an inkling that they were not to fear their captain, a mutiny would begin to brew. But as none of the men were born leaders, anarchy would follow.

Besides, he couldn't carry out his plans if his crew turned on him. They needed to stay under his control.

The lower deck was so dark it took several moments for Captain Stone's eyes to adjust.

And when they did, he smiled at the sight.

There were two iron cells facing each other on the lower deck. They had been designed for animals, not people. A bed of hay sat in the corner of one, and Georgette sat by a trough filled with water. She had not yet seen him, perhaps too set on the task at hand to notice his presence. So, he watched her splash water over her face and neck. Then she soaked her arms.

Her hair hung freely over one shoulder, the curls

damp and loose now. Her blood red gown spread across the entire floor of the cell. A wooden plank creaked under his weight, and Georgette's eyes shot up in his direction.

"I apologize, my lady," he bowed his head as he approached. "There are no maids here to assist you out of that dress."

He pulled out his knife. "I am certain you are quite uncomfortable in that tight bodice. Please allow me to…"

"No!" Georgette barked, rising to a stand. She gave him a look of defiance and her hands balled into tight fists.

Captain Stone lifted a brow. "Tell me, why the sour face? I thought we were getting along handsomely?"

Georgette's face screwed up with disgust. "You locked me up in a cage next to a dying man," she said, pointing at the cell across from hers.

Captain Stone followed her line of sight to the old pirate on the floor that he had mistaken for a pile of old rags. "Oh," he said.

He marched over to the cell, took the rusty key off the hook, and opened it with a click. The man's raspy breaths came shallow and fast.

"I couldn't sleep all night, listening to his groans," Georgette said, frowning at him. "No one has come. Why

he was locked up in the first place is beyond my understanding."

Captain Stone knelt down and pressed his hand over
the old man's chest. He was bloated and clammy. The
lights of his eyes were almost out.

Captain Stone recognized him. His oldest crew
member. Jones.

He pulled his hand away to find it drenched in blood.
He wiped it on the man's jacket and sighed heavily.

Then he took out his knife, and ignoring Georgette's
protests, sank the blade deep into the old man's chest,
right through the heart.

Death was instant, and the man let out one last
ragged breath before he left that plane of existence. It
was a sound Captain Stone had heard too many times to
count.

From the way Georgette looked at him, he realized it
was the first time she had heard it.

She pressed her hands over her mouth and staggered
back as Captain Stone rose to a stand, wiped the blade
with a handkerchief, and sheathed it. "Why are you
looking at me like that?" he asked, stepping toward her
cell door.

"You just killed a helpless man…" she said, her voice
muffled in her hands. Captain Stone frowned.

"My lady, you are quite difficult to please," he said,

dangling the key to her cell in his hand. "You complain of the noise he was making, then you complain when I put him out of his misery."

Georgette took her hands away from her mouth and scowled at him with such ferocity that it took him aback for a moment.

"You speak of him like he was an animal to put down. But he is a… was a…"

"A pirate," Captain Stone finished for her, grinning. "I thought you were brought up to see pirates as nothing more than wild animals to be put down. Surely, I was doing you a favor."

Georgette didn't speak, but she shut her eyes. Captain Stone found her reaction baffling.

"All you have to do is say the word, and I'll take you to my quarters." He held up the key as Georgette opened misty eyes.

Two giant tears rolled down her cheeks. "I think I'm safer where I am."

Captain Stone frowned and glanced back at the body of the man in the other cell. Then he looked at her and laughed. "You think I mean to kill you, too?"

Georgette averted her gaze, holding her wrist. When she did not reply, Captain Stone grabbed the bars of the cell.

"Did you not hear me last night? I have plans for you, my lady. Plans that require you to be safe and well."

Georgette lifted her eyes to meet his again.

"What do you want from me?"

The question hung in the air for a few moments as Captain Stone thought about it. Then he clenched his fist and set his jaw.

"I want you to show gratitude and to do as I say."

Georgette held his stare for a long moment, then she squinted as though in pain and shook her head. "You're despicable."

Captain Stone stuffed the key into his pocket with a disappointed sigh.

"Very well. I can be a patient man." He began to swagger away.

"Wait. You're not going to leave me here with a dead man, are you?" Georgette called out; her voice laced with panic.

Captain Stone waved a hand. "Apologies for the not-so-lively company. But as soon as you change your mind, say the word."

Then he climbed out, grinning from ear to ear at the sound of Georgette cursing him.

9

GEORGETTE

Georgette's body ached and her temples throbbed from a restless night in the dirty cell. The floor was strewn with straw, and even though someone would come and pour new water into the trough, it did not look clean enough to drink.

She glanced at the parcel of food by the cell door and the sheepskin flask propped up next to it. Untouched, of course.

How could she eat when there was an old man suffering so much in the cell across?

All night long, he wailed and moaned. Pleading God to take him.

What he got instead was Captain Stone, who ended his misery without hesitation.

Now she stared at the immobile body. It looked like a waxwork doll in a pile of bloodstained clothes.

She looked at her hands; the small strip of cotton wrapped around the finger with the splinter was soaked in dirty water. If the Captain was truly concerned about infection, he would surely not have placed her in such conditions.

His eyes were so cold and distant after he plunged his knife into the old man. The pirate had his charms, but nothing could change the fact that he was a ruthless, cold-hearted pirate.

Georgette wondered why the old man had been locked in a cell. Two pirates tossed him in and locked the door soon after Georgette was put in the opposite cage. Was it customary for pirates to leave their wounded to die alone?

Georgette asked herself what he could have done to deserve such a fate. She wondered if Captain Stone would be so ruthless if Georgette was in the same state.

This could be no life for her. She needed to escape. But she would bide her time. She touched the tip of the letter opener buried in her cleavage and took a deep, steadying breath. Then she pressed her eye to the crack in the side of the ship to look out at the blue seas.

She would escape this godforsaken ship as soon as they reached land.

But in order to navigate such an escape, she needed her strength.

Begrudgingly, she picked up the sheepskin flask and took several greedy gulps. The water was surprisingly fresh. The parcel of food happened to be a healthy slice of crusty bread, a block of cheese, and a handful of grapes.

Georgette shut her eyes and pretended to be back at the palace as she ate. She wondered what had happened to the Prince.

She had every reason to believe he was still alive. The man was a fine swordsman and captain of the Royal Navy. For whatever it was worth, she knew that he would not stop for a moment until he found her.

She washed the bread down with another gulp of water and tried to ignore the grim, damp smell stifling her nose.

Two days ago, her greatest concern was whether she would trip up or step on the Prince's foot during their dance at the engagement ball. Now she was wondering how she would break free from her captors and stay alive.

She glanced at the dimly lit cell door; the iron bars were sturdy enough, but the hinges were encased with rust.

All those hours of learning needlework and playing the piano were to waste here. She wished she had learned how to wield a sword or pick a lock. There was no dancing her way out of this predicament.

She slumped against the side of the ship and it rocked her in a smooth and steady fashion that was strangely comforting. She shut her eyes and finally allowed sleep to take over.

———

DAYS PASSED, AND CAPTAIN STONE DID NOT RETURN TO the cell. Georgette winced as she rolled over, half-asleep. The burning ache in her chest brought her to her senses.

It had been four days since her maids helped her into the dress. As it was for the engagement ball, she had instructed them to fasten the corset extra tight. A decision she bitterly regretted now.

She heard footsteps and turned quickly. A pair of dark leather boots appeared on the ladder, and Georgette held her breath as the pirate captain descended the ladder and recoiled in disgust.

He lifted a hand to his mouth with a groan. "Mr. Collins. Will you please send someone down here to dispose of this rotten corpse?" he shouted up. The affirming response was too faint for Georgette to hear, but her heart lifted for the briefest moment.

She had grown used to the dreadful smell and had

long pushed what had caused it out of her mind. She opted instead for the lie that an animal had died. Georgette rose to a stand, refusing to show an ounce of fear as Captain Stone approached.

His eyes surveyed her up and down, then he pushed a pile of clothes through the bars. She took them without hesitation, but her brows raised as she studied them.

A pair of tan cotton pants, soft leather boots, a white cotton shirt and a sheepskin jacket. Men's clothes.

Captain Stone seemed to follow her train of thought.

"We will be at the port shortly. I shall book us a room, but they won't let you in smelling like that. Plus, that gown will draw far too much attention."

The sound of footsteps above their heads picked up pace, and there was a flurry of excitement. Two pirates descended the ladder quickly and marched over to the second cage. They swung it open and picked up the body by the arms and legs.

"Heavy old blighter," one of them mumbled.

Captain Stone's glare silenced him. Georgette and the Captain stood immobile, watching as the men removed the body and lifted it to the upper deck.

Georgette was just about to ask whether they were going to bury the man when a sudden splash hit her like a punch to the gut.

She blinked a tear out of her eye and looked away.

"Are you quite certain you do not need any assistance?" Captain Stone asked, nodding to her gown.

"I'm perfectly capable of taking care of myself, thank you," Georgette said, defiant. Captain Stone sighed with a nod.

"Very well," he said. Without another word, he marched up the ladder and disappeared.

Georgette exhaled, then pulled the letter opener out of her corset. The iron scraped her raw skin, and she hissed at the sting.

She wasted no time thinking about it. The tool ripped open her gown. When she cut the ties of her corset with the jagged tip, the sudden release of tension on her chest left her gasping.

The relief was instantaneous, and she inspected the bruising all over her ribs.

She did not concern herself with the fact that she was standing naked in a dirty cell on a pirate ship. Nor did she put much thought into the fact that a pirate could walk in at any time. She picked up a bar of soap instead and scrubbed busily from head to toe, wincing as she touched the bruises on her body.

In spite of her pain, it felt good to wash off the grime from the last few days. Georgette patted herself down with her dress and pulled on the fresh set of clothes. She had to pull on the drawstring and tie it to stop the pants from sliding down her hips, and the oversized shirt had far too many ruffles for her liking. When she yanked on the boots, she was surprised to discover they were almost a perfect fit. Then she shrugged on the jacket and braided her hair back.

She could not see herself, but she reasoned that she must look like the strangest pirate.

She had never worn pants before. The clothes were so much lighter and freer than the restrictive corset and layers of skirts on a heavy gown.

She gargled some water and used a toothpick to clean her teeth. Then she peeped through the crack again.

This time, she saw sailboats. Lots of them. The sound of sailors shouting orders to each other drifted down.

Her heart leaped. This would be her chance.

She picked up the letter opener and set her tongue between her teeth as she started to work on the hinges.

But even in their rusted state, they did not bend to her will.

She wrestled with the cell door for several minutes, then slammed her fist against it in frustration. To her surprise, the cell door swung wide open with a squeal.

Georgette stood blinking with shock, but then the

ship lurched forward and threw her off balance. She scrambled to her feet, heart racing, thrust the letter opener in her jacket pocket along with another block of cheese, and ran for the ladder without looking back.

10

PRINCE EDWARD

The Victory groaned and took in water through the holes in the sides of the ship. Prince Edward's men stopped firing cannons to block the holes with crates and blankets, but the ship would not be able to continue pursuit. Prince Edward slammed his fist on the desk and stared at his maps.

The Duchess was also damaged, of that he was certain. He hummed in thought.

They would not be able to sail for too long. Prince Edward looked carefully at the few ports nearby. He reasoned the only place they could have gone was Calais, France.

He instructed his men to block up the holes as best they could and set sail for France. His heart hammered in his chest, and he had to swallow the rising nausea every time he thought about Georgette on that pirate ship.

He did not want her among those lawless tyrants for a minute longer, and with every second that passed, his stomach tightened.

He tried not to imagine what atrocities the men had in store for Georgette. It was still beyond him to understand what had possessed a crew of pirates to storm the palace and kidnap his bride. Did they intend to demand a ransom? Despite his father's misgivings, he would offer up all of the gold in the palace for Georgette's safe return. Then he would hunt down every last pirate and arrest them.

He only hoped they did not have another horrid plan for his bride-to-be.

Victory soon sailed into the French port, but his heart sank at the sight of the merchant ships and fishing boats in the harbor.

The Duchess was not there.

While his men tied the ship at the docks and began quick work on the repairs, Prince Edward pored over his maps once more.

"Where have they taken you, Georgette?" he muttered aloud.

The door to his cabin opened, and an officer stepped in. Prince Edward looked up expectantly. The officer clasped both hands in front of him and cleared his throat. "What is it?" Prince Edward barked, irritated by the posturing.

"We have a problem, Your Highness."

Prince Edward surveyed the officer. The man seemed unable to utter any more words. He opened the cabin door and stepped through the doorway again instead. "If you would be so kind, Your Highness," he said, motioning for the Prince to follow.

When Prince Edward reached the upper deck, he held in his breath.

A steel net swung from the rafters, and in it was a creature that appeared to be half-dolphin and half-woman. She stared down at them balefully, but even with the terrible scowl on her face, she was breathtakingly beautiful.

The net swung from side to side and she hissed, sharp fangs suddenly on display. The men poked at her with their bayonets.

"What is this?" Prince Edward asked, resting his hands on his hips.

"I have heard tales, sir," one of his officers said, stroking his chin. "Sirens. Vicious, violent creatures. Turn away for one second and their claws will be in your back, dragging you to the depths of the sea."

The men shuddered and aimed their weapons at the creature.

The creature had settled into silence, as though listening to their conversation. Prince Edward studied her, and the siren looked back keenly. Something in her eyes gave him pause. His hand flexed at the hilt of his sword, but he did not withdraw it.

The siren hissed suddenly, twisted, and flashed long, needle-like fingers that cut through the netting like it was butter. She landed on the deck with a loud thump and the shocked men shouted expletives as they backed away. The officers, panicked, looked to Prince Edward for further instruction.

Prince Edward remained calm. Perhaps it was the shock of encountering a creature so strange. For a reason unbeknownst to him, he could not give the order to fire at such a beautiful creature. Her naked, slender frame and free flowing black hair offered only a little modesty. The siren seemed vulnerable.

As if to disprove his assumptions, she lunged and lashed out at one of his men with her claws. The sailor's chest opened up like he'd been cut open by a bear. Huge claw marks covered his torso, and a massive crimson red stain bloomed on his chest. A profuse amount of blood spilled to the deck.

The surrounding naval officers did not wait for instruction. They opened fire on the siren. Smoke filled the air, and the siren screeched like a banshee. The sound was unbearable. Prince Edward crouched and covered his ears in pain.

The siren stopped screaming to attack again, and the Prince reached for his flintlock pistol with trembling hands. He fumbled for a few moments, suddenly out of sorts with his own limbs. A terrible wail pierced the air, and he looked up. His men were all brilliant marksmen, but there wasn't a single bullet wound on the siren's body. Shells were littered at her feet, the bullets seemed to have simply bounced off her body. Yet, one man with his wits still about him seemed to have succeeded in slashing her arm with his sword.

Her blood trickled down to the deck, and she stared wildly at them all, panting heavily.

Prince Edward rose quickly and raised a fist. His men held their fire begrudgingly.

"Steel harms them," he said, nodding to the bloody sword.

As though his words had been the permission he needed; an officer behind the siren thrust his blade right through the siren's chest with an audible crunch.

Prince Edward lurched forward, his own heart squeezing. He recovered himself at the last minute and watched the men toss the siren's dead body overboard to the sharks.

A chill ran down Prince Edward's spine as one of his men approached.

"Your Highness, we must go back and tell the King. The waters are unsafe," he said, his expression dark and brooding.

"No," Prince Edward snapped as he grabbed the railing and looked out at the open sea. "Georgette is still out there. I will not return until she is safe."

"But, sir—" The man stopped when the Prince gave him a hard look.

"I will not sleep until she is safe. Send a pigeon with instructions to bring more ships. We're going to find Miss Harrington."

If they had been trained with any less discipline, they would be grumbling. But men of the British Royal Navy had been taught to take orders first and ask questions later. Any sign of insubordination was a gross offence, so the men went about their business with the customary efficiency they had been employed for. Yet, Prince Edward could see the fear and discomfort in their grim expressions.

The Prince flexed his jaw and walked to the railing of the ship to stare down at the dead siren floating in a pool of blood.

11

CAPTAIN STONE

As the ship sailed toward the Spanish port, Captain Stone eyed the line of boats bobbing in the water. To his relief, none of the sails belonged to the British Royal Navy.

He knew there was still a risk that they had sent a message to their allies, and another attack could strike at any time.

They would need to stay on guard. The sooner the ship was repaired and back on open seas, the better.

He rubbed the stone ring with his thumb and sighed heavily as he set the spyglass down. He nodded to Mr. Collins.

"How long will it take to fix the ship?" he asked.

Mr. Collins grumbled to himself and stroked his beard. "I know a few good men. Getting the materials shouldn't be a problem. If they work round the clock, I reckon we could be back on the sea in two days."

Captain Stone groaned. It would not be a moment too soon. Every hour on the port increased the risk.

He secured his hat and looked out at the crew standing on the deck, awaiting orders.

"You have served well, now you may report to Mr. White, the quartermaster, for your earnings. Rest in good company, eat like kings. We will all need our strength for the next voyage."

A dark laughter crossed the group of men.

"Hail Perta!" someone shouted, and the rest of the crew took up the chant. But they fell quiet when Captain Stone barked at them.

"If I hear a whisper of Perta on land, I'll be having your heads. Do I make myself clear?" He gave the crew a steely glare. The last thing he needed was for loose lips to go blabbing about their plans to the locals.

The Port of Málaga was one of the busiest places to dock, and there was no telling which nosey ears might pick up such information.

As the ship reached the dock, the men sprang into action, and Captain Stone patted Mr. Collins on the shoulder. "Get your men to work as soon as you can. I'll be in the Iron Lady if you need me."

Mr. Collins' mouth curved up in a sarcastic smile.

"Speaking of iron ladies… What do you want me to do with the w—"

"Wife?" Captain Stone finished for him with a hard glare. Both men knew that was not the word Mr. Collins had been thinking of. The man nodded sheepishly.

Captain Stone straightened his jacket and cleared his throat. "She is not of your concern."

Mr. Collins had nothing to say, so he made his excuses and climbed down to join the line of men waiting to see the quartermaster.

With a deep breath, Captain Stone took the ladder down to the lower deck, then descended the next one, squinting in the dark.

He was unsure what mood the woman would be in.

She looked at him differently now. Like he was a wild lion she could not hope to reason with. But what did she expect? The old man was bleeding out, his wound was badly infected, and he was almost ninety years old.

His boots landed on the creaky floorboards and he silenced his concerns with a broad smile.

"Your chariot awaits, my lady," he said, spreading out his arms. But his eyes landed on the open cell door and cast over the empty cell.

All that remained was the red gown on the floor. Captain Stone picked it up and held it to his cheek.

The material was still warm, and it smelled of her.

Cursing under his breath, he dropped the gown and kicked the trough so hard it turned, spilling murky water over his boots.

He never thought she would run away. Where would the maiden go?

His blood began to boil at the thought of where Georgette might end up if he did not find her. But he pushed the thought out of his mind and climbed up the ladder, his heart thumping hard.

"Captain?" Mr. Collins asked, reading the look of thunder on his face. He hurried to his side. "She's gone? How is this possible?" he asked, his voice raspy.

Captain Stone ignored the man as he marched across the deck and climbed out of the ship. Mr. Collins followed close behind. "What do you need me to do?" he asked.

"Stick to the plan." Captain Stone jumped down to the dock and took in a steadying breath as he looked around at the countless faces of men at work. Now that she was in normal clothes, she would be harder to spot. He looked out for her blonde curls; they would be a sure giveaway. He only hoped he discovered her before anyone else.

"But, sir, what will you do?" Mr. Collins asked,

joining him on the dock. Captain Stone walked through the crowd, keeping his hand on the hilt of his sword. "I'm going to reclaim what is mine," he growled.

12

GEORGETTE

Georgette may not have learned swordsmanship, nor did she have the strength to fight off a man in combat, but she did have the special power all women develop from an early age—the art of invisibility. She tied her hair back into a loose braid and picked up a worn cap from the deck. She kept her head down, and it was easy to slip out unnoticed.

When her boots touched the dock, she let out the breath she had been holding. She had no time to waste. She hurried through the crowds of sailors and men, wanting to get as far from the pirate ship as possible.

Georgette had never been to Spain, but she noticed a lot of the people walking along the streets spoke in

English. She pulled her jacket tight and hugged herself as she shuffled through the milling crowds. Seagulls honked above their heads and circled the sky. The sound of the rolling tide moving in and out soothed her soul.

She tried to ground herself in the familiar sound-scape of people and water. Even a world away from home, some things remain the same.

Market stalls lined the streets with merchants standing by crates of fish. Georgette wished she had money. It would have made her escape much easier.

When she saw a pawnshop with a wonky wooden sign hanging above the door, she pushed in, and a little china bell rang to announce her arrival.

A short, elderly gentleman with a portly belly appeared behind the counter and cleared his throat. "*Buenas tardes*," he said, his droopy eyes taking in the sight of Georgette.

She pulled out the only item she had on her person. The shopkeeper jumped a little when the iron letter opener slammed on his wooden counter. "How much for this?" she asked in her best impression of a man's voice.

The man lifted a brow and gave her a discerning stare.

Then he carefully picked up the letter opener and studied it. "The crest on the handle... This belongs to the King of England. Where did you get it?" he asked in a Mediterranean accent. His dark eyes met Georgette's, and she swallowed hard. Captain Stone must have stolen it from the palace the day he captured her. She couldn't tell the man *that* story.

"A gift," she lied, keeping her voice low. The man's eyes turned into tiny slits. He was far too observant to believe the ruse, but wise enough to keep his questions to himself. He hummed deeply, picked out a few silver coins, and placed them on the counter.

Georgette didn't hesitate to take them. She was in no position to negotiate. But she did suspect the man was giving her a poor price.

"*Gracias.*"

She left the shop and followed a stream of people across the port.

A sea of sails bobbed up and down along the docks, and more boats sailed in. Georgette kept a hand in her pocket and ran her thumb across one of the silver coins. It was probably not enough to buy a crossing back to England, but it was a start.

If she could find English-speaking people, she might be able to get a job and raise the funds to buy her way home.

Staying at the port was out of the question, however.

It would only be a matter of time before Captain Stone discovered her missing.

Why was the cell door unlocked? Did he want her to escape?

She thought back to the way he'd looked at her after killing the old man. It was as if all humanity had left him. Now she knew he was a ruthless killer, there was no question of what he was capable of.

What if he found her disobedience too much to handle?

What if he didn't *want* to find her?

Hours passed by and the sun turned a deep shade of gold as it set in the sky. The tall buildings with sandy colored fronts reflected the sunset in pretty shades of red and yellow.

When she reached a quiet tavern at the very end of the port, Georgette walked inside with a growling stomach. It was unwise to spend her only coin on food, but she reasoned that a slice of bread would not cost more than two reales.

Besides, her ankles were beginning to ache, and she longed to sit on something other than a straw covered floor.

She marched in with her shoulders squared and slammed a coin on the counter. "What can you give me?" she asked gruffly.

The bartender had a long wiry mustache that reminded Georgette of her father. But she shook the thought out of her mind and matched the man's steely stare. He set a glass on the counter and poured from a bottle of cider, then he filled a small bowl with shelled peanuts and set it next to the drink.

Georgette sighed inwardly, her heart sinking. She hated alcohol, and she hated peanuts even more, but her body was weak, so she downed the drink whole and hugged the bowl of nuts to herself as she turned around in search of a seat.

The tavern was almost full of men speaking in loud voices. Some were laughing, others seemed to be in hot debate.

She found a small table in a dark corner and started to work through the nuts.

Knowing she couldn't get anywhere without a plan, Georgette pulled out the three remaining coins and plopped them on the table.

The flames of candlelight danced across the silver, and she squinted as she inspected the worn engravings.

Each of them had four images separated by a cross. She traced a finger along bird, crown, and what looked like a chapel.

The door opened and in strolled a group of sailors. They were cleaner than anyone else in the tavern; neatly combed hair tied back with a piece of cloth, and not even a speck of dirt on their boots.

Georgette sat up and listened in on their conversation as they headed for the bar.

"The ship is leaving for England in the morning," one of them said. "And not a moment too soon."

Georgette's heart quickened. She stuffed the coins back into her pocket and jumped up from her table.

"Excuse me for eavesdropping, but I hear you're headed for England in the morn," she said, trying to sound like a man. She dipped her hat down to shield her eyes and hoped her blonde curls were still hidden. The men turned to look at her. Up close, she realized how tall they were. Her head only reached the shoulder of the shortest man.

"What is it to you, boy?" a ginger sailor said, crossing his broad arms across his chest.

Georgette stiffened. She felt insulted to be addressed as a boy, but she knew it was foolish to expect anyone to see her as a man.

She coughed. "I don't suppose you have room for one more sailor."

"Sailor?" The men looked at each other, their brows raised. Georgette bristled under their stares.

She knew she needed to improve the act if she was to sell the lie. "I'm looking for safe passage to Port Harbor. I have no money to speak of, but I do have two hands and I work like a horse."

Georgette tried to keep her voice gruff and look convincing, but the tall men chuckled. One of them stooped down, and before Georgette could stop him, pulled off her hat. A cascade of blonde curls fell over her face and her long braid uncoiled over her shoulder.

The men jumped back. "It's a lady."

Georgette snatched the hat back and thrust it on her head with a scowl. "Does my sex offend you, sir?" she said, eyeing the men with as much ferocity as she could muster.

Oddly, the men were all smiles now. "No, miss. Not at all."

They exchanged looks. "You want safe passage to Port Harbor, you say?" The ginger sailor stroked his clean jaw. "What brings you all the way to Spain? Shouldn't you be at home, fixing your father's clothes?"

Georgette puffed out her chest and crossed her arms. "My business is my own. Will you allow me onboard you ship, or not?"

The men stepped back a little. Clearly, they were not accustomed to a woman speaking with such bluntness. "All right, little miss. No need to get your garter in a knot. We'll take you aboard, but the decision lies with the captain."

Georgette unfolded her arms with a relieved sigh.

"Very well. I thank you, sirs, for your hospitality. I assure you that my father shall give you a most handsome reward."

The sailors mumbled to each other while the ginger one lead the way out of the tavern. The air was cool and crisp now that the sun had set. Georgette looked up at the blanket of navy blue and stars dotted like sparkling gems in the sky.

There were far less people on the port now. An eerie stillness hung in the air as the ships loomed over them.

The sailors lead Georgette to a large merchant ship docked at the very end of the port. The tiny windows glowed yellow and flickered like candlelight.

A rush of anxiety washed over Georgette as she climbed up to the main deck. She refused a sailor's hand, opting to climb up unaided.

Something felt amiss, but she batted away the thought. Truth was, she had avoided bumping into any of the dreadful pirates, and now she was almost back on open water with a crew of decent Englishmen. Honest sailors.

Soon enough, she would be back at Port Harbor, safe and well.

The Prince would doubtless be most impressed by Georgette's bravery and tenacity, for she had not needed saving at all. She was perfectly capable of saving herself.

Her father, Lord Harrington, need not have worried about her embarking on adventures across the seas. Why, she did not suffer even a little from seasickness. In fact, the gentle rocking of the ship practically put her to sleep. It soothed her in her times of great distress.

Just as Georgette's spirits were beginning to lift, a pair of rough hands grabbed her wrists, and another pair of hands wrapped a thick rope around her. She screeched and tossed her body back and forth, wrestling to get free. But the men overpowered her. Within a few minutes, her arms and legs were tied.

"What is the meaning of this?" she cried out in fury.

The men encircled her with dark laughter. "*Sailors,* you say. What a naive little sparrow you are."

Georgette looked at the faces lit up in candlelight and her heart stopped.

She looked up at the maroon sails, and a flag waved above the helm, but not one she recognized. It was entirely red, with a black crow painted on.

"Pirates?" she whispered, horror dawning on her like she had been dropped in the Pacific Ocean in December.

"Eros has delivered us an untouched damsel to wet our sexual appetites, gents!" the ginger pirate barked.

He flicked his tongue across his bottom lip and eyed

Georgette up and down like she was a piece of meat. "It has been too long since I enjoyed an unspoiled wench."

The men chuckled, and a chill crawled up Georgette's spine.

Another man tugged her braid free from the cloth and her hair fanned out across her shoulders. The men *oohed* and *ahhed* like they were watching a firework display. Then they began to talk to each other about all the horrible things they planned to do to her.

Georgette's heartbeat drowned out their voices. Every molecule in her body trembled. As the men edged closer, she held her breath.

It was over, she thought. She had heard terrible stories about pirates and what they would do to a woman. She would be passed around like a doll. A plaything. There would be no regard for her welfare, nor whether she offered consent.

Even if the ship were to reach Port Harbor, there was no way the Prince would want to marry her then.

Hot tears prickled her eyes, but she stared at them all in defiance, refusing to give the pirates the satisfaction of seeing her cry.

A ruckus broke out above their heads.

The men stepped back and looked up to see two men standing at the helm.

The pirate captain had a large sword pressed against his neck. Its silver blade glinted in the moonlight.

Georgette blinked several times, looking at the dark figure standing beside the captain. Then her heartbeat thundered as the man roared.

"Touch my wife and I will destroy you all!"

13

CAPTAIN STONE

The ship tossed back and forth as the pirates stormed forward. Captain Stone rolled his eyes. He had expected that would be their reaction.

No pirate particularly cared for their captain. Not when they had their hands on a rare beauty like Georgette.

He kept an eagle eye on her as he slit the captain's neck in one quick motion. Then he kicked the dead pirate down and pulled out his flintlock pistol.

A few of the pirates scattered, some jumped off the ship and swam for shore, but many of them were too pig-headed and stubborn to back down.

Captain Stone's blood boiled at the sight of the men

holding his wife. She blinked at him, her eyes like two moons.

Knowing that she was watching sent another flood of adrenaline through his body and he took no time shooting and cutting down any man that came in his path.

"I *said*," he shouted as he kicked another man to his knees. "Get… your… filthy… hands… off my *wife*!" He slashed the neck of a tall ginger pirate who fell like a tree to the deck. Blood pooled out like wine around his body.

Before long, there were only two pirates left. One of them held Georgette's arms, and the other had a small knife to her neck, pressing hard enough for a bead of blood to drip onto the blade.

"Come any closer and I'll—"

Captain Stone shot the pirate in the face before he could finish his sentence. Georgette shrieked as blood and brain matter splattered the wooden beam. The knife at her neck fell along with the lifeless body of the pirate that had stood beside her.

The other pirate let Georgette go and lifted his palms. "Forgive me, Captain Stone. I did not recognize you, sir," he said, his voice shaken.

He staggered back under the intense glare of the Captain standing before him. Then he tripped over a barrel and banged his head on the side of the ship with a crunch.

Captain Stone wiped his blade on his jacket and rolled his eyes at the foolish pirate. The man had broken his own neck trying to get away.

Then he cut Georgette's bonds and cupped her face with his hands. "Are you hurt, Georgette? Did they harm you?" He searched her misty eyes.

Georgette's mouth opened and closed soundlessly. Then her cheeks paled, and she fainted in his arms.

Captain Stone picked her up and cradled her close, his chest burning with equal parts relief and horror.

The thought that she had been captured by another pirate crew made him want to hunt down the rest and slaughter them all.

His men climbed aboard. Mr. Collins marched to him and pressed a hand to his own chest. "Thank the gods," he said, lifting his eyes to the heavens. Then he turned to the rest of the men. "Fill her with dynamite and light her up gents! Let's burn this ship to the bottom of the ocean," he barked.

"No!" Captain Stone shouted. The men stopped and looked up at him, waiting for further instruction. Captain Stone caressed Georgette's cheek and brushed a golden strand of hair away from her face.

"Dispose of the bodies, yes. Prepare this ship for sail. We leave tonight."

"You mean to abandon the Duchess, Captain?" Mr. Collins said, aghast. Some of the crew took off their hats and looked at each other with shock.

It was highly unexpected news after all they had gone through to retrieve the Duchess from the British Navy. If they were to leave it at the Spanish port, it would soon be back in the hands of the Navy. None of this mattered to Captain Stone. Not anymore. There were far greater things at stake now.

"She's just a ship," he said, mostly to himself as he kept his eyes on Georgette. "Bring the supplies. I want us back on open water within the hour."

Mr. Collins nodded. "I will fetch your affects," he said, bowing his head. Captain Stone nodded to him. "I'll be in my quarters." Then he turned to look at his crew. "If any stranger even *approaches* this ship, kill him. And I want no man near my quarters unless they be wanting a chest full of iron bullets."

While that final warning rang out, Captain Stone carried Georgette up the stairs to the captain's quarters and kicked the door shut behind him.

The cabin was dimly lit with two oil lamps. One hung over the narrow bed in the corner and the other beside the desk. Georgette's breaths ran long and deep, her body heaving against Captain Stone's chest as he carried her to the bed.

He set her down carefully and removed her boots. Then he shrugged off his jacket and looked around. A jug sat next to a porcelain washbasin in the corner of the room. He poured water into the basin and dipped a rolled-up cloth in it. Then he squeezed the excess water and returned to Georgette's side.

He hesitated a moment, staring at her pretty features —her lashes resting on her cheeks. Her beauty had him under a spell. As he dabbed her face and neck with the damp cloth, he vowed to any of the gods who might be listening that he would give anything to keep her safe from harm. Even his own life, if necessary.

Slowly, color stained her cheeks, and she opened her eyes with a flutter.

Captain Stone took in a steadying breath as relief washed over him.

But then her eyes met his, and she scrambled into the corner of the bed, trying to get away from him. "You… you—"

"I forgive you," he finished for her. He set the cloth down and sat back in his chair. Georgette frowned.

"Forgive me? What could you possibly—"

"For your disobedience," Captain Stone cut in. "For

running away and stumbling into perilous circumstances."

Georgette hugged herself and began to tremble. Her eyes glazed over. Captain Stone guessed her mind was replaying the events because the color faded from her cheeks again. Then her eyes snapped wide open again, and she looked at him, mouth open. "You shot a man in the face!"

Captain Stone picked up the cloth and reached for her, but she flinched at his touch. Frowning, he put the cloth down and stood up.

"What would you have had me do?" he growled in frustration. "Stand by and do nothing? Listen to what the rotten scoundrel had to say? Shake their hands?" He started to pace the cabin. "Please, educate me on the societal appropriateness of such a situation."

Georgette lifted her chin and shut her mouth with a look of defiance. Her silence calmed him. She knew he had a point, but she would never admit it.

Captain Stone returned to the chair and sighed. "Please allow me to check you for injuries," he said, softening his voice.

Georgette stared at him for a long moment, her arms wrapped around her knees. "I am unharmed," she said, her voice weak.

Captain Stone wasn't fooled. She winced as she

straightened out her legs. "Please," he said, removing his hat. Georgette kept her eyes on his hand as he placed his hat on the table. Then he slowly reached for her face.

To his surprise, she did not flinch. His calloused fingers touched the underside of her chin. She let him lift it to expose her neck.

He peered closely at the tiny red line where the blade had cut her.

Without delay, he rolled up his sleeves and retrieved the porcelain washbowl from the stand, then set it on the floor beside the bed.

"Remove your clothes," he commanded.

Georgette's eyes widened under his stare. "Forgive me. I do not quite understand what you are asking of me," she rasped.

Captain Stone leaned in and dabbed her neck with the cloth. She hissed, and her back arched underneath him as he whispered in her ear.

"My soul will not rest until I am assured that every inch of you is unharmed," he said in a low growl. Then he pulled back to look her in the eyes. "I promise it is for medical purposes only, and I shall do nothing untoward."

"Untoward?" Georgette repeated in a startled voice. "You are wanting to see me naked."

Captain Stone's mouth lifted into a small smile. "Is it so scandalous for a husband to see his wife?"

Georgette sucked in a breath and a lump rolled down her neck as she gulped. "I assure you; I am unharmed. You do not need to—"

"Yes, I do," Captain Stone said, unable to hide the desperation in his voice. From the moment he realized that Georgette was missing, he had tortured himself with dreadful thoughts of what might become of her, should he not find her. Bitter regrets would have plagued his mind and eventually driven him to madness.

Georgette studied his face. It seemed as though she could read his mind. Perhaps his deep concern for her was obvious in his expression. Or maybe it was the tender way he held her hand that changed her mind.

Captain Stone didn't know what it was that made her do it, nor did he care to know. But his heart swelled in his chest when Georgette began to quietly undress right before his eyes.

14

GEORGETTE

Georgette shut her eyes and pretended she was home in her father's estate, and her maids were washing her. She lay on the lumpy bed, bare as the day she was born, with the heat of the Captain's eyes all over her.

She listened to his steady breaths. They soothed her. He dipped the cloth in water for the umpteenth time and wrung it.

"Turn over," he said in a low growl. Georgette's insides quivered. She did as she was told and gasped as cold droplets hit her back. The cloth plotted a cold trail up her spine and over her shoulders.

"You're too tense, relax. I will not hurt you," Captain Stone said. Georgette forced her shoulders to relax as she sank into the bedding.

She buried her nose in the musty cotton and shut her eyes again.

Doing so only sharpened her other senses. The sensation of Captain Stone's fingers grazing her skin as he washed her gave her a strange delight.

She hitched a breath when the cloth reached her bottom. He washed her with more care than she had expected, but she was not used to the harshness of his skin brushing against hers. The maids had such soft fingers.

He dried her back and legs, then commanded that she roll onto her back again. She kept her eyes shut the entire time, unable to look him in the eye as she lay naked.

She heard the cloth being dipped into the bowl of water again and held her breath, waiting for the drops to fall on her body.

But the Captain took more care. He slid the wet cloth all over her, leaving no part of her body untouched.

His hand warmed her inner thighs as he pressed the cloth to her most intimate parts, and she resisted the urge to squirm under him.

"Does this hurt?" he asked over and over. Georgette would shake her head and bite her lip as a rush of new sensations flooded her body.

His calloused hands aside, the pirate touched her as

gently as her maids. Her body began to truly relax as he dried her off. She didn't open her eyes until he covered her with a scratchy blanket.

"There are bruises on your ribs," he said, frowning as he squeezed out the cloth one last time. Georgette sat up and held the blanket to her body.

"They are only from the corset. Do not be alarmed."

Captain Stone dropped the cloth and knelt down by the bed. He studied her with such intensity, it made Georgette's heart flutter. "I will not have you sleep in a cell," he said, sounding like a dying man.

Georgette's breaths grew shallow as she struggled to make sense of the irrepressible sensations in her stomach. "Nor shall I," she said, her voice shaken. She bit her lip and looked around the little cabin. "Tonight could have gone very differently, had you not found me." For the first time, she reached out and touched his arm. Her fingers traced his bulging veins and coarse hairs. "Twice now, you have saved me."

It almost made up for the fact that he had captured her, she thought.

Captain Stone held her gaze for a long moment. Then he nodded.

"Get dressed and rest here. I shall ensure no one disturbs you."

He got up, put on his black leather hat, and headed

for the door, but he stopped with his hand on the brass knob at the sound of Georgette's voice.

"You will leave me?" she asked, panic rising.

Captain Stone turned back and gave her a piercing look. "Nay, my lady. I will never leave you. Now sleep. We have a long journey ahead of us."

The cabin cooled now that he was gone, and Georgette shivered as she dressed herself again.

She huddled under the blanket and curled up on her side, staring at the wood grain on the wall. She had been captured by a second band of pirates. Most of whom were now dead at the hands of her ruthless husband. The same husband who she had let touch every part of her body. Her toes curled at the thought.

Who was Captain Stone? How did he possess a soul so dark and fierce, and yet at the same time, so gentle?

She wasn't sure whether the pirate could be trusted, but right now, in her current circumstances, he was a far greater ally than any.

Sleep took her as she huddled in the blanket, but she did not rest. Nightmares of pirates, blood, ear-shattering bangs, and the gut-wrenching screams of wounded men plagued her.

She felt a cool hand on her forehead. It soothed. She stilled and opened her eyes, panting, and listened to the whispers of two people standing beside her bed in the dark.

"She has delirium from the fever," one voice said. It sounded like it belonged to an elderly man.

"What can be done?" Georgette recognized that voice to be Captain Stone's.

The first voice replied, "Nothing. We must wait for the fever to pass."

Georgette fell into a dark and restless sleep again, waking for only moments at a time. Sometimes, she felt a cool cloth over her eyes, or pressed to her neck. Other times, she felt her hand in a tight grip.

The third nightmare took a surprising turn.

After flashes of memories where pirates chased her through endless halls in the palace, Georgette ran into the lost prince's bedroom.

The large four-poster bed stood gleaming in the sunlight. Captain Stone sat on it, wearing his dark leather jacket and pirate's hat.

He patted the bed and commanded, "Sit."

As Georgette walked to the bed, she noticed she was wearing a long, sheer gown with nothing underneath.

Captain Stone's eyes heated her body as he looked her over. "Lay," he barked.

Georgette lay back, her heart hammering in her

chest. There was an explosion of butterflies in her stomach as he hovered over her.

He leaned in, and the bristles of his beard scrubbed her neck as he bent to whisper in her ear. She heard nothing but an incomprehensible murmur. Her heartbeat was too loud.

Then Georgette's body arched as though his heat were a magnet, drawing her to him. A hand gripped her thigh and squeezed until delicious pain zapped right to her core. She squealed.

He wrapped her leg around him and lowered his body until he had settled his weight onto Georgette's hips. The contact sent a rush of heat throughout her entire body and she squirmed beneath him, helpless but wanting more.

Captain Stone pulled back to give her a lofty grin. One of his teeth sparkled at her, and a hand slid under the hem of her gown. Georgette's breath hitched as his fingers walked their way up her thigh.

Then he nipped the lace collar of her gown and tugged it down.

Sweat collected on her brow. She shut her eyes, rolling her hips from side to side as his breath heated her breast and his fingers edged to her inner thighs.

"Oh, Captain!" she gasped, throbbed with need.

Then a sudden bolt of cold struck her neck, and she opened her eyes with a yelp.

She blinked up at the cabin ceiling and turned to see Captain Stone. The weak sunlight pouring in through the frosted windows illuminated the concern on his face as he dabbed her with a wet cloth.

"How long have I been asleep?" Georgette asked, trying to ignore the throbbing between her legs.

"Two days," Captain Stone replied. "I thought your fever broke this morning, but you are flushed again."

Georgette sat up, prompting Captain Stone to take back the cloth. "I am well, I assure you." She wiped the sweat from her brow and took a long shuddering breath, shaking the scandalous images from her mind.

The dream had been so vivid. So real. She could still feel the pressure of his weight on her hips.

"You cried out for me," Captain Stone said, his deep-set eyes narrowed. Georgette's cheeks must have gone red because his face broke into a smile. "You were dreaming about me."

It was not a question. Georgette's jaw stiffened as she tried to hide a bashful grin. She rubbed her arms, and the burning friction calmed her heightened senses, then she cleared her throat. "You said I had a fever? Was I sick?"

Captain Stone rolled his head and cracked his knuckles, as though he had been bent over the bed tending to her for the past two days. "The doctor says you were suffering from shock."

Georgette dragged her fingers through her hair and sighed. Then she looked down at the brown blanket with a frown. "I suppose that is to be expected," she said, replaying the events of the past week.

Captain Stone rose to a stand and buttoned up his jacket. "Now that you are well, I expect you to join me on the upper deck. I have something to show you."

Georgette's brows pinched and her curiosity piqued as she watched him leave the cabin. Then she yanked on her boots and followed him out to the deck.

15

CAPTAIN STONE

Captain Stone rolled his shoulders back and pretended to look through his spyglass as he heard Georgette approach.

The blazing Mediterranean sunshine beat down on them as the merchant ship sailed through calm waters. No sign of another soul for days. Being out on open water with the salty breeze washing over his face had been the only thing salving his troubled soul.

Seeing Georgette suffer nipped away at his conscience. It was entirely his fault.

He should have taken one of the maidens from Tortuga. They would have come willingly; their hearts desired adventure and freedom, after all.

The truth was, any woman would do.

He only chose Georgette because he took a liking to

her the day he saved her from the carriage. The fact that she was Lord Harrington's daughter seemed too perfect an opportunity to pass. Poetic justice to punish the man who tried to hide from his debts.

But seeing Georgette in such an ill state and being confronted by his own helplessness had made him start to doubt his choice.

The merchant vessel cut quickly through the water. They glided across the sea like a hot knife in a slab of butter. With the wind on their side, Captain Stone could already see the little Spanish island of Perta on the horizon.

He sensed Georgette's presence beside him and lowered the spyglass to look at her.

She rested her forearms on the side of the ship and looked out wistfully. The breeze tossed her stray hairs back and forth over her face and the sight of her, deep in thought, stirred something in his chest.

He handed her the spyglass, and she looked. "Is that Spain?" she asked, pointing to the island.

"Nay, my lady. *That* is the reason I brought you along on this little adventure."

Georgette lowered the spyglass to give him an inquisitive stare. "What do you mean?"

Captain Stone crossed his legs at the ankles and leaned against the ship with a sigh.

"Because you are a woman," he said, offering a shrug. Georgette remained perplexed. Captain Stone puffed out a breath as he looked out.

"Tell me what you know of the seas and the mystical creatures hidden in their depths," Captain Stone said, scrubbing a hand over his short beard.

Georgette frowned in thought. "Mystical," she repeated. Then she looked away. "Surely, you're not talking of the old children's stories?"

Captain Stone brushed her hair away from her neck and she turned her head to look at him once more. "Then you *have* heard of sirens?" he asked.

Georgette's fine brows lifted. Then she scoffed. "Sirens," she said to herself, shaking her head. "Enchanting half human, half fish..." She rolled her eyes.

Captain Stone grabbed her wrist and gave her a hard look. She shrank back.

"Do not speak ill of them," he growled. Then he cast his eyes out at the glimmering surface of the calm waters.

Georgette followed his line of sight. "Will you stop speaking in riddles and tell me what it is you'd have me know?" She wrenched her wrist out of his grasp and glared at him. Her feisty spirit only heartened him.

"Look, and tell me what you see," he pointed. Georgette huffed, but he knew she needed to see it with her own eyes to believe him.

"I too, did not believe the tales... Until..." he trailed off, looking out.

Georgette picked up the spyglass and moved it around, searching the water. Then she slammed it down with a sound of frustration.

"I see nothing!"

Just then, a beautifully eerie sound floated through the air. A sad song sung by a grieving swallow.

The crew cried out in terror and jumped into action. Captain Stone barked at them to settle down, but the men would not listen.

He watched many of them tie themselves to the ship and stuff wax into their ears.

The song grew louder, but Captain Stone grit his teeth and surveyed the seas again. "Captain..." Georgette began in a warning tone. But then she gasped and raised a hand to her mouth. Captain Stone stood very still, trying to block out the voices in the wind.

Georgette scrambled for the spyglass once more and looked out. "Good heavens, the stories are true!" she whispered. "Sirens."

The ship sailed forward just as before, but where there had been clear, calm waters, there were now hundreds of pale, beautiful women, bobbing above the surface of the water as far as the eye could see.

Their long hair flowed free, shifting over their nakedness, yet it was their eyes that held Captain Stone's attention.

As they sung their enchanting harmony, their attention was fixed solely on him. Just as it had been once before.

Captain Stone grabbed Georgette's waist and pulled her close until her hip bumped his. She yelped, but he gave her a warning look. "Last time I led my men here, we almost did not make it out alive," he murmured to her. "Let them see you."

Georgette frowned more deeply, but she looked out, her long blonde hair billowing back as the singing grew louder.

The men wailed and groaned, holding their heads as though they were in agony. Captain Stone knew they were only terrified.

Sirens were beautiful creatures, yes. But they loathed men, and pirates most of all.

With the sheer number of them now encircling the ship, the vessel could sink to the bottom of the ocean before the hour was out.

He rubbed the smooth stone on his gold ring and took deep, steadying breaths as their enchantments flowed and broke around him, as though he had a protective glamour on his person.

He held his breath and watched.

Any moment, the sirens would open their pretty mouths, bare splintered fangs and transform into monstrous evil.

Captain Stone braced for the moment of attack. It never came. The sea of eyes focused on Georgette instead, and the sirens turned suddenly to each other, whispers flying.

Georgette leaned over, her hair flowing. "Why are they looking at me?" she whispered. Captain Stone watched the sirens back away from the ship as it sailed by. Then he called out to them, keeping his voice firm and steady.

"Sirens, daughters of Isis and Poseidon… Please grant us safe passage so that my wife may not come to harm."

He wrapped Georgette in an embrace.

For a few tense moments, nothing happened.

Then, one by one, the sirens disappeared into the water. Soon, they were alone again on the vast ocean, the surface of the water as smooth as glass once more.

Georgette swiveled in Captain Stone's arms and placed her hands on his chest. "Why didn't they attack us?"

Captain Stone caressed her cheek and cocked a smile. "Because of you, my dear."

His heart squeezed as the last word tumbled out of his mouth so freely. Georgette read his face for a moment, then her stiff body melted against him. Her eyes dipped to his mouth, and she bit her lower lip. A moment later, she looked up at him again and her cheeks reddened.

Captain Stone frowned. "Are you feeling unwell again? You're flushed."

Georgette averted her eyes with a dark laugh. "You worry about me too much, Captain Stone."

Captain Stone cupped her face and urged her to meet his gaze. Her smile faded. "That is not possible. I made a vow to protect you, and I will honor that vow until my last breath."

16

GEORGETTE

Georgette's face grew hot as she clung to Captain Stone. In truth, the way he had just called her "dear" made her knees weak.

That, and the shock of seeing hundreds of sirens in the water.

"You're trembling. Come." Captain Stone stooped and picked her up in one calm swoop. Georgette's heart raced as her stomach broke out into another burst of butterflies.

He barked orders to the crew and carried Georgette back to the cabin. But she could no longer hear his words over the thumping heartbeat in her ears. He placed her on the chair and she shivered when his hands left her body. A wash of cold took over as she watched him pour a drink. Then he handed it to her. "Take heart, it is almost over."

"What is?" Georgette asked, taking the drink.

Captain Stone poured his own drink and strode across the cabin to sit in the armchair beside the desk. "There is a mountain of treasure hidden in the caves of Perta. Pirates from all the seas made an agreement to keep their plunder in one secure location."

Georgette coughed on her drink, startled. "But you're pirates. How can you trust each other to not steal the treasure?"

Captain Stone scratched the back of his neck as he stretched out like a cat.

"What do you know of pirates?" he asked, rolling his neck back with an audible crunch. Georgette finished her drink and looked down in thought.

"Prince Edward told me they are lawless, selfish men who roam the seas taking what isn't theirs and doing whatever they want to whoever they please," she said. The thoughts had tumbled out of her mouth before she could filter them. She looked up at Captain Stone with a gasp. "Forgive me. I did not mean to—"

But Captain Stone's dark laughter stopped her. "Prince Edward knows nothing." He leaned forward. "Pirates, as you call them, were privateers. We worked with the Royal Navy, sailing under false flags and posing as normal sailors." He plucked a chess piece from the table, a king, and held it up for her to see. "If it wasn't for the privateers, the war of the Spanish Succession would not have ended the way it did."

Georgette stayed quiet. She nodded, hoping Captain Stone was now in the mood to offer up some answers.

When he was done talking about the war, he set the chess piece down again. "The privateers were given ships, weaponry, and a great deal of money to sail the waters and attack enemy ships. But when the war was over, the King saw it fit to command the privateers to go back to private life."

He laughed again, but the smile didn't reach his eyes. The laugh died, and he frowned down at the chess piece. "You can imagine how these men felt about the idea of going back to land—working monotonous jobs by the sweat of their brow."

Georgette tilted her head. So much of this information was new to her. She was not entirely sure Captain Stone was telling the truth.

He dragged a hand over his face with a sigh. "Pirates, as you call them, are democratic. We are governed by our own code, and in the beginning, we were honorable. So, we decided to keep our treasure in one place and share it out fairly."

Georgette gripped the edge of her seat. "Where do the sirens come into all of this?"

Captain Stone picked up his drink and downed it in one. "For reasons unbeknownst to me or my crew, sirens have taken up residence around the island for the past month." He set his drink on the table and gave Georgette a piercing look. "Every vessel that attempted to sail to Perta ended up in Davy Jones' Locker."

Georgette hugged herself as a wash of cold flooded her body. The idea of sinking to the bottom of the ocean was too much to think about.

"Which is why you are so valuable, my dear," Captain Stone said, his face creasing with a smile. Georgette's heart fluttered at the word *dear* again.

But a realization dawned, and she bit her lip with a frown. "So, I'm nothing more than a siren repellent, and you need me every time you want to collect your treasure. Is that it?" She stood. She was not sure if it was the liquor fueling her anger, but she clenched her fists and paced the room. "You capture me, force me to marry you, and for what? So I can make sure sirens do not attack?"

Captain Stone rose to his feet with a deep growl and knitted brows. Georgette did not back down. She squared her shoulders and held his stare.

After a few moments, he opened his mouth to speak,

but the ship lurched, almost knocking Georgette off her feet.

Without hesitation, Captain Stone grabbed her by the arms to steady her. He bent to hold his face close to hers. "We shall finish this conversation later."

Then he let her go and opened the cabin door. "Come. We've got a long walk ahead of us."

THE ISLE OF PERTA WAS NOT AS BIG AS GEORGETTE HAD expected it to be. Especially considering that all the pirate treasure was said to be hidden here.

Sticks crunched under her boots as she followed the Captain through the forest. The wind rustled the leaves above their heads, and soon Georgette could no longer decipher whether the sound was from the ocean or the wind. The line of pirates walked like an ant colony behind them, and Georgette could just make out the conversations the few closest to her were having.

The morale of the men had risen significantly now that the sirens were no longer a problem and their treasure was within reach. Georgette smiled to herself as she listened to them talking about the many things they intended to do with their money.

"I'm going to Calais, and I shall ask for the finest bed

in the inn, with the finest company," one of them said. Sniggers followed.

"I shall fetch myself a whole barrel of wine from Italy," another man said. "Then I shall drink myself to an early grave, laying on the sandy shores with two ladies in my arms."

The third pirate almost shouted his response, his excitement rising to a pitch. "I am going to buy a house in Tortuga and have a different maiden bathe me each night."

Georgette looked back to scowl at them. "Is it all about women and wine with you?" she snapped. The pirates looked at her like she had just spoken a foreign language. The shortest one in the middle shrugged. "What else is there?"

The three of them sniggered again as Georgette turned away, huffing. "It seems as though your crew is plotting their retirement, Captain Stone," she muttered. Captain Stone was busy inspecting a large rock previously covered by large banana leaves.

"We're here," he announced, brushing the leaves away to reveal a small opening. Georgette sucked in a nervous breath. "We're to go in there? It's hardly big enough for a small child to fit through!"

Captain Stone chuckled. "It is fortuitous that you are not wearing one of your gowns, my lady." He glanced at her body. "I am most certain that you will fit. Do not worry, it gets wider."

He held a fist in the air and the trail of pirates stopped. "Weapons and outer clothing off, gents."

He tossed his jacket on the ground, along with his sword and pistols. Finally, he dropped his hat and inspected Georgette, who did not fancy the idea of removing any clothing.

"Your jacket, my dear." He held out his hand to her. Georgette hesitated. She could feel an icy blast of air wafting out of the cave, but now that the pirates were ready, she shrugged it off and tossed it to him, then crossed her arms over her chest.

She felt wildly exposed in the thin cotton shirt with no corset to keep her modest. Captain Stone took her hand and bent low to murmur in her ear, "No one is looking at you."

"How can you know that?" Georgette whispered back, glancing at the long line of men behind her. Captain Stone's stubble grazed her cheek as he moved closer. "Because they know that I will gorge out the eyes of the man who so much as glances at my treasure."

He drew back to give her a knowing look. Georgette's stomach flipped. She nodded and followed Captain Stone inside the cave.

Luckily, he was correct. After the tight spot, the

mouth of the cave opened out and the rocky path descended deep into the ground.

A cold breeze washed over them as they urged forward, and the men's excitable voices echoed around Georgette. She gritted her teeth and tried to ignore their lewd conversation, keeping an eye on the rocks and trying to keep her footing.

After an extended period of time, the ground was damp. Before long, their boots splashed in deep puddles. The cracks above their heads let in weak streams of sunlight, but it was not enough to see very far.

Just as Georgette was about to ask how much farther they would have to go, the ground levelled out and the water became ankle deep. They walked into a huge cavern.

Green and blue lights flooded the cave ceiling. Georgette looked around with a keen eye and saw that it was the reflection of pools of water near the edges.

When the crew filled the vast cave and looked around, the air grew heavy and tense. "It's gone!" one of them shouted.

Captain Stone's hands balled into fists as he marched back and forth. He peered into the water as though he was checking for drowned treasure.

"Where is it? Where has it gone?" another pirate said, his voice echoing around them. Georgette's chest tightened as she watched the men grow agitated with confusion and anger.

"Enough!" Captain Stone barked. His voice thundered around the cave like a roar. The men stopped and looked at him for instruction, but Georgette noticed that their eyes held no fear this time. They watched Captain Stone with tight jaws instead, like a pack of wolves ready to pounce at any given moment.

"As you can see, the cave has been emptied," he said, his voice firm. Georgette could see a hint of worry on his face, and a spark of fear lit within her. "Someone has stolen from us, and mark my words, we shall find out who has done this. We will——"

"You have led us all to ruin!" A tall pirate with burly arms pushed forward through the crew, pulling a fist back. Mr. Collins, the first mate, jumped in the way and scowled at the pirate. "Back down, Hawksy, unless you want to have your soul ripped from your body."

The tall man gave Mr. Collins a filthy look, but stepped back and didn't say another word.

A voice spoke suddenly. It seemed to come from everywhere and nowhere at once. Every living soul in the cave cowered. "If you want that which is yours..." the voice sang. "You must sail to Imerta and return that which is hers..." A slender, dark-skinned siren had surfaced a few paces away. The entire crew took a few steps back. Only the creature's head and shoulders were above the water, but Georgette could see glimpses of her long, silver tail glittering in the depths. The siren's chestnut brown hair floated like it had a mind of its own.

Captain Stone went down on one knee and leaned forward. "Do you mean to tell me that Isis has taken the treasure? All of it?"

The siren turned slowly and set her deep brown eyes on Captain Stone. She nodded. The other pirates backed away even more, holding their breath. Georgette wondered why they were so afraid.

The siren spoke in a pure, lilting, sing-song tone, but there was something distinctly familiar about the sound of her voice. It almost felt as though she had heard that voice before.

"You have stolen from her, but Isis is forgiving. Return it, and she will return what she has taken from you."

Without another word, the siren lowered herself into the water and disappeared.

There was a beat of shocked silence as everyone processed the information. Then Hawksy charged for Captain Stone. "This is all *your* fault!" he screamed. Spit flew in Captain Stone's face. Georgette stumbled away in horror as the man grabbed Captain Stone's shirt and punched him square in the jaw.

Mr. Collins tried to wrestle Hawksy off the Captain, but the pirate kicked him in the shin, then in the head. "Stay out of this, old man."

Then he turned to Captain Stone again, his nose a mere inch from his. Captain Stone stood mute, a hand on his jaw and his eyes on the water as though searching for a missing tooth.

"Thanks to you, we have no money and no ship. Now the formidable goddess Isis is sending her army of sirens to destroy us."

Georgette's heart thumped as she watched the menacing pirate threaten Captain Stone. Her husband. If he were to be killed, what would become of her?

She stepped forward. "And what have you stolen from Isis?" she asked.

"Surely, you must know." She looked out at the rest of the pirates, who all glanced at each other. Her heart sank at the sight. In actual fact, it appeared none of them were the wiser.

"Shut up, wench," Hawksy said. His foot flew out to kick her, but Georgette jumped back just in time and Captain Stone punched him in the gut. The pirate staggered backward, but reposed himself and balled his fists.

He was not fast enough.

Captain Stone growled, and Georgette could see that he was trembling. "How dare you threaten me? How dare you insult my wife?" He charged, grabbed the pirate's head with both hands and yanked until a deafening crack echoed in the cave. The tall pirate dropped dead to the floor, his head at an awkward angle.

Captain Stone stood, his shoulders rising and falling as he panted like he'd just run a marathon. He turned to the others, his dark eyes blazing like a furnace. "Any pirate with mutiny in their heart, step forward now," he bellowed. The pirates stood still, staring at him ashen-faced, their chests heaving. None of them even dared look at the fallen pirate.

"Good, then. We shall head back to the ship and set sail for Imerta at once."

No one argued.

The long trek back to the shoreline was eerily quiet and uneventful. Georgette kept close to Captain Stone's side and did not so much as look in his direction. Once again, she was reminded that he was ruthless, cutthroat. She was not sure if it gave her comfort or dismay. One thing was certain, though. If one man had to die in that cave, she was glad it was Hawksy and not her husband.

Tensions rose again as everyone boarded the ship. The tide was high and the rolling seas were tumultuous, as though the water sensed their unrest.

Captain Stone started to shout orders for the men to take their places and make preparations for their next voyage, but one of the men wielded his knife and jumped down from the top deck with a roar to land on Captain Stone. Georgette screamed as she watched the pirate sink his dagger into Captain Stone's back.

To Georgette's surprise, the men cheered. Had they had been silently conspiring this whole time?

Captain Stone grunted and twisted like a cat. The attacking pirate fell hard and remained on the ground. He appeared stunned from the impact of his fall. The rest of the crew fell silent.

Captain Stone flexed his shoulders and put a hand back to pull out the dagger. He pulled the blade free. The crew stared with wide eyes as Captain Stone examined the weapon and shook his head as though he had merely been stung by a bee. Then he turned to the rousing mutineer.

"Frederick Martins. I hereby sentence you to death," he declared. Then he grabbed the shocked pirate by a lock of his hair, lifted him up, slit his neck, and tossed him overboard before he finished bleeding out.

The men winced at the sound of the pirate's gargled yelps and jumped at the deafening splash.

Whispers flew around the ship.

"The rumors are true."

"He cannot be killed."

"God save us. He is a demon."

Georgette ran to Captain Stone. He didn't flinch when she touched his back to inspect the wound. There was a tear in his shirt, but the skin underneath was perfectly intact. She could not even see a bruise.

"I saw the blade go in. How is this possible?" she whispered to him.

Captain Stone glanced at her for a moment, but shouted to his crew.

"I thought we settled this back in the cave, but perhaps I was not perfectly clear," he said, wiping his blade on a cloth. "We are sailing to Imerta, where we shall fight."

"But Isis is a goddess. She cannot be harmed!" Some brave soul shouted what everyone was thinking.

Captain Stone raised his palm. "And I cannot die," he barked. A hallowed silence followed. "Listen carefully," he added with a steely glare. "You must do exactly what I say, or you will wish you were fed to the sharks before I am finished with you."

17

PRINCE EDWARD

Prince Edward leaned against the mast of the ship with his arms crossed as he squinted into the dark night, straining his ears for any unusual sounds. The cry of a bird, a splash in the water announcing the unwelcome presence of danger, or heaven-forbid, the screams of Georgette, held captive and desperate to break free.

He had already begun to grow sick with worry for her. With each passing day he refused sleep, his mind raced with several worst-case scenarios. Fatigue pulled at his limbs as he stubbornly stayed upright, but his blinks grew long and slow.

When he finally closed his eyes, his imagination constructed terrible images. Georgette's lifeless body in the water, like the siren he had seen tossed overboard like an unwanted catch from a fishing trip.

Or finding her with a bloodied face and arms full of bruises.

He pictured himself binding the arms and legs of her captors and sending them all to the noose for a satisfying public execution. Justice would prevail, he would make sure of it. But time was flying, and he did not want Georgette to pay the price for his incompetence.

He scoured the seas for any clues of her whereabouts. If the Duchess had not docked at the French port, his next guess was southern Spain.

His men had patched up the ship as quickly as they could and set sail for their next target.

Prince Edward nodded and jerked awake, cursing as he realized he had nodded off. He dug his nails into his palms and started to pace at the helm of the ship, letting the icy snap of the night wind wake him up again.

A slight whimpering sound reached him. He paused and strained his ears as he followed the sound and looked out.

The whimpering led him to the side of the ship. He leaned over and squinted into the darkness... The whimpering came again.

Prince Edward strained some more, and suddenly,

the darkness morphed into the shape of a head and shoulders bobbing in the water.

"Help! Help!"

Alarmed, he pulled back, heart racing. Then he leaned over again. He could make out bright blonde curls now. They framed what he suspected was a face. A woman. His heart leaped.

He gasped. "Georgette."

Without hesitation, he tore off his jacket and belt. His gun and sword fell to the wooden deck with a clang. Several men jumped, startled by the noise. Before they could ask him what he was doing, Prince Edward dove off the edge of the ship.

Their cries rang out, and several of his men rushed to the railing. Prince Edward paid them no mind as he swam as fast as his tired limbs would carry him.

"Help me!"

Her voice was laced with panic. Prince Edward finally reached her. Now that he had reached her, however, the woman's soft blonde curls were fiery red. A smattering of freckles covered her cheeks and nose.

Prince Edward frowned as he treaded water. Then he took in her milky shoulders and bare breasts. The clouds parted for a moment and a sliver of moonlight illuminated the vast, glittering fin in the water.

The Prince lurched back. "A siren!" he choked, trying

to swim away. The siren launched forward and grabbed him by the shoulders. The next thing he knew, her cool hand was on his cheek.

A rush of tingles shot through Prince Edward's body, and he found himself smiling.

The siren edged closer, her breasts touching his chest. He gulped.

Though he was certain she was going to kill him, he could muster no negative emotions in that moment. A resignation washed over him. He was not sure if the siren had him under a spell, or if he was so sleep deprived that he was still hallucinating. He did not have the motivation to be concerned about either possibility. He merely floated in the siren's arms and smiled at her beauty.

Nothing mattered. He swallowed again and stared into the glowing eyes of the mystical creature.

"Tell me, lady. What is it you want?" he asked dreamily.

The siren's hand was still caressing his cheek. She looked into his eyes with curiosity. Then her pretty lips parted and she spoke in a voice that tinkled in his ears like a melody.

"No man has ever called me a lady," she said, not answering his question. Prince Edward was inclined to ask again when a large net scooped them both up and out of the sea.

The siren cried out and hugged her small frame as though the net was made of blades. Prince Edward snapped back into intelligent consciousness. The thin strands of the net were made of steel.

As the net swung round by a crane at the side of the ship and was lowered to the deck, the men kept their bayonets aimed at the siren. Someone pulled the Prince out.

Two of his men ran forward and asked if he was well, but Prince Edward waved them off and turned back to the siren still cowering in the net.

"Why are sirens roaming the seas and launching attacks?" he demanded. The siren's spell was weakening, but even now he felt an insane urge to go to her.

The siren hugged herself, her eyes wide, glancing around the Naval officers with their weapons aimed at her.

Prince Edward motioned for his men to back down and stepped closer to the net. The men obliged warily.

"I will not harm you, my lady," he promised, keeping his voice soft.

The siren's frown faded as she studied him.

He could not be sure, but Prince Edward thought she smiled at him.

In a flash, she was scowling again.

"A man has taken something precious from the

goddess Isis, and she wants it back," she said with a hiss. The men flinched at her words, but Prince Edward's mind raced.

He turned to the men surrounding them. "Leave us."

The men exchanged looks and hesitated, but when Prince Edward squared his shoulders and repeated the instruction, they scattered.

When they were alone, he turned back to the siren, who flinched again in the steel net. The clouds parted once more, and he could see the pink lines along her arms where the net had grazed her skin.

Horrified to see her bruised, he spread the net and picked her up in one swoop. The siren wrapped her slender arms around his neck and stared wide-eyed at him as he strode across the ship and took her to the side. The siren sat on the railing, her fin out over the water. She held onto a thick rope and studied the Prince with curiosity.

"Why help me?" she asked.

Prince Edward sucked in a breath. "No woman should be enslaved."

The siren's eyes bulged. Then she settled into a charming smile and began to play with her long, red hair. "Your kindness will not go unnoticed," she said. Then she touched his cheek. "I will make it known to my sisters."

Prince Edward shrugged. "I know not of the thing that your goddess is seeking, but I too am in search of something precious."

"Or someone," the siren corrected. She tilted her head to the side as though she could read his mind. Prince Edward nodded.

They stared into each other's eyes for a long moment, and Prince Edward felt they shared a mutual understanding. Then the siren flopped over the side of the ship and splashed into the water. When her head reappeared, she waved to him.

"I shall ensure my sisters do not harm you. I wish you well on your search," she called up to him with the sweetest voice. Prince Edward rested a hand over his heart.

"Maybe we shall meet again. I am Edward. Will you tell me your name?" he asked, not knowing why he bothered. It was as though the siren had him under a spell again, but her cheeks flushed. She turned her back to him, but then whipped round to give him a cheeky grin as though she had changed her mind. She uttered one word as she disappeared into the dark waters.

"Serena."

18

CAPTAIN STONE

Long days passed at sea. The crew seemed to have fallen in line, but it was clear that tensions were still rising.

Captain Stone trusted no one other than his first mate, Mr. Collins—the old man had served under him from the privateering days. He was loyal, to be sure. But even with the gift of immortality, Captain Stone needed a crew. He could not sail the seas with only his first mate.

The Island of Imerta appeared on the horizon on the seventh day at sea and a prickling sense of foreboding set the hairs on the back of his neck on end. But he ignored it, putting the sensation down to anxiety.

With Georgette at his side, the sirens would not be a concern.

So long as the crew followed his orders, he would soon have Isis locked up and out of the way.

The treasure would be reclaimed and the numerous pirate captains who were out for his head would receive their lost treasure.

Despite his concerns, Captain Stone felt lighter. As if for the first time in a long time, he did not carry the weight of the world on his shoulders.

He ordered Georgette to stay with him in the cabin, out of sight of his motley crew. For the most part, she did as she was told.

Sometimes, however, he would find her sneaking to the deck to look out at the sea. She kept her head down and pretended to be working alongside the other men so as not to be noticed, and her ability to become invisible seemed to work on most of the crew.

Captain Stone bristled at the sight of it. He wanted to keep her as far away from the wretched men as possible, especially now that they knew he was immortal. Georgette would never be safe around them.

He looked up from his papers as the door squealed open and Georgette returned with her head low. When she took the worn hat off, her golden hair fell in soft waves over her shoulders—a sight Captain Stone was sure he would never tire to see. He resisted the urge to smile.

"You look troubled," he remarked, picking up on the line between her brows. "Why?"

Georgette set her hat down, marched forward, and rested her palms on the desk to give him a hard look. "The crew is restless again."

Captain Stone cocked a brow. "Mr. Collins assures me they are in good spirits. Are you telling me my first mate is a liar?"

Georgette scowled under his discerning stare. "I'm saying your first mate is telling you what you want to hear. My question is, is that what you want to hear from me?"

She held his stare. He was not sure what had lit the fire in her eyes, but he approved of it. Georgette possessed a stronger backbone than any of his men. No one would have been able to hold eye contact with him for so long. Neither would they dare tell him the truth. Not even his first mate, it seemed. He rubbed his chin in thought.

"I value your honesty," he said at last. "What do you know of their restlessness?"

Georgette picked up his flask and took several greedy gulps before she replied. "They do not believe you will deliver the goods. They think you will fail and they will surely die."

Captain Stone slammed a fist on the desk. "They *will* die if they continue to speak such things." He rose to his feet but paused under Georgette's hard stare. She pointed at him. "There is another way…" Her eyes dipped to his hand and Captain Stone frowned, suspicious. He remained silent while she paced the cabin. "It's the ring, isn't it?"

Captain Stone held his hand as if it were a newborn baby, and rubbed his thumb over the stone. "What are you suggesting?"

Georgette stopped pacing and laughed to herself. "I've been watching you. Wondering how you could have survived that attack unscathed. It got me thinking about the mysterious object you supposedly stole from a goddess."

She pointed at Captain Stone's hand. "It's an immortality ring, isn't it?"

Captain Stone's mouth cracked into a smile for a flicker before he frowned again. Then he walked around the desk to approach Georgette and brushed her hair away from her shoulders. "It appears there is more than meets the eye with you, my dear." He caressed her cheek and her bottom lip protruded in the most alluring way. But her eyes were dark with fury. He wished she would not look at him like he was a monster. He sighed. After the things he had done right in front of her, he supposed it was unrealistic to expect anything else.

"Yes. This ring belongs to Isis, and it bestows me with the power of immortality. But I did not steal it. Nor shall I give it back."

He began to stride out of the cabin, but Georgette grabbed his arm and he stopped. "Please. Consider what you are saying. You are leading an entire crew to their deaths."

Captain Stone could not deny that her words cut him. "After everything we've been through, my lady, still you have so little faith in me?"

He held her arms and gave them a squeeze. "Fear not. My plan will work. All is well."

THE ISLAND OF IMERTA SEEMED NOTHING MORE THAN A floating volcano to the human eye. Captain Stone knew better.

Those who braved a landing would find lush, green trees, and exotic flowers growing strong and in great quantity in the fertile volcanic soil of the island. But not many men could afford the privilege of witnessing the island in all its glory. The waters were teeming with sirens.

Captain Stone had seen it once, a very long time ago. He was lucky then to have escaped unscathed after the sirens ripped apart the ship.

That was when he had discovered the secret power of the ring. The siren's claws could not touch him, nor could their fangs. It infuriated them. He would never forget their banshee-like screams as they struggled against his protection.

After that, he had resolved to stay as far away from the island as possible. Now their goddess left him no choice.

The pirates wanted him dead for losing their treasure, and even though the stone ring would stop him from suffering such a fate, they could harm the one treasure he cared about—Georgette.

He shook his head to stop any more dark thoughts from entering his mind and gripped the edge of the ship to stare at Imerta's foreboding silhouette instead.

It was dark as they approached—thick clouds shrouded the moon. Their only light was the soft golden glow of the oil lamps on the ship.

"Imerta, Imerta," one of the crew began to sing quietly. "Bare us your fertile fruits." More men joined in the ancient song. "Imerta, Imerta, anchor our spirits with your iron roots."

Georgette joined Captain Stone and gave him an

inquisitive stare. He smiled at her. "You haven't heard the song of Imerta?"

She shook her head.

Captain Stone leaned against the ship, staring at the huge volcano looming over them. "It is said that Isis, the Egyptian goddess, is particularly fond of music. The rumors are that if you sing to her, she will grant you mercy."

He removed the stone ring and held it up for Georgette to see. "She possesses magic unlike anything anyone has ever seen. But what I find most interesting is that she is the goddess of rebirth."

He took Georgette's hand and slid the ring onto her finger. She stared at him with wide eyes. "I thought you said the plan would not fail."

Captain Stone winked at her. "Exactly."

A bold voice suddenly thundered through the silence of the dark night.

"*You come like thieves in the dead of night with vengeful hearts!*"

The men began to panic, dropping to their knees and begging for mercy.

"*There is penance on your lips, but no remorse in your souls,*" the voice said.

Captain Stone looked over the side of the ship to see

thousands of faces looking up, eyes twinkling like stars. It was as though the sky had fallen. As he looked upon them all, a deep sense of regret flooded his body.

"Draw your weapons," he barked at his crew. "To the cannons!"

Georgette began to tremble next to him. "The sirens… Their fury is like nothing I've ever felt."

Captain Stone grabbed her arm and frowned at her. "Felt? You feel their fury?" he asked.

There was no time to talk. The sirens darted through the water, throwing themselves at the belly of the ship like bolts of lightning. The men shouted to each other, knowing there was no other option than to fight. Every man drew his pistol.

"Captain Stone, there are too many of them," Georgette urged. Her warning was in vain. He was already aware, but there was no way his pride would allow him to turn back, and Isis would not allow him retreat either. Not without the ring.

Gunpowder filled the air as pirates and sirens battled. They were no longer beautiful, but now vicious creatures more deadly than sharks. Some of them began to climb the sides of the ship. Once aboard, they dragged men over and into the water with a human wail and a monstrous screech.

The metallic scent of blood filled Captain Stone's nostrils as a tail hit him hard on the back of the head. For the first time, he fell with a thud and the pain vibrated from his chin all the way down his spine.

Georgette hurried to him, and the siren backed off. "You're hurt," she whispered, touching his chin. She removed her fingers and crimson blood came away with them.

Captain Stone staggered to his feet, disoriented. "Nay, it is but a scratch!" he said, emboldened with adrenaline. Mr. Collins fought gallantly, slicing the air and keeping the sirens away, until he was able to reach one of the rowing boats. "Captain, we must leave this godforsaken ship. The sirens are ripping her apart."

Captain Stone did not argue. He had Georgette jump into the little boat before he followed. Mr. Collins lowered it to the water and climbed down before he cut the ropes and took up the oars.

As sirens approached, Georgette lifted the ring in the air and shouted with authority. "Grant us safe passage."

The sirens backed away, creating a free path.

They rowed through quickly.

The sounds of dying men and the groaning ship being torn to pieces carried on the air.

"You have paid the price for your foolish attack," Isis' voice thundered from the sky as Mr. Collins rowed as fast as he could. "The next time you come here to betray me, I shall not be as merciful."

The pain in the back of Captain Stone's head splintered suddenly and ran all the way down his neck. He slumped in Georgette's arms, succumbing to the darkness of sleep.

19

GEORGETTE

Georgette's hands shook as she tried to block out the screams and focus. The unconscious Captain Stone lay stone-still in her lap. She tore the ring from her finger and slid it onto his, praying to whatever god might deem it fit to save him now.

As soon as the ring sat snug on his finger, the seeping blood stopped and the slit on his chin closed up.

Within moments, the captain was healed. He opened his eyes and blinked up at her. Relief flooded Georgette.

Without thinking, she pulled his head to her bosom and squeezed his body with a big hug.

"I thought I'd lost you," she whispered.

Captain Stone sat up and caressed her cheek. It was too dark to see his expression, but judging by the tilt of his head, Georgette supposed he was incredulous. "And you cared?" he asked.

She nodded, and he embraced her.

There was a long moment of silence as the two held each other. Mr. Collins finally cleared his throat, and they broke apart.

"Apologies for breaking up such a tender moment," he said, not sounding sorry at all. "But we have company."

Georgette turned and gasped at the giant ship sailing in their direction. The sky had turned a soft blue as the sun began to rise, and there was just enough light to see the sails. "The Royal Navy," she said, shocked.

Georgette's heart jolted as she thought about who might be on that ship.

Prince Edward.

She had long given up hope of any rescue. Now that it was here, she didn't know what to feel. But there was no time to lose. She waved her arms and shouted for them until Captain Stone grabbed her waist and pulled her to him. A rush of heat flooded her core.

"What are you doing?" he growled.

Georgette frowned. "Do you really think we'll get to shore alive in this?"

She pushed his hands off her. "Do as I say, and you'll come to no harm. I promise," she said.

Captain Stone gripped her wrist and gave her an odd smile. "So, that's what it is? You'll go running back to your prince and think you can demand that the Navy does not slaughter a couple of pirates?"

Georgette leaned in until her lips hovered an inch from his. "You cannot die, remember?"

Captain Stone looked down at his hand and frowned. "I gave it to you," he said, as though in disbelief. Voices shouted overhead from the ship, and a rope ladder dangled above their heads as they rowed close.

Georgette averted her eyes from Captain Stone, her heart squeezing. "You need it more than I do."

Then she climbed the ladder, her heart thumping wildly in her chest.

When she flopped over the edge of the ship, a crescent-shaped line of soldiers aimed their bayonets at her. She raised her palms. "My name is Lady Georgette, daughter of Lord Harrington..."

"...and my fiancée. Stand down, men." Prince Edward marched through the line of soldiers, and the next thing Georgette knew, she was in his arms and up in the air.

"I thought I had lost you," he whispered into her hair. When he pulled back, Georgette could see that the Prince had collected a few more lines on his face that were not there before. She traced one between his brows with her fingertip. "Do not fear, my prince. I am unharmed."

Prince Edward's face relaxed. Before Georgette could stop him, he kissed her.

His lips were smooth, and the kiss was chaste, lasting no more than a few seconds. But an earth-shattering roar flooded the air, followed by several loud explosions.

Georgette whipped round to see Captain Stone stood on the side of the ship, his leather jacket billowing out like a cape. The Navy fired at him, but the bullets rebounded, dropping to the deck like hail.

"No. Please, stop!" Georgette shouted, watching with horror as Mr. Collins fell face forward and landed with a terrible thump.

A pool of blood seeped around his head like a red halo.

For a moment, Captain Stone shut his eyes, as though to compose himself.

Then he jumped down and withdrew his sword.

Georgette lunged forward to run into the firing line, but Prince Edward grabbed her arms and forced her back.

"Let my men deal with the pirates, my lady. We need to get you to safety," he said, over her protests. He picked her up, carried her to the captain's day cabin, and locked the doors.

"Please, Edward. Let me talk to him," Georgette begged.

Prince Edward frowned and rested his hands on his narrow hips. "To whom? The pirate? You want to speak to the wretched fool who captured you?"

Georgette shook with fear. "You don't know what he's capable of. He can't die. He will kill you all," she burst out.

Prince Edward rubbed his thumb along his chin and frowned more deeply.

"I'm not lying," she pressed.

The sounds of gunshot grew louder and closer, and Georgette hitched a breath as the Prince touched the hilt of his sword. "Stay here," he ordered. "I'll come back for you when it is done."

Georgette tried to follow him out, screaming at him to stop and listen, but the Prince was too fast. He locked the door behind him and Georgette could only slam her fists against the frosted windows.

Captain Stone would not hesitate to kill the Prince. Of that, she was sure. And even though she couldn't fully process the way she felt anymore, she knew she didn't want either man to die.

For the second time in what was beginning to feel like an eternity, Georgette was locked in a seaman's cabin and hard-pressed to escape. She looked around the room.

An oil lamp stood nearby. She smashed it and dripped the oil on the hinges of the door, then took her knife and rammed it into the crack.

The door frame splintered until the hinges broke free. She gave it one hard kick, and the door fell to the ground with a bang.

Piles of bodies lay on the deck and Georgette's boots splashed through puddles of blood. She didn't stop running until she could see the Prince and Captain Stone in a sword fight on the main deck.

"Stop fighting! Stop!" Georgette screamed.

Wounded soldiers tried to grab her, warning her to get away, but she jumped out of their clutches. "For the love of all things holy, will you please stop fighting?" she bellowed.

Captain Stone's sword sliced Prince Edward's thigh.

Knowing that Captain Stone would stop at nothing until every man on the ship was dead, and that Prince Edward could not kill him, Georgette climbed the side of the ship and screamed as loud as she could.

The two men stopped and looked up at her for the first time, their faces identical for a moment. "Georgette, get back to the cabin!" Prince Edward shouted up.

"What are you doing?" Captain Stone wailed; his voice laced with devastation.

Georgette held her knife to her own neck and glared at them.

"If you do not stop fighting, I will slit my own throat and fall to the bottom of the ocean," she said.

The two men dropped their swords and raised their hands. "Please, come down from there," Prince Edward said, softening his voice.

Captain Stone rested his hands on his hips. An odd sense of *déjà vu* washed over Georgette at the sight, but she shook it out of her mind and focused on the task at hand. Finally, she had their attention.

"You will take us to the nearest port," she said, looking at Prince Edward. "And you will allow myself and Captain Stone to disembark this vessel without any harm."

Prince Edward looked at her like she had slapped him. "You mean to stay with the pirate?" he asked, his face was awash with sheer horror.

Georgette bit her lip. He was so close.

Her rescuer had come for her, but he had no idea that Captain Stone was too powerful. Too ruthless. Too stubborn.

If the Prince somehow got her away from the Captain, the pirate would sail the seven seas searching for her—killing anyone and everyone who got in his way. She couldn't bear the thought of that.

Neither could she hope for any harm to come to the Captain.

"I do," she said, keeping her voice firm. "What will it be? Will you agree to the deal? Or am I to…" she motioned to slit her throat and the two men jumped forward with a gasp.

"Fine, fine! I shall do as you wish," Prince Edward said, lowering his head. He turned to Captain Stone. "As long as you agree to leave me and my men alone."

Captain Stone gave a curt nod, and the two men shook hands. Georgette exhaled the breath she had been holding and climbed down to the deck.

The adrenaline left her body in a rush and she sank to her knees, looking at the destruction around them.

Hot tears prickled her eyes. "What is to become of me?" she whispered. "Is this my life now?"

20

CAPTAIN STONE

To Captain Stone's surprise, Prince Edward kept his word. He and Georgette disembarked at the nearest port. The deep crease between his brows was the only giveaway that he was not happy about the agreement. Georgette kept quiet, barely looking in Captain Stone's direction. He carried Mr. Collins' body over his shoulder, and they walked in silence as they weaved through the streams of people on the docks.

In any civilized country, it would have been noted that Captain Stone was carrying a dead man. This, however, was no ordinary port. This port, in fact, was well known to have frequent travelers of morally gray intentions. The locals had learned that if they wanted to keep their lives and safety, then they could not ask any questions, and the sight of a dead man was not as unusual as one might think.

Captain Stone's heart was heavy as he carried the body of his first mate—a man who had stood at his side from the very beginning of their privateering escapades. It hit him that his entire crew was now dead. He glanced at Georgette. She had not so much as glanced in his direction since they left the English ship. Did she see him as a monster? Did she think he was too cold and cruel?

He wanted to tell her everything, but there was so much to say that he wasn't sure where to start. Besides, an important task remained at hand, and that needed his utmost attention.

When he bought a rusty spade in exchange for one of his golden rings, Georgette did not ask any questions. He thought perhaps she knew what was going through his mind, as it seemed that she was able to read him so easily. They walked for a long time until the crowds thinned out and they ended up on sandy Egyptian soil.

Without a word, Captain Stone carefully laid out Mr. Collins' cold body. Then he took the rusty spade in both hands and set to work digging in the sand.

Georgette watched in solemn silence. Several hours passed by before Captain Stone shrugged off his jacket and loosened his shirt, sweat dripping down his body.

The air hung heavy.

Several times, Georgette opened her mouth as though to ask something, but then promptly closed it again. Captain Stone was glad for her silence. The sorrow and fatigue he felt were almost more than he could bear. He felt sure that if Georgette spoke, he might snap an insensitive response that he would regret later.

The truth was, they were now very alone.

On the one hand, it was a relief to be rid of his mutinous crew. But he now faced the daunting task of finding a new crew with no money and a list of enemies that was growing longer by the day.

When he felt satisfied with the grave, Captain Stone rolled Mr. Collins' body into it. The corpse landed with an uncomfortable thump.

It took hardly any time at all for him to cover the body with earth and fill in the grave. Soon enough, a mound of sand was left to mark the place he had laid his first mate to rest.

Georgette marched into the woodland and returned with two large twigs held together with strands of her hair. She placed the makeshift marker at the head of the grave.

She turned to Captain Stone with teary eyes. "Would you like to say a few words?" she asked. He frowned deeply.

He considered himself a man of action rather than

words, and an uncomfortable tightness formed in his throat at the thought of what one ought to say at an old friend's burial. He could not form a syllable.

Sensing his struggle, Georgette offered to speak on his behalf. He inclined his head and listened as Georgette recited a poem he had never heard before. She ended with a beautiful hymn, and tears came to his eyes as he recalled the simple but haunting melody. A vague memory came to him of a time long ago, when he had been a little boy in church.

They stood in silence for a while, and Captain Stone eventually looked up to see that the sun was now casting a warm, amber light on Georgette's face and hair.

He looked out sharply at the setting sun and a new sense of urgency took hold.

"We need a boat and a crew," he said to Georgette.

She nodded, pale-faced. "May I be so bold as to suggest a slice of bread? I cannot remember the last time food has passed my lips. You also need to eat, after all that hard labor."

Captain Stone thought on it. It must have been two days since their last meal. So much had happened in such a short space of time.

He nodded. "Very well. Come with me."

It was dark when they returned to the docks. The golden glow of gas lamps lit the path as they walked in silence, and Captain Stone listened as the tide rolled in and out, grounding him.

One of the port masters was busy talking to a captain who had just disembarked his ship. Captain Stone noticed the small leather pouch sitting innocently on his desk.

Without hesitation, he pocketed it, ignored Georgette's disapproving frown, and led her down the street to an old inn.

They settled for a bowl of stew, two crusty bread rolls, and a jug of beer. Captain Stone then guided Georgette up the creaky stairs to their room.

The soft murmur of other patrons nursing their drinks and exchanging stories of the sea reached them through the floorboards.

The combination of a full stomach and newfound privacy seemed to offer Georgette the courage to speak her mind. "You planned for the sirens to attack, didn't you?"

Standing beside the wash basin, Captain Stone unbuttoned his shirt and peeled it off. He avoided her discerning stare, poured some warm water into the basin, and washed his face.

"I've been thinking about everything that happened…" she continued. "How we got into this situation," she added, removing her outer clothing with a sigh. Captain Stone glanced at her. She was now loosening her braid. Her soft golden waves fanned out over her shoulders.

When he didn't speak, Georgette took it as permission to share her theory. "I couldn't understand why you would sail to Imerta, give me the immortality ring and let those sirens tear the ship and the crew to pieces." She shut her eyes and flinched as though the memory hurt her.

Captain Stone grit his teeth and washed his upper torso with a damp cloth.

"You saw what they did at the Isle of Perta," he said bitterly. "All of them turned mutinous and tried to kill me... The things they would have done to you if they had succeeded..."

Horror flooded his body, and he shook his head.

Georgette dropped her hands and stared at him open-mouthed. He met her wide blue eyes. To his amusement, they flickered downward. In spite of her chastity, she could not stop herself from taking a glimpse at his nakedness.

She nipped her bottom lip and looked at his eyes again. "You killed your crew... For me?"

Captain Stone charged across the room so fast, the basin crashed to the floor and sent water flying. Neither Georgette nor Captain Stone paid it any attention. He found her hands and gripped them like his life depended on it.

"Make no mistakes, my lady. I will burn this entire world down to keep you safe," he growled. The air between their bodies was charged with an electric heat.

Georgette's breath hitched, and her eyes grew even larger. Captain Stone even thought he caught a glimpse of a smile dart across her pretty lips.

21

GEORGETTE

Georgette listened to the soft snores coming from the chair in the darkest corner of the room. She couldn't sleep.

Not while she wrestled so savagely with her thoughts.

She had been in the Prince's cabin, *this* close to going home.

She touched her lips, remembering the Prince's chaste kiss. She was not sure what she was more worried about, the Prince finding out she was now married to a pirate, or Captain Stone discovering the Prince had kissed his wife.

His bellowed words echoed in her mind from the day he rescued her.

Touch my wife and I will destroy you all.

She shuddered. Going with him was the right thing

to do. Prince Edward would be dead otherwise. Captain Stone would not have wasted a moment of hesitation. She had seen him kill before.

Now she was in a foreign land with her enemy, with no hope of rescue. Running away already proved futile— she had no experience in the real world. She would surely end up in danger again.

Captain Stone's promise came back to her then.

I will burn this entire world down to keep you safe.

The man was a cold, ruthless criminal, but for some unknown reason, he was committed to keeping her safe.

She sighed and tried to sort through her confusion.

There was the fact that he had never forced her to be carnal with him, even though he had forced her into marriage and was entitled consummation by rights. Even when he told her to show him her nakedness and washed her down, he did so with surprising tenderness.

The heat of his hand lit up a fire in her that day. It continued to simmer, even now, as she lay in the tiny inn bed.

He had vowed that he would not do anything to her until she got down on her knees and begged for it, and so far, he had kept his word.

She rolled over with a huff and frowned at the wall. She may have had a slight curiosity as to what the man could do to her, and how that might feel… But she was far from begging to find out.

She decided to list all the reasons to hate the man. They included every dastardly act he had done, starting with when he stormed the castle and captured her.

Slaughtering all those pirates like pigs. Sending his own crew to oblivion…

Another voice suddenly intruded on Georgette's reverie.

He did those things to keep you safe, didn't he? The pirates were going to do terrible things to you, and his crew was going to do the same.

She bit her lip and buried her face in the musty smelling feather pillow, trying to douse the insensible flames of desire rising within.

She could not possess feelings for her captor. What kind of life would that be?

In any case, staying with him was her best shot at surviving in this world. While she figured out a way to return to her Prince without getting him killed, she needed Captain Stone.

Her core throbbed at the thought.

THE NEXT MORNING, CAPTAIN STONE SEEMED IN A GOOD mood. He hummed to himself while he bathed and dressed by the sink basin. Then he winked at Georgette before he left the room, leaving instructions for her to get dressed and meet him downstairs.

Georgette washed as quickly as she could and weaved her long hair back into a braid. She hopped on one foot as she pulled on a leather boot, and her hands trembled as she fasted the ties on her cotton shirt.

She had no idea what awaited her, but she did not like the idea of leaving the little room at the inn. She had already grown attached to its simple comforts. The tiny log fire with just embers burning now. The creaky wooden bed tucked between a bookcase and a night-stand, with nothing but the Bible on its shelves.

She cast her eyes around the room one last time as she rested a hand on the brass knob.

When she entered the tiny bar downstairs, the innkeeper greeted her by the name "Mrs. Stone." It took her aback to be addressed by that name, but what surprised her even more was that it made her smile.

"Good morning," she said, trying her best to hide the shock in her voice. She glanced around the room of patrons and frowned. "May I enquire as to the where-abouts of my husband?" she asked, putting on her formal voice, again. Her stomach flipped at the word husband.

The innkeeper nodded to the door. "He stepped out for a moment. I have taken the liberty of making your breakfast. If you would like to take a seat…" He gestured to a small table laden with more food than Georgette had seen in a long time.

She thanked the innkeeper and wasted no time tucking into the food. She tore off a chunk of freshly baked bread and the smell flooded her nostrils, expelling a sigh from her body. Then she gulped down the beer, forgetting about airs and graces as hunger took hold.

"You should try the bananas; they are quite delicious in these parts of the world."

She jumped at the sound of Captain Stone's voice. He stood silhouetted in the doorway to her left, framed in sunlight with his hands on his hips.

Then she looked at the table. A plate of bananas sat untouched on a plate with all manner of grapes.

Captain Stone chuckled and opened his satchel. "We will take all of it with us. We have a long journey ahead."

Georgette dabbed at her mouth with a handkerchief while she watched Captain Stone load up his satchel until it was brimming with food. Then he tossed a large sheepskin flask to the innkeeper, who caught it with ease.

"You know what to do," he said, nodding to the man. He turned back to Georgette with a cheeky grin and plucked a grape from its stem. He rolled it between finger and thumb as he regarded her. "You are looking quite beautiful this morning, my dear." He leaned forward and planted a kiss on Georgette's cheek.

She resisted the urge to lift her brows at the kiss, but could not suppress a giggle. The bristles of his beard tickled her cheek in the most delightful way. He pulled back, and she caught sight of the roomful of strangers ogling them.

Now she understood. He had told the innkeeper to address her as Mrs. and he was now claiming her as his wife. In other words, he was telling the room of men to steer clear of Georgette.

He held her eye and grinned. As though he could read her thoughts, he gave her a nod. Then he popped the grape into his mouth and moaned. "I must say," he said, helping Georgette to her feet. "I am rather partial to grapes. I like the way their juices burst over my tongue." His eyes lingered on Georgette as he said it. For some reason she could not name, her cheeks grew hot.

"Pray tell, what has got you into such a fine mood?" Georgette asked as Captain Stone collected a now-full sheepskin flask. He secured it over his shoulder and took her hand with a broad grin.

"I have secured us a method of transportation," he declared as they walked outside. Georgette squinted and raised a hand to shield her eyes from the blazing sunshine outside. That was when she saw the tall, golden-haired animal chewing lazily on some straw.

Her eyes widened at the sight of its massive hooves and the two floppy humps on its back.

"What is it?" she asked as Captain Stone loaded the bags on the beast.

He looked at her with surprise and pointed at it. "This? You do not know what a camel is?" He laughed. "There is so much for you to learn."

Then he picked her up, lifting her until his head was pressed against her crotch. She squirmed in his arms, the heat of his breath lighting up the inner fire again. "Put your foot in the stirrup. Go on," Captain Stone's muffled voice directed her. She did as she was told and after a few moments of awkward attempts, she was on the saddle. The camel made a guttural noise and stepped forward, but Captain Stone shushed it and climbed on with ease. He settled in front of Georgette and took her hands, placing them on his stomach. "Hold on tight," he muttered, then he instructed the camel to start moving.

With every step, the saddle swayed, and Georgette wobbled, giving her no choice but to slide right up to Captain Stone's body, her breasts pressed against his back while she held him in a death grip.

Captain Stone started humming to himself and vibrations flooded her body.

"You're too tense, my lady," he said, patting her hands. "We have a long journey ahead, and I do not want your muscles to be sore before we get to the next port."

Georgette tried and failed to soften her grip as she wobbled with the camel's movements. "If I may," she shouted over his shoulder, already breathless. "But if I were to sit at the front and hold on to the reins…"

Captain Stone's chortle made her stop. "It is better this way; you do not want me poking you in the back."

Georgette frowned, not understanding his meaning. But she did not argue. She tried to change the subject instead, so she could ignore the fact that she was riding a camel.

"You mentioned a port. Is that where we are headed?"

Captain Stone hummed. "Indeed. We are going to see an old friend."

"And then?" Georgette asked.

Captain Stone caressed her arm. "My friend has a ship and a crew. Sailors, you'd be glad to know." He fell silent for a few minutes, as though he had fallen into deep thought. Finally, he cleared his throat. "And then we reclaim what is mine."

"The treasure?" Georgette asked. "You want to go back to Imerta? We almost died."

"You didn't. You had the immortality ring, remember?" Captain Stone pointed out. Georgette tightened her grip around his waist.

"But if you die, I die," she said, voicing her worries. Without his protection, she was not going to last very long.

Captain Stone twisted to give her a look she couldn't read. It was a mixture of fury and amusement.

"Well," he said, turning to face the front again. "I do believe that is the nicest thing anyone has ever said to me."

22

PRINCE EDWARD

P rince Edward ached with the agony of how close Georgette had been. Once again, he had lost her. He was so close to taking her home. So close to having her back in his arms.

Her scent lingered on him, and he touched his lips at the memory of their kiss. He had not planned it, but the relief of seeing her again had overwhelmed him.

He felt her stiffen, and he wanted to reprimand himself for forgetting his manners, but he could not bring himself to regret his actions.

He was happy to see her alive and unbroken. Whatever had happened, it was not so terrible that she lost the sparkle in her eye.

What he did not understand was her insistence on

leaving with Captain Stone. It crushed his heart to see her go.

He could not fathom what lies the pirate must have told Georgette for her to stand up for him. But he knew one thing: he would get her back.

He looked at the lines of wounded officers bandaged and moaning as they lay in their bunks. He walked to the end of the cabin to speak to the doctor who was cleaning a particularly nasty wound on an officer's knee.

"What is the situation?" Prince Edward murmured to the doctor.

The old man wiped the sweat from his clammy brow with a heavy sigh. "Fourteen injured. Three dead. The main concern is infection."

Prince Edward nodded and made his excuses to leave. He headed for the captain's quarters and surveyed the maps on his desk.

A buildup of frustration exploded suddenly, and he slammed his fist on the desk. Two of his men walked in then, seeking instruction.

Without looking up at them, the Prince rested both palms on the desk and breathed deeply. "Do we have any carrier pigeons left?" he asked.

"One more, Your Highness," one replied.

Prince Edward opened one of the drawers of his desk

and pulled out a piece of parchment. Then he took his pen and scrawled a note.

"Send this at once," he said, sealing the letter with wax and pressing his ring to make an outline of the crown.

He handed one of the men the letter. Both officers wore inquiring expressions.

"I believe Captain Stone is going to visit an old, mutual friend. This man is only loyal to money, so if we get to him first, this could play out in our favor."

The officers shifted their weight and looked uneasy. "Forgive me, Your Highness, but what makes you think the pirate would go to such a disloyal man?"

Prince Edward scoffed. "Captain Stone's list of allies is growing smaller by the day. He has no ship, no crew. He's desperate."

The officers glanced at each other, awkward, then one of them struck up the courage to ask the question that seemed to be on their minds.

"But you made a deal with the pirate. You will surely not go back on it?"

Prince Edward walked around his desk and squared up to his officers. They stiffened under his stare and the blood drained from the officer who dared to question Prince Edward's plan.

"If you think I am going to stand idly by while that

blood-thirsty pirate has his filthy hands on my betrothed, you are a fool. Now, any more questions? Or are you going to get back to work?" he asked. He did his best to keep his voice level, but his hands shook with anger.

The officers nodded and marched out of the cabin.

Now alone again, a single tear rolled down Prince Edward's cheek. He shut his eyes and thought of Georgette, praying it would not be long before he could have her in his arms again.

23

CAPTAIN STONE

Georgette's body grew limp and heavy against Captain Stone's back. They spent the day riding the camel's back. The journey was slow and the scenery vastly empty—nothing but rolling sand dunes and tufts of brown weeds for miles. But Captain Stone was happy to be out of the hustle and bustle. Now alone with his thoughts and a sleeping woman pressed up against him, he thought it was all not so bad. Though as minutes of solitude turned to hours, his mind began to take him to dark places. Mr. Collins was dead—one of the last men on Earth Captain Stone could trust. With his list of allies growing small, he knew it would only be a matter of time before his demons would catch up to him.

He held Georgette's thin arms tight with one hand at

his stomach and kept a firm grip on the reins with the other hand. The zing of her skin against his sent a rush of calm, soothing his worries while the camel walked on lazily. He knew it may have been quicker to ride a horse, but camels were considerably easier to purchase in Egypt.

Besides, a camel was much better suited to long journeys, able to stroll along the desert plains all day and night, if needed. They also required far less water.

Speed aside, the only downside to riding a camel was the smell. Captain Stone tried to breathe through his mouth and ignore the putrid stench.

The sky grew orange with a magenta tinge to it as they reached the port. A rush of salty sea air washed over them, and Captain Stone inhaled deeply. He did not like to be far from the sea. The fresh air cleansed his troubles, lifting him out of despair and promising him the only thing that mattered to him: freedom.

A short black man paced back and forth as they approached. His tan colored pants and shirt made him camouflage in the scenery. He looked up and waved a gray handkerchief as though to flag them down. Georgette stirred as the camel halted and she moaned into Captain Stone's back. He squeezed her arms reassuringly, then nodded to the man who had now joined them.

"Good to see you again, Mr. Dixon."

On closer inspection, the man's brow was shiny with a

film of sweat and his thick brows knit together as he watched Captain Stone and Georgette get down from the camel.

"I got your message. You can't stay here. If what you say is true, then you're not safe here." His dark eyes flittered to Georgette, who stared back with a puzzled look.

Captain Stone set his jaw and inhaled as the salty sea breeze washed over him. Then he clapped a hand on Mr. Dixon's thick shoulder. "Worry not, my friend. We have no intention of staying long. Is the ship ready?"

The tension in Mr. Dixon's shoulder eased a little as he gave a curt nod. "They're stocking the rest of the supplies as we speak. Come with me."

Mr. Dixon led Captain Stone and Georgette to the docks and took long strides through the throng of people milling around. Captain Stone had to pick up a run to keep up with the man, who was surprisingly fast for someone so short. Georgette hurried alongside and kept quiet, but to his surprise, her hand curled around his bicep and she clung onto him.

Captain Stone's mouth curved upward for a moment, but he forced a serious expression when their eyes met. Finally, Mr. Dixon turned and headed for a small alley between two wooden buildings.

The sun was weak now, casting long shadows across the sandy floor. A sudden sense of foreboding rushed down Captain Stone's spine as he followed Mr. Dixon up a flight of creaky wooden steps and into a small dwelling above a tavern.

Once inside the dark room, which comprised of only a bed, a moth-eaten couch and a tiny basin in the corner, Mr. Dixon bolted the door shut, blocking out the last of the sunlight.

He secured the shutters and lit an oil lamp while Georgette looked around the place, stilling holding onto Captain Stone's arm.

"For goodness sake, Dixon. What has gotten into you?" Captain Stone asked, dropping his bag to the floor. He peeled off his jacket, prompting Georgette to let him go. Mr. Dixon's soured face glowed in the flickering lamp light. "How could you be so foolish, Stone? Bringing *her* with you? Have you no idea the hell you've brought on me?"

Georgette hugged herself as she shivered. Without hesitation, Captain Stone pulled her close until her hips bumped his, and wrapped an arm around her waist. "What are you talking about?" he asked Mr. Dixon, who had set the lamp down and picked up a bottle. He unstopped it with a popping sound.

With a gruff sigh, he dragged a hand over his bald head. "Georgette Harrington. She's betrothed to the

Prince of England, is she not? Everyone is talking about it. The whole bleeding Royal Navy is after you."

Captain Stone and Georgette exchanged looks. News certainly traveled fast, although he supposed it had been almost two weeks since he took Georgette from the royal ball. Sailors talked. They would have noticed the ships scouring the seas for their lost princess to-be.

But that was not Mr. Dixon's main concern. Captain Stone could see it in his eyes. The man chewed his tongue and looked from left to right, his face scrunched up into a tight scowl. "You and I both know you're not worried about the Royal Navy, Dixon. What is really troubling you? Spit it out."

Mr. Dixon took a long swig from the bottle and wiped his mouth. Then he jumped as though hit by a sudden thought. "You must be exhausted from your journey. Here," he handed Captain Stone the half-full bottle, then he headed for the door. "I will return with food."

Before Captain Stone could stop him, the man had left. The door slammed shut behind him.

Georgette exhaled deeply, as though she had been holding her breath since they arrived.

"There's something about that man…" she whispered, her eyes flashing. "I know you say he's an old friend, but—"

"No, I feel it too. He's not acting himself," Captain

Stone said, frowning back. Georgette headed for the couch and he let go of her. She collapsed into it. A puff of dust flew into the air, and the musty smell made her cough. Meanwhile, Captain Stone held the bottle and sniffed.

"What are you doing?" Georgette asked, watching him.

Captain Stone set the bottle down and picked up the sheepskin flask from his bag instead. "Something is wrong. I suggest we do not consume anything he offers us."

Georgette tilted her head to the side as she loosened her braid and ran her fingers through her wavy hair. "You think he'd poison us? Why would he do that when he's your friend?"

Captain Stone drank the stale water from the flask and handed it to Georgette. "I'll bet there's a pretty penny to be had from delivering us to the Royal Navy," he muttered, joining her on the couch with a sigh.

He slumped forward and rested his elbows on his knees. Georgette took several long gulps of water.

When she lowered the flask to the floor, Captain Stone sighed again. "I'll be glad when we're back on open sea."

Georgette hummed as though to disagree. "You think the Navy isn't going to search every ship and vessel they come across? What makes you so sure we'll be in less danger out there?"

Captain Stone turned to give her a smirk. "Who said anything about it being less dangerous?"

His eyes lowered to the swell of her breasts, dewy in the lamplight. She exuded a sweet scent, and her tangled hair rested over her shoulders in messy waves. Captain Stone resisted the urge to rake his fingers through it. Then he looked up to meet Georgette's pretty eyes once more.

Even with dark rings under her eyes, she remained the prettiest woman he had ever laid eyes on.

Her pouty lips drew his attention, and he had suddenly forgotten all about Mr. Dixon and the Royal Navy.

Right now, he was alone with Georgette, his wife. A different appetite drew him to lick his lips.

Georgette must have noticed and read his thoughts because her mouth fell open with a small gasp of affront. "How can you look at me like that... When we could be in terrible danger?"

Captain Stone wanted to laugh at how little she knew about the workings of a man. He took a lock of her hair and rubbed his thumb over it with a smile. "I must confess, your innocence is quite becoming."

Georgette frowned. "I am not innocent," she snapped

out the word as though it were an expletive. Then she placed her hands on his chest and lightly dug in her nails. Captain Stone shut his eyes as his blood traveled south at her touch. He groaned and opened his eyes to see Georgette trying to read him. Did she understand the torture she was putting him through?

Could she see how much he wanted to rip her shirt off and lick every inch of her exposed skin?

He broke into a sweat at the thought and tugged on the drawstrings of his shirt, hoping for some air on his clammy chest.

The cracks of the window offered very little relief.

Georgette's fingertips grazed his skin when he tugged his shirt down and she yelped, drawing back as if she had been struck by lightning.

Captain Stone grit his teeth, trying to ignore the tension in his pants. He throbbed for her.

"Don't do that," he said, almost pleading. He picked up her hands.

"Do what?" she whispered.

Captain Stone placed her hands on his bare chest again and sighed as a flood of delightful tingles flooded him once more. Then he caressed her cheek and looked into her eyes. "Don't look at me like I'm your enemy," he said. "I can live with the whole world thinking I'm a monster. But not you."

Georgette nipped her bottom lip and lowered her eyes to his mouth for a long moment. Her sweet smell grew stronger and the tension between the two of them was almost tangible. It encircled them and flooded the room.

He wanted her. More than all the treasure in the world.

For the first time, he could see in Georgette's eyes that she was thinking it, too. Her eyes found the unmistakable bulge in his pants and her chest heaved.

She dug her nails into his chest again, like a cat bedding down.

Finally, her gaze met his, and Captain Stone moved his hand from her cheek to grip the back of her neck. She squeaked, but he did not see fear in her eyes. He found something wild in there instead.

He wasn't sure if it was the fact that they both wanted to escape their situation or break the rising tension, but something had Georgette moving to his mouth like a moth to a flame.

He waited for her, determined to make sure he wasn't going to do anything she didn't ask for or—judging by the way she gripped his shoulders and yanked him forward—*demand.*

"How long do you think Mr. Dixon will be?" she whispered against his mouth as they hovered barely a hair's width apart. Her hot breath tickled his lips. When he smiled, his mouth grazed hers.

"Does it matter?"

The answer was, apparently, no. Georgette closed the space, climbed into his lap, pressed her body up to his, and kissed him.

Captain Stone groaned in sweet agony as she moved in his arms. Rushes of heat and pleasure scoured through his entire soul. Her mouth was wet, salty. She tasted like the sea. When Captain Stone began to explore her with his tongue, a purring sound escaped her.

Kissing a woman was the perfect antidote to stress. Captain Stone's mind emptied of all thought, and his body moved on pure instinct.

He dragged his hands through Georgette's hair while her hips rolled over his, massaging him in the most satisfying way.

The tension mounted as all of Captain Stone's senses magnified. Now he knew what her mouth tasted like—and that it was tantalizing—he longed to taste all the other parts of her with his mouth. He began to kiss along her jawline. She threw her head back. Then he traced a line of rough kisses down her neck to her collarbone. Georgette began to tremble in his arms, and when Captain Stone tugged on the strings of her shirt, she raked her hands through his messy hair and rocked in his lap with a long moan.

He took it all back. This woman was not innocent after all. Georgette knew what she wanted, and she was going for it without hesitation. She was wild. Feral. He *loved* it.

She must have forgotten their surroundings and the fact that Mr. Dixon would walk in at any moment, because she clawed at his shirt, picking it up at the hem and yanked it over his head.

They broke apart, panting for a moment. Captain Stone searched her face for any sign that she didn't want this to happen.

He dipped his head to give her a grin as his hand slid under her shirt briefly, but then he pulled back. Georgette sucked in a breath with a hiss.

"No. Don't stop," she said, her voice dripping with need.

Captain Stone's grin widened. "Are you begging me?" he asked.

A flash of annoyance crossed Georgette's face. It was the worst thing he could have said, because whatever spell had been cast was suddenly broken. She scrambled away from him, panting.

"What are we doing?" she whispered, her eyes darting to the door. "This isn't real, I'm still dreaming."

She dragged two hands over her face as Captain Stone moved closer. He reached round to her pert bottom and gave it a hard pinch, to which she promptly yelped.

"That hurt me! Why did you do that?"

Captain Stone chuckled. "You are not dreaming, my dear. But there are more pleasurable places that I can pinch, if you would allow me…"

He lifted a suggestive brow, but Georgette was already tying the strings on her shirt and smoothing out her clothes.

"We cannot do this."

Captain Stone's smile fell as her words landed like rocks in the pit of his stomach. "I respectfully disagree," he said, biting against the pain of his arousal in his pants.

When she continued to make herself more presentable, he frowned, deflated. "You don't want this, do you?"

Georgette scowled at him. "Of course I don't. This… This whole situation is nothing but a fantasy."

"Fantasy? That means you liked it," Captain Stone said, his spirits lifting. Georgette's face broke into a slight smile for a moment before she shook her head with a deep-set frown. "We can't. Not here. Not like this."

Before Captain Stone could argue, a sound startled them both. The creaky steps alerted the arrival of several people.

"What are the chances that is Mr. Dixon and a couple more of your old friends?" Georgette whispered, her brows lifting.

Captain Stone's heart sank. He threw on his shirt, tiptoed to the door, and bolted it. Then he peered through the spyhole.

In the darkness, he could only make out shadowy figures, but he strained his ears and made out whispers.

"Do what you want with the lady, but don't kill *him*. We want him alive."

Captain Stone swore silently and grit his teeth. Then he picked up his bag and looked at Georgette. "We need to leave. Now," he whispered.

Georgette shrugged. "How? You've just locked our only way out."

Captain Stone tiptoed to one of the shutters and yanked it open. The rush of ocean air filled his lungs to the max, and he sighed with relief. He climbed out and stood on a narrow ledge, then he helped Georgette out and they closed the shutters silently.

"Do not look down and you will be fine," Captain Stone muttered as they edged along the narrow ledge.

"I am afraid it is too late for that," Georgette mumbled back. She proved nimble on her feet, however, and followed Captain Stone as he climbed up onto the roof.

A throng of people surrounded the building. Luckily, no one appeared to be looking up. But they needed to move fast. Once they broke into the room, the place would be crawling with men.

They scrambled over the rooftop to the other side and climbed to the ground like two alley cats.

"Come on," Captain Stone whispered, as they made their way through the dark to the silhouettes bobbing at the docks.

Knowing that Mr. Dixon had sold them out, Captain Stone chose the closest ship and snuck onto it.

The ship was vast and full of English-speaking sailors.

At best guess, he thought they were sea merchants headed for England.

It was not the best course to be on, but Captain Stone thought the alternative was much worse.

He took Georgette's hand and the two of them hurried breathlessly, cloaked in the night, to hide among large crates of fish.

As soon as they settled, Captain Stone's heartbeat calmed, and he glanced at Georgette, who was gulping for air. "And you wanted to…" she whispered. Captain Stone lifted a brow.

"And you didn't?"

Georgette shut her mouth and frowned. Then she

shook her head like she was clearing her mind. "Never mind that. Your friend just sold us out, and now we're stowaways on some god forsaken ship going to who knows where. We need a plan."

Captain Stone smiled. He had a liking for this feisty side of Georgette. "You're right," he murmured. He peered over a crate, watching the line of sailors filling the ship. "They are about to set sail. We'll wait until we're on open water, then commandeer a small boat and sail to Imerta."

"You still want to go there? With no ship, nor crew?" Georgette asked, her voice raspy.

Captain Stone squeezed her hand. "I've got all I need right here."

Georgette frowned at him. "Why do you want that treasure so badly? What do you think it will get you?"

Captain Stone looked at her with a thoughtful smile. Her eyes shone like two jewels in the moonlight. He could still taste her on his tongue. He swept a strand of hair from her face and grazed her bottom lip with his thumb. "Freedom, my lady. Freedom."

24

GEORGETTE

G eorgette and Captain Stone hid from the merchants as the ship set sail. They remained undisturbed for many hours. Captain Stone held Georgette close as they huddled in the shadows among the crates, and she melted into his arms, burying her face in his chest. The steady *thump-thump* of his heart-beat against her ear while the ship swayed soothed her. She shut her eyes, listening to the muted voices of the sailors going about their work and—for a time—forgot all about their situation.

Captain Stone's scent enveloped her. Behind her shut eyes, memories flashed across her mind. The taste of his mouth and the graze of his stubble on her neck. The way he had squeezed on her curves. She swallowed and squirmed in his arms, grinning into his shirt.

Had they been somewhere more private, she would have let things go further. He was her husband, after all.

He had also been her savior on countless other occasions. She found herself developing all sorts of confusing feelings toward him the more time they spent together.

She frowned while she thought about it. The man was a ruthless killer. A pirate. As if that wasn't enough, he possessed a magic ring that gave him immortality.

He made a formidable enemy. Submitting to him and staying on his good side was crucial to survival.

Georgette tried to reason that her feelings were purely biological. Right now, he was the alpha male in her life. And he'd forced her into marriage. She belonged to him.

Of course, the roughness of his touch and the way he looked at her had her stomach doing flips. She never considered herself to be the kind of woman who would enjoy being told what to do, but from the very first moment they met, when he growled "good girl" in her ear, she was weak for him.

Sometimes, the thought angered her. She was not weak. Nor was she submissive.

If they had sex, he would have claimed her and all the power she had over him would have been lost.

She gritted her teeth, vowing to stay strong. She

would not beg for him, even if every part of her soul wanted him. She would resist. She had to.

That did not mean she could not secretly enjoy laying in his arms, however... Or craning her neck to catch a glimpse of his sleeping face. His breaths came out in slow, hot puffs that tickled her cheeks as she stared at him.

The man had barely slept. She could tell by the dark rings under his eyes. Now asleep, his face relaxed, leaving faint lines around his eyes and cheeks. Something stirred inside her as she stared. The soft moonlight illuminated his face, and she memorized every chiseled part of it.

He was defenseless as he slept, but his hands rested heavily on her waist. Georgette walked her fingers down his bare arm, grazing the bulging veins and landing on his broad hand. She glanced at his face as she picked it up, but he did not stir. His breaths continued to come out long and slow.

She wondered how the man could sleep so peacefully while they were surrounded by strangers. Then she remembered he loved the sea as much as he loved treasure. Perhaps he was being lulled by the gentle rocking of the ship. It could also be the calming cleanse of the salty sea air, flooding their lungs with the purest fuel.

She entwined her fingers with his and slowly moved his hand up over her body to rest on her heart. She sighed and rested her head on his chest again, looking at the stone ring two inches from her eyes. The center of the stone swirled with different colors in the moonlight. Only now, up close, could she see its ethereal beauty. To anyone looking at it from afar, it seemed to be nothing more than a rock. Under the moonlight, it was obvious the ring was magical.

She wondered how it worked. How could something so small offer immortality? She could still hear the steady *thump-thump* of Captain Stone's heartbeat as she snuggled into his chest and let a wave of sleepiness quiet her curious mind.

Rest would not be so easy, however.

Just as she fell into a slumber, the fearsome thunder of a fired cannon roared through the night. A ground-shaking collision followed, then several outcries of fury.

Captain Stone woke in an instant and clutched Georgette tight as he whipped round, trying to see the attackers. He swore.

"Pirates," he spat.

Georgette felt cold fingers climb up her spine.

More cannon fire, ceaseless now, flooded the air with smoke and screams. Before long, the ship groaned. A crew member screamed that it had begun to take on water, and as if to confirm the report, the ship began to dip sideways into the sea.

Captain Stone stood and lifted Georgette with him, then marched forward, ducking and forcing her down just as a cannonball whizzed by. "Stay close, don't engage, and you will be safe."

Georgette kept a sharp eye on him and soon felt assured that he knew what he was doing as she followed him around the edge of the ship. He had fixed his gaze on the dark ship anchored next to them as he marched forward. A scrawny young man, barely out of teenage years, landed on the ship brandishing a rusty blade. Before he could so much as raise it in the air, Captain Stone stuck his own knife deep into the boy's chest. Georgette saw the lights disappear from the young pirate's eyes as he slumped forward and fell dead on a crate. Georgette stared and Captain Stone yanked on her arm. "We need to keep moving," he said.

Terrible sounds flooded the air, and Georgette's ears rang. Bones crunched. Flesh ripped. Grown men screamed in agony. The most terrible sound of all was the cannon fire ripping through the ship and tearing it to pieces.

Captain Stone helped Georgette down the side of the ship to a dingy. He cursed the gods when they settled in and found that it was damaged. Another pirate swung overhead from a rope and landed on the damaged boat, looking at Georgette like a cat eyeing a rodent. Without thinking, she thrust her knife into his shin. The metal went in with a sickening crunch. The pirate howled for a moment, then Captain Stone slit his throat and kicked him overboard.

The pirate howled like a wounded wolf all the way down until he was silenced by a splash.

"I daresay you are getting the hang of this," Captain Stone said to Georgette, the corners of his mouth turned up in amusement.

She frowned back at him. She did *not* want to get the hang of injuring and killing. Even if they were pirates.

There was no time to argue. The ship lurched violently, knocking them both off the damaged boat. They fell like two rocks to the water.

Georgette shut her eyes as she fell, anticipating the depths and the freezing cold. But she felt Captain Stone grab her roughly by the forearm, and she looked down to see the tips of her boots just grazing the surface of the water. Captain Stone was above her, clutching her forearm in a grip like a vise. "Hold on to me!" he barked. His other hand held on to a thick rope.

Georgette grabbed his waist and clung to him as tight as she could, trying to ignore the fact that her face was now buried in his crotch.

Captain Stone swung them forward once, twice, and then they were swinging onto the lower deck of the pirate ship. Georgette let go of the Captain's hand, tumbled, and coughed, struggling to recall what it meant to breathe.

"Stay here. Stay hidden," Captain Stone muttered. He stepped over her and charged forward.

Still gasping, winded by their landing, Georgette gripped the handle of her knife. Her life certainly depended on it.

She shuffled into a shadow and huddled there, listening to the shouting above. Then she watched the merchant's ship beside them give one final groan before it sank into the sea. Cheers followed briefly before a succession of screams splintered the victory. Georgette's heart raced, and she strained to hear any approaching footsteps.

When they came from her left, she kicked over a barrel, sending the approaching attacker off the edge of the ship and into the water.

Another pirate rushed forward, but Georgette was ready for him. She drove her knife into his middle and yanked it out again, drenching her fist with hot blood. She did not see the pirate's face before she sent him after his comrade over the edge of the boat.

Her stomach lurched at the sound of his cries of anguish, but the moment passed as soon when she heard more footsteps.

Georgette moved on instinct. She had come too far to be killed in the shadows by some pirates. Her will to survive was too strong.

A roar echoed in her ears and she looked up, listening out for Captain Stone. She could not quite make out what he was saying, but she knew he was barking orders.

Suddenly, a hot piercing pain spread over her left thigh. In a flash, she swung and stabbed the pirate that had snuck up on her. Her blade landed on his neck. The man gargled on his own blood, choking as he slumped forward, his heavy body forcing Georgette to fall.

She landed on her back and the pirate's blood began to spread out over her. She gasped for air, scrambling to get him off, but the pain in her thigh only intensified with her movements and before long, the sounds of the chaos around her grew faint. Her body grew limp, and all went dark.

25

CAPTAIN STONE

"Your enemies are growing, Manny," the man sneered at Captain Stone. "The pirate lords have placed a bounty on your head. Mark my words, there's nowhere for you to run now."

Captain Stone withdrew his sword from the belly of his final attacker and watched grimly as the man sank to his knees and fell face first on the deck.

Crimson blood soaked the wooden planks and flowed under Captain Stone's leather boots.

Something flickered in the corner of his eye and he turned sharply to see a young man trying to sneak off the ship.

He charged forward and held out his sword to stop him. The pirate was visibly shaken. When he turned, the moonlight exposed his ashen gray face.

He was just a boy. Captain Stone set his jaw. What kind of soulless captain recruited young boys?

"You. Give me your name," Captain Stone growled.

"S-S-Smith, sir."

Captain Stone lifted a brow, unimpressed by the boy's lack of originality. If he was to lie about his name, he could have at least come up with something more convincing.

He pressed the blood-stained blade to the boy's chest, and the lad raised his skinny palms in the air.

"Please. Don't kill me. I don't mean no trouble, sir," he begged, his knees knocking.

Captain Stone leaned forward to give the boy a hard look. "I'm not going to kill you, but you will do something for me."

The boy nodded; greasy blond hair flopping like a mop on his head. "Yes, sir. Anything, sir."

Captain Stone withdrew his blade and gestured to the bodies littered on the deck. An eerie silence blanketed the scene and Captain Stone could see the whites of the boy's eyes as he surveyed the dead men.

He dug into his pocket and tossed the boy his compass. "You're going to take a boat and head to the nearest port. Then you're going to find the pirate lords and pass on the message I will give you now."

The boy held the compass like it was a stick of dynamite. He stood wide-eyed, trembling. Captain Stone stepped closer. "You tell them what happened here. Tell them that I, Captain Stone, will bring hell and brimstone down on any pirate who wishes to do me harm."

He planted a hand on the boy's thin shoulder. "You will pass on this message for me, will you not?"

"Yes, sir. I promise." The boy nodded. As he made to leave, Captain Stone tightened his grip on his shoulder. "And Mr. Smith… If our paths cross again, I shall not be so merciful. Remember that."

After the boy left, Captain Stone strode across the ship, smiling darkly to himself. Though the dying pirate's warning rang in his ears like the bells of Notre Dame, he was satisfied to be home.

He dragged his hand along the smooth railing, looking at the worn steps leading to the upper deck. Huge gray sails billowed above his head.

The fates had brought him back to his ship—a sign that perhaps, they smiled on his mission. He wiped his blade on his pant leg and sheathed it.

Then he leaned over the side of the ship and called out to the small boat full of sailors. They turned their oars frantically, trying to row away. Captain Stone watched them for a few minutes.

"I am looking for a crew," he bellowed suddenly. One of the men on board the small boat nearly dropped his oar. Captain Stone chuckled to himself. "I can hardly sail this ship on my own," he continued. He spread his arm wide. "What say you?"

The sailors paused their escape and exchanged wary looks. Then they put their heads together and began to mutter to each other. Captain Stone drummed his fingers on the ship patiently. They pulled apart again, and must have decided that their chances of survival were better if they boarded the ship, because they turned the boat around and headed for him.

When they climbed into the ship, Captain Stone barked his orders and the men set to work immediately.

Sailing to Imerta was now a highly pressing matter.

But the thought of Georgette flashed through his mind and he jolted.

He rushed to the lower deck and returned to the place he had left her, only to find a dead man.

Heart racing, Captain Stone shouted Georgette's name as he whipped around, looking from left to right. A faint mumble landed on his ears like a thunderclap. He looked at the dead man again and saw him shift slightly.

Captain Stone knelt and wrenched the man away, revealing a white-faced Georgette, her eyes closed.

"Georgette," Captain Stone breathed. He started to

lift her, but she yelped, reaching for the rusty handle sticking out of her thigh. A pool of blood had drenched her pant leg. Captain Stone's chest throbbed in agony as he silently cursed all the gods.

His beloved Georgette was hurt.

26

PRINCE EDWARD

The air grew heavy as the ship sailed through eerily still waters. The hairs at the back of Prince Edward's neck stood on end. He could sense death all around him.

Sure enough, as they broke through a cloud of fog, a watery graveyard presented itself.

Scores of lifeless bodies floated face down amongst a wreckage.

The Naval officers muttered quietly to each other as they sailed through the destruction. Many removed their hats in respect.

Prince Edward gripped the edge of the ship and gritted his teeth as he surveyed the damage.

No sign of blood anywhere. Prince Edward had no doubts about what could cause such a scene.

As though on cue, a flash of red caught his eye. He marched to the starboard side to get a closer look.

Serena shot out of the water and landed on the deck of the ship.

She slithered upright, and her long fin flicked playfully like a cat's tail as she smiled at Prince Edward.

"Have you found her yet?" she sang, stroking her fingers through her locks. The Naval officers around them stumbled backwards. Their muttering grew louder. A few men groaned in terror. None made a move as Prince Edward edged closer to Serena. She flicked back her hair cheekily, thrusting soft, pert breasts forward.

Prince Edward resisted the urge to remove his jacket and cover her up. Several gasps from his men put him on edge, but Serena grinned. She seemed greatly amused to see so many men squirming at her nakedness.

Prince Edward had never seen a woman so confident and free. All of his life's training told him to avert his eyes as a flush of heat rose to his face. But her question rang in his mind, and dread was building in the pit of his stomach.

She was beautiful. Unbelievably so. He hated himself for even looking at another female when his darling Georgette was still in terrible danger but what man could help admiring a creature like this?

He shook his head and looked down at the wooden planks of the ship.

Serena hummed softly.

"Wait here," she said. Prince Edward looked up at the sound of the splash and saw that Serena had disappeared.

She was gone for fifteen minutes before ripples of water announced her return.

"She's with a pirate named Captain Stone, correct?" Serena called up to him. Prince Edward leaned over the edge of the ship, his heartbeat picking up speed. "How do you know—" he began, but stopped when Serena chuckled.

"I can hear you from across the ocean. Pining for your Georgette and cursing her captor, Captain Mannington Stone," she teased. Prince Edward bristled, but ignored the rush of humiliation. He knitted his brows and attempted to look serious despite his burning cheeks. "Have you found her?" he asked, unable to hide the hopeful tone in his voice.

Serena's smile widened. "I can give you the co-ordinates, if you wish."

Prince Edward's heart leaped, and he grinned back. "That will be incredible. Thank you, Serena."

After she passed on the co-ordinates, Prince Edward

frowned. "But why are you doing this?" he asked, wondering what heavy price he would have to pay the siren for such valuable information.

With another splash, Serena landed on the deck again, her heaving chest now mere inches from Prince Edward's. He swallowed hard and kept his gaze on her eyes. Upon closer inspection, they were like two hazelnuts with flecks of yellow.

"I, too, long to be loved," she purred, stroking his face again.

Prince Edward kept his hands very still, aware of how close he was to the mystical being. He got the impression that she was playing with him, like a cat might play with its prey before devouring it whole.

"I am indebted to you, Serena. Thank you," he murmured. She cocked her head to the side and clasped her hands with a giggle.

"If you need me, handsome one, just whisper my name," Serena said, looking at the Prince's mouth. "I will be listening."

Prince Edward swallowed again, then watched as Serena flipped backward and dove back into the water. Her musical laugh echoed in his mind.

After a shocked moment, he shook himself and directed his men to set a course.

Emboldened, he picked up his spyglass and looked out at the horizon. Georgette was within his reach. Even though he knew it was unlikely she would come with him without a strong reason, he had a plan to get Captain Stone on his side and reclaim Georgette all at the same time.

27

GEORGETTE

G eorgette blinked in the darkness and frowned. She was on a narrow, lumpy bed that felt strangely familiar.

She wondered if the past few weeks were a dream. Perhaps she was home, waking on the morning of her engagement ball.

She pictured herself walking downstairs to meet the maids in the kitchen, telling them about her strange dream.

One of them would remark on Georgette's fantastic imagination. Georgette would agree.

Her governess would stride in and put a stop to the silly conversation, commenting sagely that Captain Stone was merely a result of eating cheese too close to bedtime. And the swashbuckling adventure, wherein she killed pirates, was just her mind facing her fears of marrying a prince and becoming a princess.

Georgette would not argue. It made so much more sense than the idea that a menacing crew of pirates stormed the palace during her engagement ball and captured her.

So much more sense than the idea of a lady being forced to marry a pirate captain—a cold and ruthless, but also fiercely protective and passionate man.

She stirred, and a dull ache spread over her thigh. Georgette frowned in the darkness and patted herself.

She was naked under a thin cotton sheet. Someone had wrapped the painful part of her leg in a bandage.

All the memories came rushing back in a flood. Georgette realized why her surroundings were familiar. Her eyes flew around the murky darkness of the room wildly. She could make out a desk, a small chest, a chair… She didn't know how it was possible, but she was back in the captain's quarters on Captain Stone's ship.

Her fingers brushed with something hard and warm, and a gasp made her jump.

There was a rustle of movement, then a flash of light. Georgette squinted, blinking as her eyes adjusted, then she saw two blue eyes shining in her direction.

"You're awake," Captain Stone said.

There was a surprising softness to his voice. Georgette smiled.

"I'm naked," she replied without thinking. A rush of heat flooded her cheeks as soon as the words came out, but Captain Stone did not smile.

He had concern etched deeply on his face. The line between his brows seemed to be permanent now.

"You lost a lot of blood. I should never have left you."

Georgette lay still and let Captain Stone hold her hands as he knelt by the bed. Then she noticed the stone ring glinting on her wedding finger. She did not remember Captain Stone putting it on her. "What happened?" She looked to the Captain's bright eyes for an explanation.

"I returned for you," he said, his shoulders sagging as though they bore the weight of the world. "And when I did, you had hardly any life left in you. I thought I was too late."

Georgette followed his line of sight; he was looking at the ring. Then she remembered what she had seen it do to him. "After the attack at Imerta, you were hurt. But when I put the ring on you, you healed. Instantly." Captain Stone met her inquiring stare and allowed a tiny smile to cross his lips. "I had hoped it would do the same for you. Unfortunately, your healing has not been so instantaneous."

Georgette withdrew her hands from his grasp and held the sheet as she tried to sit up, but her thigh throbbed and she winced.

Captain Stone shushed her and stroked her hair. "You must rest. Your body needs more time."

Georgette dragged a hand through her hair. It was soft and silky, like it had been carefully brushed while she slept. She eyed Captain Stone's wiry locks; she hadn't supposed he even owned a comb.

"None of this makes any sense. I thought…"

Captain Stone's caressed her cheek, and she fell silent. "Worry not, my lady. All is well."

But Georgette could not stop the barrage of questions filling her head.

"How long have I been sleeping? Where are my clothes? Did you brush my hair? Where are we going now?"

Captain Stone rose to a stand with a chuckle and walked to the other side of the cabin. The floorboards creaked under his boots. For the first time, Georgette noticed the room was swaying from side to side. She held the sheet to her body as she wriggled back and forced herself to sit up. When Captain Stone returned, he placed a pile of neatly folded clothes beside her.

"I was concerned about the risk of infection, so I took it upon myself to keep you meticulously clean."

Georgette swallowed as she took the bundle and held it to her chest. She recalled her finger and looked down at it. The one that had caught a splinter. Captain Stone had been meticulous about getting it out... With his mouth.

Her insides squirmed and chills swept over her at the thought of his mouth touching other parts of her. The Captain cleared his throat. "I assure you; I have been most respectful."

Georgette snorted before her brain could stop it. Then she blushed. The idea that Captain Stone was a gentleman was too amusing to resist a laugh. Captain Stone scowled.

"You may have forgotten, my lady, that I made a solemn vow to protect you... Even from me."

He turned his back and paced the quarters while Georgette yanked the soft cotton shirt over her head. She dressed quickly, wincing as her muscles throbbed against her movements.

She tucked her shirt in. "And to whom did you make this vow?"

Captain Stone turned around to face her. His blue eyes were considerably darker.

"Your father."

Georgette scoffed and began to braid her hair. "I do not believe you," she said, avoiding his eyes. There was no conceivable reason to. Her father and Captain Stone had never met. Not even at the ball.

Her breath hitched as she thought about the night of the engagement ball. She had not seen her father anywhere. She was not certain if he was even alive.

"I do not need you to believe me," Captain Stone said grimly as he picked up a jug of water. "I have more pressing concerns on my mind." He poured a drink and handed it to her. The water was stale and warm, but she appreciated it all the same.

It seemed that now he was not as concerned for her, another worry was taking center stage. "What is it?" she asked, clutching her glass.

Captain Stone poured himself a drink and knocked it back like a shot of whiskey. "The pirate lords have placed a bounty on my head."

Georgette gulped. "But you have the ring. You'll be fine."

She made to pull the stone ring off her finger, but Captain Stone placed a heavy hand over hers, stopping her. "No," he said, his voice firm. "Keep it on for now. At least, for one more day." Then he scratched the back of his neck with a sigh.

"If there is a bounty on my head, it means that you are in more danger than ever. You are my wife, after all."

Georgette's heart squeezed at the word wife despite the terrible news.

She was his wife. That was true.

And if Captain Stone's enemies wanted him dead, they would want her too. If not to kill her, then to claim her as their prize.

Her stomach lurched at the thought. "Why have they placed a bounty on your head? What did you do?" She pushed off the bed and came to a stand, trying to give him a hard look, but she wobbled on her feet. His rough hands found her waist and steadied her.

"Are you strong enough to walk?" he asked, lifting a brow.

Georgette was not sure, but she didn't want to look weak. She gritted her teeth with a nod. But she bent to pick up a boot and the room began to spin. She stumbled into Captain Stone. "I may need to hold onto you, if you do not mind," she confessed.

Captain Stone helped Georgette to the deck.

The crisp sea air whipped at her, and she inhaled its salty freshness. It felt good to be out of the stuffy captain's quarters.

She watched the crew going about their business. The air was subdued and quiet, and only a few glowing lamps offered light in the dark night.

The sky was black. There was not even one tiny star

to be seen. Georgette took in her surroundings and felt a chilling sense of foreboding course through her body. The hairs on her arms stood on end.

She gripped Captain Stone's arm for comfort as they walked. When they reached the edge of the ship, she gasped at the sight of the black sea—like an ocean of oil surrounding the ship.

Captain Stone bowed his head and rested his fore-arms on the rail.

"Long ago, when the privateers were out of work and started to sail under the name pirates, there was an agreement... To live under democracy." He looked out at the vast blackness. Georgette suspected he was replaying the events of the past in his mind's eye.

"The captain of each vessel was named a pirate lord. We agreed to work together in mutual understanding so that everyone would follow the code."

"The code?" Georgette asked.

Captain Stone nodded. "The code of the brethren. They are... A set of rules. Imagine the Ten Commandments, but for pirates."

Georgette failed to stifle a laugh at that. "Surely, one of those rules is not to put a bounty on a fellow pirate's head?"

Captain Stone hummed in thought. "It was agreed that our spoils and treasure would be stored in a single location. Secure. Far from the reaches of men. And that it would be shared out equally."

Georgette frowned as she thought back to the deserted cave. "So, the treasure that Isis stole from you…"

Captain Stone met her stare and gave her a nod, the white of his eyes shining in the lamplight. "She did not only take my crew's treasure. She took it all. The pirate lords hold me responsible."

"But why? You didn't tell Isis…"

"It was my idea to store all the treasure on that wretched island," Captain Stone spat, looking out at the sea again. "As long as that bounty is on my head, I fear that I cannot keep you safe."

Georgette looked down in thought. "I finally understand why you are so determined to go back to Imerta… Why you said getting that treasure would grant you freedom."

He positioned himself in front of her hips and pinned her against the railing. She looked at him. His breath fanned hot on her neck, and she closed her eyes as he growled into her ear.

"Make no mistake, my lady. I do not care for gold and material things. There is only one treasure I will die for, and I am looking at her right now."

Georgette's stomach flipped as he pulled back to give

her a hungry look. They were exposed at the helm of the ship, but the blanket of darkness gave her a sense of security. She held her breath, stiff against his hard body. The next thing she knew, her hands were on his chest.

"Captain…" she whispered. He gripped her hips and squeezed as he gave her a rough kiss. His short beard grazed her cheeks. Then his tongue found its way into her mouth and she melted against him.

Georgette's body lit up with a burning sense of need. Her back dug into the railing and the captain cupped her bottom as she wrapped her legs around his waist.

The ring must have completed its job, because her thigh no longer throbbed. A new ache had replaced the pain in her thigh. It grew in her midriff as she let the Captain explore her mouth with his tongue.

She rolled her hips and sent a flood of tingles through her core. When he left her mouth to kiss her neck, she threw her head back.

His hand grabbed her braid and he tugged on it. "Tell me what you want, my lady?" he growled in her ear.

Georgette shut her eyes and whispered her most secret thoughts.

"I want to forget about everything. I want every moment to feel this good." Captain Stone put her down and turned her around, bending her over the railing.

Georgette hitched a breath as his hands roamed the front of her body. She could hardly breathe as every atom buzzed. She grew lightheaded.

She could not understand why the Captain's rough touches were setting off such a chain reaction in her body. When he took her from the engagement ball, she could have never imagined a time that she'd allow him to touch her this way. Now she was grabbing his hands and guiding them under her shirt. The skin-to-skin touch scattered her thoughts, and a flood of good sensations took hold.

His calloused fingers brushed her skin in the most delightful way. He pinched her again, and this time it was like a lightning bolt shot through her. It hurt, but in a good way.

Then his other hand slid down her pants, caressing her inner thigh. She arched back and rested her head on his shoulder, giving herself completely to him.

In that moment, she was his. She would let him do whatever he wanted to her. Indeed, she *hoped* for it. Her breaths came out short and fast and her body jerked all on its own as Captain Stone worked on her body with his hands and mouth. He sucked on her neck and bit down until it stung, then he swept his tongue over the bite as though to make it better.

All the while, his hands moved expertly all over her.

He seemed to know exactly what to do to make her body react.

Just as the pleasure reached its peak, Captain Stone withdrew his hands from her body.

Georgette frowned at the abrupt conclusion to her euphoria.

She turned to look at him and protest, but noticed the sour look on his face as he stared at something in the distance.

"We have company," he muttered. Slowly, she followed his line of sight and squinted at the dark silhouette of another ship. The thick clouds parted then to reveal silver moonlight, and she saw the ship's sails clearly. She recognized them in an instant.

The Royal Navy.

28

CAPTAIN STONE

C ursing, Captain Stone ripped his hands from Georgette and climbed to the lower deck, barking orders to his new crew. The men jumped into action without complaint, but the hope on their faces was unmistakable. He knew they had no loyalty to him.

The sailors were not pirates, after all. To them, the Royal Navy's arrival was a miracle. He knew that as soon as the Navy boarded the ship, they would drop their weapons and abandon him.

He was not certain if Prince Edward was aboard that ship, or whether the Prince had made their deal known to the Navy. But he was quite sure there would be no leniency this time. Even if he somehow managed to escape with Georgette, one thing was certain; they were not going to Imerta.

The way he saw it, they had two options. The first was to order the men to the oars and try to outrun the British Royal Navy. A most foolhardy plan, to be sure.

The second option was to allow them take Georgette, his ship, and his crew. Let them lock him up in the cells below deck. Then he'd break out and escape on a dingy with Georgette as soon as they reached France.

Plan B was equally foolish, in his mind.

He gripped the hilt of his sword and set his jaw as he glanced up at Georgette's figure above his head. She still had the immortality ring, and the ship had reached them before he could get a chance to climb back up to her.

Authoritative shouts cut through the eerie silence and several ropes swung in the air, followed by Naval officers landing like cats on the deck.

Captain Stone's crew of sailors fell into a line and dropped their weapons like they were made of lava. Every one of them surrendered and muttered their praises for being saved.

Captain Stone stood in the shadow of the sails, glowering at his unwelcome guests. The whites of his knuckles were on show on the pommel of his sword.

The only silver lining to the situation was that the men had not yet seen Georgette standing at the helm.

Nor had the crew revealed his identity to the officers. It would likely only be a matter of time before they did.

Captain Stone tried to think quickly. There was no plausible way the Navy knew he had reunited with his ship. After all, before Captain Stone had taken it back, it was teeming with blood-thirsty pirates.

Just as he was starting to think he could simply get away with hiding in plain sight, another man landed less than two feet away from him.

A pair of ocean blue eyes bore into the depths of his soul.

He squared his shoulders as he held eye contact with the man. The stranger stepped closer, and the moonlight illuminated his face. Clean and well-kept as ever. Dark hair pulled back into a ponytail under his hat. Not a speck of hair on the bottom half of his face, and when he sneered, a set of straight pearly whites flashed through the grin.

Prince Edward had his knife pointed directly at Captain Stone's heart when Georgette's panicked shout made him look up.

Seizing the opportunity, Captain Stone kicked the Prince in the gut, prompting him to bend over with a grunt. The two men broke out into a sword fight.

Blades clanged and clashed as they swiped at each other. The two men seemed a match for each other. This was not the first time Captain Stone had crossed swords with Prince Edward, and he felt in his bones that it would not be the last. His arms moved as though on muscle memory, and he sidestepped in time with the Prince.

It was not until Georgette landed nearby and put herself in the middle of them that the fighting stopped.

"Edward, please," she cried.

Captain Stone flexed his jaw, thinking she should not have to beg the Prince. But Georgette's utterance of the Prince's name seemed to soften his resolve. Prince Edward lowered his sword.

"I thought we had an accord," Captain Stone murmured to him, watching like a hawk and waiting for him to lash out again.

The Prince tossed his sword to the ground and raised his palms. "We do. I am not here for any trouble. In fact, I am surprised to see you two aboard this ship."

The royal gave Georgette a wanting look and his hand flexed as though he thought about grasping her arm. He seemed to decide against it at the last moment.

"Are you well?" he asked her, his voice lowering. His gaze dipped to Georgette's mouth and Captain Stone's stomach clenched.

Georgette did not so much as glance in Captain Stone's direction as she nodded back. "I am. But

Edward, you must let us go. We are all in terrible danger."

She placed a delicate hand on his shoulder and Captain Stone ground his teeth. He did not like the way the Prince and Georgette were looking at each other. Such fondness. Such tenderness. It was a way he had never seen Georgette look at *him*.

Their long history was plain. Captain Stone wanted to be rid of the Prince as soon as possible. Prince Edward grimaced and looked at him with his brows knitted together.

"I know. Like it or not, I do believe I need your help."

Captain Stone stepped back in surprise. "My help?"

Prince Edward gave a curt nod and motioned for them to follow him. "Come quickly. We can talk about it in my cabin."

Captain Stone and Georgette exchanged looks before they followed the Prince aboard his ship.

The men were talking at top speed to the naval officers, some of them pointed at Captain Stone as they passed.

"What will you do with my crew?" he murmured to Prince Edward.

The prince glanced back at the men and scoffed. "You call that a crew? Pitiful, Manny. You need not concern yourself with them."

Georgette's face snapped in his direction and her eyes narrowed at him. She mouthed *Manny?*

Captain Stone shook his head, silently rebuffing her questions. True, Georgette and the Prince may have had a history, but Captain Stone and Prince Edward had more between them.

Not that he cared to tell her about it.

When they reached the main deck, Prince Edward guided them to the group of officers standing guard over a bundle of rags.

They reached them and the Prince nodded. One of the officers promptly pulled back the rags to reveal the stone face of a dead man.

Georgette gasped and threw her hands over her mouth. Captain Stone grunted. Georgette's reaction was an exaggeration for the Prince's benefit. She was already settling into her role as the damsel in distress. The lady had killed, talk less of being exposed to more than her fair share of bodies.

Captain Stone ignored her melodrama and scrubbed his chin instead. "Am I supposed to recognize this man?" he asked, looking at the Prince.

The Prince nodded to the officers, and they covered up the corpse once more. He strode to the captain's cabin in silence, and they followed him. He did not open his mouth until the door was secured behind them after they had walked inside.

"There is not a single scratch on that man's body," he said. Walking around his desk. He slammed a fist on the outstretched map.

"Six vessels have sunk in as many days, and the seas are littered with those bodies."

He looked up to give Captain Stone a look. It was the meaningful kind that said more than any tongue could manage in a split second. Captain Stone frowned back. "What are you suggesting?" he asked.

Prince Edward rolled his eyes, then planted his weight on his palms, squaring his jaw. "Ships torn apart. Lifeless bodies of only men. No women. No children."

Georgette's eyes widened as she seemed to catch onto what the Prince was saying. "Sirens," she whispered, and the Prince looked at her, his expression softening. He cleared his throat and stood straight again. "The seas are not safe," he said, eyes flitting between Georgette and Captain Stone.

Captain Stone scoffed and crossed his arms. "You say it as though they have not always been perilous."

Prince Edward gave him an incredulous look, then tore off his hat and tossed it on the desk. "Now is not the time to be pedantic, Manny."

Captain Stone stiffened at the sound of his name.

From the corner of his eye, he saw Georgette give him an inquiring stare once again.

"What do you want me to do about it? Ask Isis to kindly call off her sirens from human men and their boats?"

Prince Edward dragged a hand over his face with a huff. "I had hoped you would know why the goddess of the sea and her mermaids are so active at present. They've always been somewhat hostile, yes. But they're moving now, Manny. It seems as though nowhere is safe."

Captain Stone shut his eyes as the tension built up in his body. How was he to navigate such a conversation with Georgette present? Without revealing too many details… Details that would surely unravel her.

He picked up the glass decanter and poured himself a drink to buy time. He offered Georgette and the Prince a drink, but both declined, busy exchanging furtive looks. The sight prickled Captain Stone even more.

"Isis is looking for something that belonged to her," he said finally, avoiding Georgette's big eyes.

Prince Edward gave him a hard look, like a father looking at a disobedient son. "What did you steal from her?"

Captain Stone downed his drink in one and smacked his lips together as the comforting heat burned all the way down. "That." He pointed at the ring on Georgette's hand.

Prince Edward followed his line of sight, frowning, while Georgette gasped and lifted her hand as though she had never seen the ring before. Captain Stone was impressed by her acting skills. She had the Prince completely fooled that she did not already know this information.

Meanwhile, the Prince walked around the desk and took her hand, peering at the ring on her wedding ring finger. Then he looked at Captain Stone, his eyes flooded with conflicting emotions. Captain Stone smirked at the sight of him figuring it out.

"You married her?" he said, his voice raspy, as though the words cut the back of his throat.

Captain Stone could not hide his delight at the Prince's pained expression. Prince Edward rested his other hand atop Georgette's and looked deeply into her eyes. "Tell me it is not true," he whispered.

Georgette's bottom lip rolled inward and she bit down. Then she began to tremble, though Captain Stone sensed this too was an act. He wondered what game Georgette was playing. "I had no choice in the matter."

"Nay, that is not true." Captain Stone slammed his hand on the arm of the chair with a thump. Georgette looked at him, her eyes blazing with fury. "You threatened to kill my father," she hissed.

Suddenly, Captain Stone was not so certain that this was an act. Perhaps, he wondered, the true act was the way she had been with him all this time?

He inwardly shook the thought away, too disgusted by the idea.

"But you did have a choice," he said, lifting a finger.

Prince Edward's face twisted into a scowl as he made a noise of repulsion. Then he cleared his throat. "Leave us."

Captain Stone's frown deepened. "I beg your pardon?"

Prince Edward squared his shoulders and stepped up to Captain Stone. The Captain rose out of his chair and the two men began a staring contest, their chests puffed out. "I said," the Prince growled. "Leave us."

Captain Stone was about to smack the Prince across the face when Georgette's voice froze him.

"Please."

He gave Georgette a baffled look. "You think I am going to leave you with…"

"Oh, for goodness' sake, Manny. You know very well that I will not harm her. You have no reason to worry."

"It's not her safety I'm concerned about," Captain

Stone replied, his mouth lifting into a grim smile. Then he looked at Georgette one last time.

Her soft curls were frizzy and wild, but her eyes were bright again, as though his comment was the most delightful thing she had heard all year.

Then Captain Stone sighed and set his glass on the table. "As it turns out, I am overcome with the urge to stretch my legs and speak with my crew."

With a mixture of pride and heartache, he strode for the door and gripped the handle a little too hard as he yanked it open.

He did not turn back as he walked out, but just before the door shut again, he heard the soft, pleading voice of the Prince uttering two words that sank like rocks to the pit of his stomach.

"Dearest Georgette."

29

GEORGETTE

Prince Edward's seafoam blue eyes bore into Georgette's for several long moments while he grazed his fingertips along her bare arm. His spiced cologne washed over her with a sense of familiarity, and his touch sent a confusing rush of emotions through her. At this point, she could not be sure how much more confusion her mind would be able to take.

The devotion and concern in his gaze were clear. His hands found hers and he held them tight, making her stomach knot with guilt.

If he knew what she had been doing with the Captain just moments before, she was certain he would not want to be anywhere near her.

For now, it was like old times. She could not deny there was something soothing about being in his presence again. It took her back to the safety and innocence of Port Harbor—stealing a private moment in the parlor of her father's house... The way he would hold her hand, his heaving chest hovering mere inches from hers.

She reached up and caressed his smooth cheek, then dragged her finger down to his jawline, where she caught sight of a small ink tattoo just under his hair. "I've never noticed this before," she whispered, studying the anchor etched into his skin.

Prince Edward took a long breath, as though her touch offered him a peace he had been long searching for. When he opened his eyes again, he met Georgette's inquisitive stare with a shrug. "My brother had this birth-mark... It looked like an anchor to me."

Georgette listened intently. In all the years they had known each other, she had never heard him speak of the lost prince. It was strictly forbidden to talk about him. Present circumstances appeared to have loosened his tongue on the matter.

"You miss him very much?" she asked, sweeping his hair away from his brow. Prince Edward gave her a strange smile that she could not read. "After he was reported lost at sea, I thought it was fitting to get the tattoo." He puffed out another breath and leaned forward.

Georgette bit on her lip until it stung. Prince Edward

moved in and planted a soft kiss on her cheek, his skin cool against hers.

He lingered, and she savored the moment. But then she felt him jerk and her heart stopped. A million fears went through her mind at once. Could he have smelled Captain Stone on her? He dropped one of her hands and, before she could stop him, brushed her hair away from her neck. He pulled back, frowning so deeply, his brows had knitted into one bushy line.

"This bruise..." he muttered, touching her neck. Then he searched her eyes. "Did *he* do this to you?"

Georgette was certain if she bit any harder, her lip would bleed. She swallowed her guilt and cleared her throat. But she did not reply.

She could not. How could she tell the Prince, to whom she was betrothed, that her captor had sucked on her neck so hard it left a mark?

And she *liked* it.

She groaned inwardly. The thought of the Captain's rough kisses and the marks they had left made her stomach do flips. Like she had swallowed a fish whole. She resisted a smile and looked at the Prince's shiny shoes instead.

He was impeccably dressed—not even a spot of dirt on him; his Naval uniform neatly pressed. It was as though he had walked straight out of the palace. No one would have thought he had just been in a sword fight. In fact, it marveled Georgette how calm and collected he was, considering the circumstance. Of course, now that he had seen the bruise on Georgette's neck, his disposition darkened. He let her go and started to pace the cabin.

"I'm going to kill him," he growled. Georgette's heart skipped a beat. He clutched the brass hilt of his sword and gave her a piercing look.

"My dearest Georgette, I make this vow to you. I will kill that beastly pirate, and you will be free."

He lowered himself to one knee and looked up at her with misty eyes. "I will save you, Georgette. And you will be mine."

Georgette stiffened and her stomach knotted, but she forced a smile. "You said you need him, am I mistaken?" She covered her neck with her hair again. "If you kill him, what will you do about Isis and her army of sirens?"

Prince Edward rose and grabbed her shoulders. "You have the ring," he said, his voice barely above a whisper. It crushed Georgette's heart to see the hope in his eyes. His breaths came out short and fast, tickling her cheeks. "I shall kill him, we will return the ring to Isis, and this nightmare shall end. Then I will take you home and we can be wed."

Before Georgette could utter a word, he scooped her

up in his arms and pressed her against himself. When he kissed her, she kept her eyes open, too stunned to move. His eyes were shut, and he moaned into her mouth.

This kiss was more than a simple peck on the lips. It was fueled by passion and longing. He squeezed her body as though making her a promise that he would never let her go again.

When he released her, she stood frozen on the spot and her brain worked overtime, trying to conceive a plan.

The truth was, the idea of Prince Edward killing Captain Stone made her nauseous. But they couldn't sail to Imerta with no crew. With the British Royal Navy in tow, perhaps they stood a chance at getting out alive.

She chewed the inside of her cheek for a moment. "I've seen those sirens attack. I have been to Imerta with him," she said, giving Prince Edward a hard look. "Whether you like it or not, my lord, we need Captain Stone. He is the only person who can take us to Isis."

Prince Edward's jaw jutted out as he hummed in thought. "Are you asking me to keep him alive? After all he has done to you? To us? Do you truly believe he will simply hand over the ring?"

Georgette lifted her hand and the stone ring sparkled like a diamond. "He already has." Then she gave his arm a gentle squeeze. "Tell me, Edward. How much do you detest pirates?"

Prince Edward's face twisted into a scowl. "I loathe them to the highest degree."

Georgette nodded along. "And what would you say if I told you I could ensure that all the pirate lords and their crews will be in one place at the same time?"

Prince Edward cocked his head to the side and gave Georgette an odd smile. Like he had found a puzzle too difficult to solve.

"What are you suggesting?"

30

CAPTAIN STONE

Captain Stone's blood boiled as he watched the Prince kiss Georgette through a crack in the door. He could not bear to leave them alone for too long. When he returned, he could just make out a few tender exchanges between the two before the Prince made his move.

To his utter disgust and disappointment, Georgette did not reject him. In fact, it sounded as though she was plotting with the Prince. Plotting against *him*.

When the door finally opened, Georgette's flushed cheeks came into view. She gave him a grin. Her smile would have lifted his spirits at one point, but now his stomach lurched. He wondered how he could have been so foolish to believe she possessed feelings for him.

Of course she'd plot with the Prince to bring him to ruin.

He gritted his teeth as he smiled back. "Prince Edward and I have an idea," she announced, inviting Captain Stone back into the cabin.

Captain Stone glowered at the Prince, who blinked several times with a neutral expression. Captain Stone was relieved the man had enough sense to not gloat about kissing Georgette.

In fact, sensing the mood, Prince Edward began to edge out of the cabin.

"I need to give my men instructions," he muttered before disappearing through the cabin door.

Now alone, Captain Stone turned to Georgette. She rubbed her arms and gave him a sheepish smile. "We shall sail to Imerta and take back the treasure," she said. When Captain Stone did not respond, she quickly added, "With the full support of the Royal Navy, of course."

Captain Stone lifted a brow. "And you think that stealing from Isis will stop her attacks?"

Georgette frowned. "No. Obviously, we will need to give her this…" She held up the stone ring.

Captain Stone hummed in thought as he slid the delicate ring off her finger and inspected it in the light. "Did I ever tell you how I came to obtain this ring?" he asked.

Georgette's hair swooshed as she shook her head from left to right.

Captain Stone took a seat behind the captain's desk and sighed.

"I won it in a game of cards." He leaned back in the chair and rested his boots on the desk with a thud. "A unique fellow, Twitchy. I'll never forget his wiry mustache." He looked up from the ring to inspect Georgette's expression. She hovered by the door, still hugging herself. Her smile had vanished.

"You cannot surely be talking about…"

Captain Stone chuckled darkly. "Love makes a person do remarkable things, my lady." He held the ring up to the light. "It is said that Isis fell for a human once. She crafted the immortality ring with her own magic so that she could be with her love for all of time."

Georgette dropped her arms and approached the desk with a frown. "What happened?"

Captain Stone surveyed her over the ring. "The fool lost it, enraging Isis. She has been searching the seven seas for the ring ever since."

"And the man? What happened to him?" Georgette asked, looking at him wide-eyed. Her innocent stare prickled Captain Stone. He wondered if this was also part of an act. Was she trying to manipulate him again?

He slid the ring onto his finger and watched a flash

of annoyance cross her face. Then he shrugged. "Dead, probably. But that's not my point." He leaned forward and slammed a fist on the desk. "Love makes you do things. Foolish things."

Georgette frowned at him. "What are you telling me?"

Captain Stone snorted. "Your father is a gambling man. Did you not know?" He smiled at her blank stare. "Of course, you didn't know. How could he tell his sweet, innocent Georgette, his only daughter, that he gambled away his wealth and sold her to a pirate?"

Georgette's cheeks flushed. "You're lying to me. My father hasn't played a game of cards in all his life. You must have threatened—"

Georgette stopped at the jarring sound of wood scraping across the floor as Captain Stone jumped to his feet. She backed away as he strode around the desk. He cornered her and pinned her to the wall with one hand at her neck.

"I may be many things," he growled, glaring at her with his nostrils flaring. "A pirate, a murderer, a thief…" he listed each word slowly and her eyes flashed at each word. "But I am *not* a liar."

Georgette's hands flew to his wrist and he loosened his grip on her neck, stepping back. "I've made good on my vow, have I not?"

"What?" Georgette gasped, rubbing her neck with a frown.

Captain Stone started to the pace the cabin. "Have I not kept you safe from harm? Even after you deliberately disobeyed me and ran away?"

"That was only so I could be your siren repellent," Georgette spat.

Her words hit him square on the chest and he walked right up to her, but she kept her expression steely, and they stared each other down. "Is that what you think?" he asked. "That's all you think you mean to me?"

Georgette's face grew crimson, but she continued to scowl. Captain Stone was not sure whether to be aroused or irritated. He chose the latter.

"Of course, I'm nothing more than a siren repellent. Only, the last time we were around sirens, they seemed more than happy to attack while I was aboard. So I suppose now that I've lost my charm…"

"You'll go running back to your prince?" he sneered.

Georgette lifted a hand to her cheek and looked at him like he'd slapped her. "What has any of this got to do with—"

"I saw you," he forced out in an acid whisper. "I saw him. Both of you."

He couldn't bring himself to say the words, but Georgette seemed to know where he was going.

"He kissed me," she said blankly.

Now it was Captain Stone's turn to flush. "Right. Yes." He raised a palm and started to pace again.

He stopped at the sound of a snort and whirled to face her. "Pray tell! Is something amusing?"

Georgette's face broke into a grin as she shook her head. "Forgive me, my lord. I knew you to be possessive, but I never took you for a jealous man."

"So, you do not deny it?" Captain Stone asked, his fury rising once more.

Georgette shrugged. "If you saw it, how can I possibly deny it? Unless, of course, you cannot be sure of the thing you saw and are thereby placing me under this ridiculous interrogation in order to ascertain what thing you saw exactly and thereby punish me for it." She crossed her arms. "So? Which is it?"

Captain Stone's head spun as he tried to follow, but before he could muster a reply, Georgette walked right up to him and stopped with her chest kissing his. "Tell me, Captain. Does it kill you?" She slid her fingers down his body to the hard bulge in his pants.

"What?" he grunted, trying to hold perfectly still while his blood traveled south with her hand. Georgette's pretty lips curved upward.

"That I possess all of the power," she whispered, before she cupped him. He lurched forward and gripped her arms. "Do *not* play with fire, my lady. Unless you wish to get burned."

Georgette rolled her eyes back and sighed, arching her body against him. Then she hooked a leg around his waist and placed her palms on his clammy chest. "I was convincing the Prince to spare you," she whispered.

"Spare me? How merciful," Captain Stone said, losing track of his thoughts as his body throbbed with need. He *needed* to claim his wife.

She suddenly pushed him back and dropped her leg.

The air cooled rapidly between them.

He stared in dumb silence.

"Let us say we go to Isis and return the ring in exchange for the treasure, and all the pirate lords are there to see it."

She cocked her head to the side, twisting a lock of her hair between her fingers. Captain Stone had to swallow hard to focus on what she was saying. "What benefit does that bring me?" he asked.

Georgette crossed her arms. "The entire Navy fleet will be there too. So, while the pirate lords and the Navy are busy fighting…" She walked up to him again with a smile. "You and I can take a boat and…" She waved a hand. "Sail away to freedom."

"Freedom," Captain Stone repeated.

Georgette leaned in to whisper in his ear. "The pirate

lords will see that you have single-handedly delivered their treasure from Isis, stopped the siren attacks, and brought the Navy into a trap. They will not only remove the bounty on your head." She chuckled and shook her head. "Nay. I daresay they might make you pirate king."

Her hand wandered downward again, but Captain Stone grabbed her wrist and placed her hand on his chest. "So, that is your plan?" he asked, studying her face. She grinned at him, eyes sparkling like two jewels. Then she stepped back.

"Are you in, Captain?" she asked, resting her hands on her narrow hips. Captain Stone frowned at her. "Does the prince know about this plan?"

Georgette's smile faded before she gave a shrug. "A version of it."

She avoided his stare and started to play with her hair again, and suddenly Captain Stone was even less confident. "How can I be sure that you're not trying to manipulate me?" he asked.

Georgette met his accusatory stare and—to his surprise—grinned. "Good old-fashioned trust, Captain Stone."

31

GEORGETTE

G eorgette looked out at the sunset as the ship sailed across the vast waters. It had been four days since she negotiated with the Prince. He did not try to kiss her again, much to her relief. She was certain that if he did, Captain Stone would not have shown any restraint. The pirate would have killed the Prince, and that would have been the end of her plan.

She knew she was playing a dangerous game.

Prince Edward believed she was leading Captain Stone into a trap. Once he handed the ring back to Isis, he would become mortal again. Then if the pirate lords didn't kill him, the Navy would. Georgette would be free to go home with him and become his wife.

She felt at odds with herself as she watched two seagulls swoop across the sky. She did not want the Captain to die, but she was not entirely sold on the idea of navigating life as a pirate's wife. Especially one who spoke of her father with such disdain. She pulled out the golden locket from inside her shirt and opened it up to stare at her parents' portraits. She wondered what had become of her father since the ball. Was he wracked with grief? Did he join the search party? She wondered if he was somewhere over the horizon, looking for her.

As she thought about her father, she longed for home. The Governess, though cold and distant at the best of times, must surely be missing her. Ever since Captain Stone captured her, she had been in terrible danger. Going home with the Prince was not only the right thing to do; it was also the safest choice.

She closed the locket and pushed it back between her breasts with a sigh, wondering why the thought of going home, even as she longed for it, stirred up a sickly feeling from the pit of her stomach.

There was a part of her that had never felt more alive. The sensation of adrenaline coursing through her veins from the constant threats to her life could prove addicting. Captain Stone was a dangerous man, to be sure, but there was a quality to his roughness that drove her senses wild. His calloused hands squeezing her and his guttural growls in her ear claimed her on a biological level. She swallowed as she thought about him.

Prince Edward's hands were soft, and his smooth cheeks were tender against her skin as he kissed her. The two men were polar opposites, though there were some similarities. She turned around and watched them on the deck. Captain Stone was looking out on the starboard side with his spyglass. He stood firm and authoritative, with his feet planted hip-width apart, while his long, dark jacket billowed out behind him. Over on the port side of the ship stood the Prince, mirroring Captain Stone's stance.

The two men had barely exchanged two words over the past four days. Tensions were high and they kept their eyes on the seas, braced for another siren attack—or worse, a pirate ship.

Every now and again, Prince Edward would glance at her. She'd give him a quick smile to reassure him, and then he would return his gaze to the sea. Then the Captain would steal a glance.

It had happened so many times, Georgette lost track of who was who at one point. Though the two men were vastly different in their apparel and manner, there was something remarkably similar. For the life of her, Georgette could not quite work out what it was.

Perhaps it was their intense protectiveness. Or their need to make sure she was safe at all times. The pirate and the Prince were two sides of the same coin, wanting the same thing: Georgette.

She hugged herself and shook the thought away. She was not used to this much male attention. She had spent all of her mature life spoken for. No suitor ever even had a chance to look in her direction. No one dared look upon the Prince's betrothed. Now, if anything untoward were to happen and their truce ended, the Captain wouldn't think twice before slitting the Prince's throat.

She did not want Captain Stone dead, but she hated the idea of him slaughtering the Prince even more.

"What in the name of Poseidon is that?"

Georgette looked up at the cry of one of the Naval officers. He pointed and Captain Stone marched to the port side. A flood of men rushed over. Georgette stood up and leaned over the railing to get a closer look.

"Poseidon indeed... It appears as though Isis has summoned him to send us all to our watery graves," another officer said, his voice hollow in the wind.

"Where is your courage, Godfrey?" Prince Edward snapped. But the echo of a terrible roar reached them. The sound seemed to be increasing in volume, and in the distance, a thunderous tower of water was headed in their direction. Prince Edward looked to Captain Stone, who was observing it through the spyglass. "Is this anything you have happened to come across before?" he asked. He had to raise his voice over the steadily rising rumble. Captain Stone lowered the spyglass and gave him a grim look. "Maelstrom."

The word sent a shiver through the officers on the deck, and Georgette knew why. Her heart jolted at the sound of it.

Her father had spoken of a maelstrom before. It was said to be the most unforgiving natural disaster, claiming the lives of any souls in its path. It was the very thing that had claimed her mother's life.

Before long, the sky grew black. Storm clouds were taking over. Without hesitation, Prince Edward barked orders to the officers, telling them to steer the ship away from the pillar of water headed for them.

Captain Stone seemed to have other ideas. He scowled as rain started to pour, and headed for Georgette.

"Come on," he said, grabbing her wrist. Georgette tried to wrestle out of his grip, but he was too strong. "What are you doing?" she said, blinking heavy rain-drops out of her eyes.

The roar grew louder, and she gulped on air as she looked at the giant maelstrom headed for them. The wall of water was almost at the ship.

"If we stay on this ship, we will die," Captain Stone

said, his voice firm. "If you want to live, come with me. Now."

"Where are we going?" Georgette shouted back as the rain grew heavier. Before long, she could hardly see through the torrential downpour. It took her a moment to realize this was not rain but water coming off of the moving maelstrom.

Officers and crew members cried out, but every voice was now lost in the roar. Georgette tried to search through the sea of faces for the Prince, but Captain Stone dragged her to the back of the ship. He untied the dingy and coaxed Georgette onto it. "How is this the safer option?" she shouted as the boat filled with water. It was already ankle deep when she stepped inside. Captain Stone did not reply. He simply climbed in with her and began to work the rope to lower them into the water.

"Georgette!"

The Prince's shout was faint. Georgette pushed wet hair out of her face as wind and water slapped her cheeks. "Edward!" she shouted back. She grabbed Captain Stone's arm. "We have to go back for him," she said. But it was clear the Captain had no intention of turning back.

When the boat hit the water, he rowed the boat to the Duchess. Once on his ship, he cut the ropes tying her to the Naval ship. Georgette took deep breaths as her senses went into a frenzy. The cold water had drenched her to the bone. She climbed the thick rope to the upper deck of the ship like a drenched rat.

The pillar of water had reached the ship. With a groan, the Naval ship lurched sideways. Georgette watched with horror while Captain Stone busied himself at the wheel of the Duchess.

"Captain... They're all going to die!" Georgette shrieked as she watched the mast splinter. It suddenly snapped like a twig and landed with a soul-shaking creak and crash. The Duchess soared forward through the water like a hot knife in butter while the Naval ship groaned and crumbled into millions of fragments. Hot tears flooded Georgette's eyes as she screamed for the Prince. It was no good. Before long, the Maelstrom had swallowed the Navy ship up whole, drowning out the last of the crew's screams.

Georgette ran to Captain Stone, who was wrestling with the wheel. "We have to go back! The ship is down! The Prince..."

"He is gone, my lady. If you do not wish to suffer the same fate, I suggest you let me work," he snapped over the roaring seas. "Hold onto something."

Georgette's arms trembled as she wound a length of rope around her arm and tied herself to the helm. There was no time to dwell on the fact that the Prince was dead, and Captain Stone was right. The maelstrom had taken the Naval ship; now it was headed for the Duchess.

She took deep, steadying breaths as the ship rocked violently from side to side, but even though it groaned beneath her feet, Captain Stone steered the ship through the storm as an expert. It seemed as though he knew exactly which way to go to avoid being claimed by the force of nature.

But it did not stop terror rising in Georgette as she wondered if she was fated to meet the same end as her mother.

She clamped her eyes shut as another wave of water pelted her body, and clung to the side of the ship with all her might.

Hours passed by and still Georgette clung on. Meanwhile, the Captain steered his ship through the storm, never losing focus. Not even for a moment.

He stared into the storm, unafraid and determined. But Georgette knew that even Captain Stone had his limits. She did not know how long he would be able to keep steering the ship through the storm. But one thing was certain, there were no other survivors. No one could have lived through that storm.

Just as Georgette was beginning to think the storm was about to claim their souls too, the ship lurched sideways and crashed onto its side. Captain Stone knocked into her as they landed, and a mixture of water and sand flew up into the air.

Soon, the elements began to calm. Georgette blinked into the chaos, and saw a weak moonlight peeping through the clouds. They were no longer on the sea.

She nudged Captain Stone, who groaned and rubbed his head. Then he looked around.

"We've crashed on land," Georgette said, coughing sand out of her lungs. Captain Stone helped her up and the two stumbled out of the shipwreck onto the sandy shores. The dark island loomed over them in the night's sky and Georgette couldn't recognize it.

"Is this Imerta?" she asked. Captain Stone shook his head, raking his hands through his wet hair and squeezing it out. "No, but it looks as though one of the gods wanted us to land here. If that is true, we should keep our wits about us."

Georgette swallowed hard. "I thought the gods do not interfere with human affairs?"

Captain Stone laughed darkly. "What tales has your father been telling you about the gods? They *love* to interfere with humans."

When Georgette gave him a blank stare, Captain Stone shrugged. "They're immortal and incapable of killing each other, what else have they got to do with their existence?"

Georgette frowned deeply. "Are you telling me they just killed Prince Edward... For fun?" The words cut the back of her throat like razor blades and her eyes prickled.

Captain Stone shrugged again. "Perhaps Poseidon is on my side. He did us both a favor, after all."

Georgette looked at him incredulously for a moment. When she could not find an ounce of remorse in his expression, she scowled. "You are despicable!" Without another word, she stormed off into the dark tree line.

As Georgette stomped, her boots squelched in the ground and her body shuddered in the mercilessly cold night. Nothing could distract her from the horror that her Prince was dead. His screams haunted her memory: the last sounds of his voice. He was calling for her.

She clamped her eyes shut, screamed and shook her fists to the heavens, cursing the gods. Now her plan was truly ruined. She was shipwrecked on an unnamed island in the middle of nowhere, with no means of escape. Pirate lords and sirens were still hunting them, and she was stuck with a pirate captain who did not seem to possess a single compassionate bone in his body.

She hugged herself and shivered in the darkness. The tall trees towered over her with twisted branches, but for the first time, she was not afraid. Not even when she heard the rustling of leaves from behind. Nor the snapping of a twig as someone approached.

"Listen," she said crossly. "I just need you to leave me alone for a moment—" Georgette began, turning around to glare at Captain Stone. When she turned, he was not there. She saw a small boy instead. Before she could say anything, he raised a wood pipe to his mouth and blew. She felt a sharp scratch on her neck, and the next thing she knew was darkness.

32

CAPTAIN STONE

The sky grew clear and twinkling stars looked down on the island as Captain Stone wrung out his shirt and shook the excess water from his hair. He muttered to himself, thinking about Georgette's words.

Ungrateful woman!

He saved her from the most unforgiving maelstrom he had ever seen, and she called him despicable. He knew she had feelings for the Prince, but he thought she could have, at *least*, shown the Captain some gratitude for saving her life.

Now she had stormed off into a dark woodland all alone in the dead of night. He admired her spirit, but he could not ignore how foolish she was.

He had decided to wait for her to cool down and come crawling back to him. He was certain she would turn back once she realized there was nowhere to go. Then, perhaps, she would come to her senses and realize he was not her captor after all, but her savior.

The smell of smoke reached his nostrils.

He paused, then whipped around in the direction of the scent.

Deathly still and straining now, he could hear faint sounds coming from deeper in the forest. He could just about make out tribal cries.

His heart sank.

He knew those cries.

He had heard whispers across the sea of tribes that took shipwrecked sailors, roasting and eating them for sport.

Of all the islands to crash into. He shut his eyes for a moment and wondered why, of all the island on the seven seas, they had to be wrecked on an island of cannibals. Had he been saved by Poseidon, only to become the next victim on this barbarous race?

He tore through the forest, chewing on his lips and praying to goddess Athena for a cunning plan to fight his way out. The smoke smell grew stronger, and he slowed so as not to alert them. Following an amber glow that was now visible through the trees, he came upon their campfire.

He had not thought it possible that his heart could sink any lower, but it dropped all the same.

Georgette was a limp form tied to a post. A pile of wood was smoking at her feet. Captain Stone deduced the wood had just been lit. These were not cannibals, he realized. They meant to burn her. Probably as an offering to their gods.

The tribe sang and danced to the beat of drums, while the pyre at Georgette's feet took flame. Georgette awoke, probably from the heat below her. She blinked at the flames and began to scream.

Captain Stone was not going to stand by and watch his wife burn alive. He was struck by an idea. If the tribe worshipped gods, he would become their god.

He roared with authority as he stepped into the light and withdrew his sword. A sea of faces whipped around in his direction, and several of the indigenous people picked up their wood pipes. Captain Stone stormed across the camp and walked right onto the pyre.

There was a hush, and everyone watched with bated breath as Captain Stone became engulfed in flames. Tongues of fire licked his body and set his sword ablaze. "I am Hephaestus!" he roared. "And I command you to release this woman!"

No one moved.

Captain Stone did not intend to wait for them. He cut Georgette's bonds in one swift movement and she fell into his arms. He walked through the fire once more and she clung on to him as though for dear life, burying her face in his chest.

The stone ring shone in the light of the flames as he walked out. Captain Stone set Georgette down and the two looked around at the gathered tribe in silence. Slowly, every man, woman, and child went to their knees and bowed, singing a solemn but unintelligible song of what appeared to be worship.

Captain Stone and Georgette waited for them to finish. When enough time had passed, Captain Stone raised a hand. A hush fell.

The plan was working, he thought. The tribe truly believed him to be a god, as he had known they would. For how could they have known that the stone ring was the only thing that kept them both from being burned? Now he needed to get Georgette away from them.

A tall tribal man with a headdress made of feathers and twigs stepped forward.

"Lord Hephaestus! We beseech you to end our suffering! Allow our rivers to flow pure, and our make our soil fertile again," he said, bowing. Captain Stone looked about at the people. Scrawny children with swollen bellies looked back at him dolefully. The adults and young people were skin and bones. After a second examination, Captain Stone realized the chief who had spoken was not just tall, he was gaunt. They looked like they had seen a decent meal in a long time. Wide, hollow eyes stared at him with hope. It was then that he saw their humanity. They were simply mothers and fathers, trying to bring about a miracle so that they could feed their children. He wished then that he was a god so that he could solve all their problems. What he did have, was a grounded ship stocked with food and water. He was certain they would be able to salvage enough from the wreck to feed themselves for a few weeks at least.

He nodded. "I have seen your sacrifice and I shall show mercy for your pain," he said, raising his hands. The light of the flames danced in the eyes of the people as they watched him in awe. "Give me three nights with this woman, and I shall open the heavens in the morn and bless this land to bring forth fresh fruit."

The tribe cheered and chanted, and the drums picked up again as the people danced. "This way, my lord. Please." The chief took them through the camp to a treehouse. The winding steps leading to it creaked beneath their feet but held firm. Inside, Captain Stone was impressed. The treehouse was a big and sturdy structure. Two women entered, throwing soft white and pink petals all over the bed and floorboards. Another woman walked in with a large pot of murky water.

Without another word, the women stripped Georgette and Captain Stone out of their damp outer clothes. Then they offered dry sack cloths. Captain Stone and Georgette thanked the women, who backed out of the treehouse, bowing and nodding.

"Rest, our lord. We shall wait for you to return to us," the chief said. Then he shut the door, leaving them alone.

There was a beat of silence while Captain Stone listened to the creaking steps below, then the faint murmurings of the tribe. Georgette turned to him, her eyes wide and teary. "Why do you keep saving me?" she asked fiercely. He wrapped his arms around her and pulled her close. She struggled against him for a moment but settled down in resignation a moment later. "I will always save you," he muttered into her hair before kissing her head. "I will never stop saving you."

Georgette broke down in tears. Her body shook so violently, Captain Stone had to tighten his grip. He stroked her hair and let her wail against his chest. She seemed to be trying to say something amidst her tears, but it did not matter. He knew she was releasing all of the frustration and fear that had built up in her since the night of the engagement ball. It was his fault. Everything that had happened to her since he stole her from her home was his fault, and she deserved this time to be upset about it.

So he held her and waited. Waited for the time when she had stilled and no more tears came. Sure enough, she slumped in his arms as her knees buckled.

Captain Stone picked her up and carried her to bed. "I'm so tired," she said, her eyes bloodshot and slitted. Captain Stone shushed her, ignoring his own aching body. He set her head on his elbow and let her body melt into his own while they lay in bed. "Sleep, my love. Nothing will happen to you, I promise," he whispered in her ear before kissing her temple. Georgette did not need to be told twice. Soon enough, she fell asleep. Captain Stone stroked her arm and matched her breaths with his own. The gentle rise and fall of her shoulders as she slept in his arms was as soothing being at sea. He did not allow sleep to come. Not yet.

He strained his ears, listening to the music and dancing below them, keeping alert just in case the tribe changed their mind and chose to devour them both.

After several hours, the music died down and all was quiet. He nestled into Georgette and rested his chin on her head as she slept. He was not sure what game she had been playing, and if the real reason she was so upset at losing the Prince was because she planned to run off with him. But it didn't matter anymore.

The Prince was dead. Of that, he was sure.

He sighed.

It was not yet clear to him how they would get off the island, but Captain Stone knew one thing: Georgette was his once more.

As he finally succumbed to sleep, he did so with one single thought.

He was not going to lose Georgette again.

When he woke, the first thing he saw were Georgette's ice blue eyes staring at him. Her face was framed in daylight and the air was stifling. Captain Stone yawned and noticed that Georgette's hand was on his cheek. She scratched his short beard with a smile. The sight flooded Captain Stone with warmth, but then she frowned and looked downward, and he knew she was thinking about the Prince again.

He frowned back.

He knew she would not simply move on.

She had feelings for the Prince, that much was clear.

He cradled her face.

"I'm sorry," he whispered.

The words prompted a look of surprise from her. He realized this must be the first time she had heard him offer an apology. In truth, it was the first apology he had made in a very long time.

"I'm sorry I couldn't save him," he said. And it was true, but Georgette could not have known that. Nor was she likely to believe it now.

Georgette sat up, looking perplexed. "Who are you?" she whispered, tucking hair behind her ear.

Captain Stone sat up. "You know who I am," he said, combing the tangles out of his hair with his fingers.

Georgette chewed her lip and looked down in thought for a moment. Then she edged closer and smoothed Captain Stone's hair away from his forehead.

"No," she said softly. "Who *are* you…?" she asked again, studying his face. Then she tucked his hair behind his ear and ran a finger across his jaw. She seemed to be searching his face for something, and Captain Stone tensed. She put a finger under his chin, and after a stiff moment of hesitation, he let her lift his chin. Her finger traced something on his neck, near his jawline.

"This birthmark…" she whispered, meeting his stare again.

Captain Stone was not sure how she could have known about it.

He drew away and cleared his throat.

Georgette stared at him open-mouthed and her eyes

grew misty. "You're the lost prince," she said in a faint voice. She turned her back to him and hugged herself.

Captain Stone swallowed hard. "How did you know?" he asked, scratching the back of his neck.

Georgette did not move. "I think I have known for some time now."

She sighed. "From the moment you caught me in the lost prince's room, I should have known." She turned to look at him, soft tears rolling down her cheeks. "And the Spanish man said that letter opener belonged to the Crown."

Captain Stone frowned. "What?"

Georgette sniffed and wiped her eyes with a laugh. But then her face fell. "Prince Edward. He's... He was your..."

"Baby brother," Captain Stone finished for her. Then he sighed heavily and dragged a hand through his hair. To say it aloud after all these years was like lifting a weight from his shoulders.

Georgette stood and started to pace the room. Then she whipped around. "Why did you fight him?" she burst out.

Captain Stone shrugged. "We had a complicated relationship," he muttered. Georgette held her face in her hands and laughed weakly. "Complicated indeed." She turned to him again. "The king declared you lost at sea; everyone thinks you are dead."

Captain Stone nodded. "Aye, and that is exactly what I wanted everyone to believe."

"But why?" Georgette hugged herself again. "How could you put your family through so much pain? How could you abandon your people?"

Captain Stone scoffed at the question. "I have already told you, Georgette. Freedom means everything to me."

Georgette lowered herself to the bed again, nodding slowly as though dazed by the information. "You're the lost prince," she said again, barely above a whisper.

"It does not change anything," Captain Stone said, placing a hand on her shoulder. She lurched away. "It changes *everything*!" she said hotly, throwing her hands in the air.

"Why?" Captain Stone asked.

Georgette shook her head and shut her eyes as though struggling with something in her head. "Because... It means you're not just a..."

"Pirate?" Captain Stone finished for her. Georgette's eyes snapped open, and she nodded. "You're a prince. And now..."

Captain Stone set his jaw as he studied Georgette's hopeful expression. "Now, you're married to a prince.

Not just a ruthless, lawless pirate," he finished, disgust rising.

He spread his arms wide. "I chose this path, Georgette. I walked away from that life. *This* is who I am."

"But it doesn't have to be," Georgette said, edging closer. "We can go home. You can take up your rightful place in the palace and…"

"No," Captain Stone said firmly. Georgette opened and closed her mouth silently as she glared at him. His glare remained steady. Finally, she shut her mouth and crossed her arms with a huff. "Well, it's all a moot point, I suppose. How we are to get off this forsaken island is beyond me. We shall have to keep pretending you're a god and live out the rest of our days in this treehouse."

Captain Stone smirked at her sulking.

He approached her, and when she didn't turn away, he reached out and pulled her hair away from her neck. Then he moved closer and planted a trail of soft kisses down to her collarbone. "Would that be that so terrible?" he asked, reaching for her face. Her frown broke into a smile as he cupped her face in his hands and slid round to grip the back of her neck.

"I suppose…" she whispered as he moved in. But he didn't wait for her to finish before he kissed her. She moaned against his mouth, but she didn't push him away.

Instead, she parted his lips with her tongue and her hands gripped his shirt, urging him closer.

When her body pressed up against his chest, a wonderful shudder ran through Captain Stone. Everything zinged as her skin brushed against his and he took great delight in tasting every part of her mouth.

Georgette pushed him down on the bed, climbed into his lap, and rocked her hips against him as her hands roamed over the muscular landscape of his back. Feeling her weight on his hips was enough to throw the pirate's mind into a spin. He gripped her waist and squeezed as she rocked back and forth. Every atom in his body was charged as she picked up the pace and began to kiss him with more gusto.

Suddenly, she was shimmying out of her clothes. Her heat set Captain Stone's body ablaze with need. He trailed his hands down her bare back, then tangled them in her long hair while she started to kiss his neck.

The woman knew exactly what she was doing. He was certain of it. Every brazen touch set off a chain reaction in his body. He did not doubt that she had never been with a man, but her instincts were driving her. It took all of Captain Stone's resolve not to flip her over and force his way into her there and then. But he wanted her first time to be slow… Gentle.

She was acting confident now, but he knew that her first time would hurt if he wasn't careful.

He let her hands explore him and he kissed her back, nipping her skin and licking it better, all while she moaned in the most delicious way.

His ears pricked at an odd but far-off sound and he ignored it. She had just begun to nibble on his neck.

The sound came again, and this time, it gave him pause. Georgette went on busily…

Then a loud explosion shook the treehouse. Georgette shrieked and the two held on to each other in alarm.

Another tremble, then shrieking villagers.

A series of loud booms followed.

Captain Stone got to his feet.

Georgette's eyes were wild. "What is it?" she asked him.

He could hear faint screams and the sound of a horn. Captain Stone began to pull on his clothes. "Get dressed," he told her sharply.

"Where are you going?" she asked, breathless.

Captain Stone pulled on his boots and peered out of the tiny window.

A ship with black sails had grounded itself next to the shipwreck. A black wave of men poured out like ants and charged toward the locals who had dashed to the beach.

Captain Stone grimaced and turned back to Georgette. "One of the pirate lords has found us," he said. Georgette's face went ashen-gray. Captain Stone knelt at her feet and took her hand to his lips. "I will slaughter every single one of them, then I will come back for you," he vowed. Georgette took a breath and nodded. "I'll be here."

Captain Stone gave her another quick kiss, picked up his sword, and ran out of the treehouse without another word.

33

GEORGETTE

Georgette's heart raced as she waited in the treehouse for Captain Stone's return. Before long, she tiptoed to the window to see what was going on.

She could just make out the tiny dots of men on the beach. A great battle was in progress, and a scattered line of men were infiltrating the woodland.

It was then that she heard the crunching of sticks snapping under the treehouse. She paused to listen and knew instantly that it was not Captain Stone. She got to her feet shakily and yanked on her jacket, now dry from the sun. The stairs creaked, announcing the arrival of an unwelcome guest. Georgette gripped the handle of her knife and watched the doorway.

The door swung open, and Georgette braced herself…

In walked a young, olive-skinned woman, dark hair pulled back into a tight bun at the top of her head. "You must come, my lady." She gestured with both hands, reaching for Georgette. "It is unsafe," she hissed.

Georgette sheathed her knife and followed the woman out of the treehouse. The sounds of battle grew louder, and Georgette stopped for a moment to stare in wonderment as she watched the tribal men climbing the trees. Each one had a knife clamped between his teeth.

Then she saw the pirates heading for the camp.

One by one, the tribal men dropped down to bury their knives in the backs of the pirates. Their screeching rang out through the trees.

The woman grabbed Georgette's hands and urged her to keep walking, snapping her out of her reverie. They soon joined a small group of women and children heading deeper into the woodland. Then they began to run.

Georgette ran as hard as she could, until her legs throbbed and her lungs screamed for air. Eventually, she couldn't take it anymore.

She stopped and bent over gasping, trying to catch her breath. The group ran on, and soon, Georgette straightened to find that she was entirely alone in a tiny clearing.

When she had fully recovered, she tried to determine what direction the women had gone. The ground was too dry to pick up any tracks, not with an untrained eye at least.

Terrified, Georgette staggered forward, looking wildly around and listening out for any sign of human life.

A twig snapped, and something hard hit the back of her head. Her knees buckled. Before she hit the ground, a pair of rough hands grabbed her and then she was surrounded by voices.

Pirates. The world went dark again.

Murmurs. Laughter.

Georgette woke in a dark, dirty cell with a blinding headache. She rubbed her temples and scowled into the darkness for several long moments as her mind registered that the room was swaying.

She groaned and leaned against the bars of the cell, too distracted by the throbbing pain in her head to care about the fact she was locked up.

Shadows moved above her on the deck. The floorboards creaked, and the men walking around spoke in low voices. But not too low that Georgette could not hear them.

"Sad, pathetic cod... Did you see him crying on the

beach when he saw us take the wench on the boat and sail away?"

Dark laughter followed.

"The man may be possessed by a devil, but we didn't need to kill him. He's marooned on that godforsaken island, and we have his wife."

"We'll all have her, too."

More dark laughter. Georgette gripped the bars of her cell and grimaced at the cracks between the floorboards while the pirates talked.

She patted herself down and cursed. Her knife was gone.

A black rage overcame her, and she began to imagine all the different things she would do to them with her bare hands.

She thought about what they said about Captain Stone. Had he really seen her being taken away? If that was true, she was not sure what he would have done. She needed to get back to him. Of that, she was sure.

She looked around the cell door, looking for weakness. It was not dissimilar to the one she had been in on the Duchess. These hinges were well-oiled, however, and someone had successfully locked the door this time.

She paced the cell, hating the fact that she was nothing more than a sitting duck. The pain in her head was unbearable.

She had just lowered herself to the ground and put her head in her hands when a strange but familiar sound filled the air. The laughter and conversation ceased immediately. An eerie silence fell.

The ethereal singing cut through the air again.

"Oh gods. Poseidon deliver us!" someone on the deck cried.

Georgette raced to a crack in the side of the ship and squinted. Only one creature she knew of could sing so beautifully and still put the fear of gods into the hearts of men.

Sure enough, several glittering fins crossed her view, while more voices picked up the song. Georgette took several steadying breaths.

If the sirens attacked this ship, it was very likely Georgette would drown, but she had never been as relieved as now to see the mystical creatures.

She picked up a small wooden crate from the dusty floor and smashed it against the iron cell door. Someone banged the floor about her head.

"Stop that, wench!" a pirate barked at her. The rest of the crew remained silent. Besides the creaking of the ship, no one made a sound.

Even the waters seemed to calm.

Georgette picked up a broken nail from the pile of broken pieces of crate and started to chip away at the crack in the side of the ship. It was a long shot, but she wouldn't sit around and wait for death. The drive to get back to the Captain was too strong.

Then the singing turned into hissing, and everything happened at once.

It was like the ship was struck by lightning from all directions at the same time. The floor beneath Georgette's boots shook, and she fell to her knees. Meanwhile, cracks appeared in the side of the ship and began to grow bigger. Georgette stumbled to her feet and kicked at the weak points, determined to break out of the cell. Panicked footsteps overheard told Georgette that the pirates were now under attack.

The ship lurched side to side, there was a thunderous crash from the upper deck, and Georgette guessed the mast had broken. The hissing continued and thousands of heavy strikes continued to hit the sides of the ship until water began gushing in.

It rose fast.

Georgette's heart picked up speed as she thought about how easily she could drown. The water was already up to her calves by the time she got up again. She peered out of the large crack and caught sight of one of the sirens lining up to strike again.

"Hey, you!" she shouted. "Do you think you can get me out?"

The siren locked eyes with Georgette, and for the first time, she was completely unafraid. The siren's expression remained totally calm. As though it was entirely normal to be spoken to under these circumstances. Then the siren rushed forward, and Georgette jumped back just in time for the siren to claw her way into the cell. When she burst inside, a wave of water flooded the cell and Georgette stood frozen in awe of the whimsical creature.

Her long fin was dazzling, the scales glittered like her lower body was made of millions of diamonds. The woman's long, red hair flowed over her upper body like a dress.

The water level was now at Georgette's neck. She gulped air as water continued to rush inside the ship.

High-pitched screams cut through the air. The ship took on more water. Outside, the sirens were positioning themselves for one last, fatal blow.

The siren grabbed Georgette's wrist and she jumped at the cool touch. "Come," said the siren, her voice gentle but authoritative. "You belong with us."

Georgette frowned and made to speak, but water had filled the cell. The siren pulled her out into the open sea.

Georgette could not swim.

The siren let her go, and the water pushed her down into darkness.

She scrambled her arms and legs, trying to reach the

light above her head, but her body sank lower. Scores of sirens floated all around her, watching. In Georgette's struggle, they seemed mildly entertained by what they were watching. The red head that had pulled her out of the ship reached out and touched Georgette's cheek. "Breathe in the water," she said.

Georgette frowned and bound her mouth together on reflex. She guessed this was how the sirens were able to kill people without leaving a scratch. By fooling them to fill their lungs with water.

Georgette's lungs burned. No matter how hard she tried to kick her feet, her body sank like a boulder. Deeper and deeper.

She looked up at the fading light of the water's surface and then she grabbed her locket and shut her eyes, thinking of her mother.

A sadness washed over her as she thought about dying. But she reasoned that she would, at least, be reunited with her mother soon. There were still sirens gathered around her, watching. Perhaps they were waiting for her to die. The redheaded siren that had saved her hovered and stared.

When her body refused to hold breath any longer, she opened her mouth and gulped the water, waiting for death to come.

It did not.

The water entered her body like crisp morning air and flooded her with the most invigorating energy. In an instant, every atom in her body began to tremble. She took in more breaths, feeling lighter every time. The sinking sensation was gone. She felt light as the air she had been struggling for a moment ago.

She did a small flip and let out a squeal.

Something brilliant rushed past her as she did so.

It was then she realized she no longer had legs.

Georgette looked down at the long silver fin flowing below her waist. She moved it left, then right.

"What is happening?" she asked, and she was surprised to hear her own voice so clearly. A wave of laughter surrounded her. She looked around. The sirens were laughing.

"Come, sister," the redheaded siren said with a giggle, reaching for her. Her heart soared, and she took the siren's hand.

They zoomed through the water at lightning speed. The ocean rushed past, whipping her hair back. The most thrilling sensation she had ever felt coursed through her veins.

She laughed at how free she was in this moment. All these years, she had been terrified of the water. Her father had told her that she would drown. Did he know the truth?

As these thoughts came to her, the sirens seemed to follow them.

"You must come with us, sister," they seemed to say telepathically. Georgette followed them, and the group of sirens sped through the waters at an impossible speed. Georgette laughed as her long tail propelled her forward. She reached out and her fingertips seemed to be able to sense all the creatures in the sea.

They passed a sleeping whale. A school of tiny fish scattered as they sped past. A pair of white sharks sniffed with curiosity as they went by.

Georgette swam free and fast, gleeful and playful. For the first time in her life, her existence made sense. In the sea, she had no expectations imposed on her. No cruel men had power over her now.

She beamed from ear to ear as the realization hit her like a spark.

"I'm a siren!" she said.

The surrounding sirens laughed, and when Georgette joined in, she found that their chorus was the most beautiful sound. They moved as one, instinctively knowing which way to go.

"Mother is waiting for you," one of the sirens said to her. Georgette stopped and hovered in the water, frowning. "My mother is dead."

The laughter bristled her this time, but only for a

moment. "No, sister. Do not believe the lies of an old man. Mother is waiting for you."

As if woken from a spell, Georgette shook herself and thought about Captain Stone. He had told her lies about her father... Or so she thought. Truly, her father had kept secrets from her. Secrets like the fact that she was a siren. And that her mother was alive somewhere out at sea.

She pictured Captain Stone deserted and alone on the island, and her heart ached. "I have to go back," she said, turning around. The sirens exchanged looks. "Men are bad, sister," the redheaded siren echoed in her mind. "Come with us and be free."

Several of them tried to reach for her arms, but Georgette jerked away and shook her head. "No."

She started to race back in the other direction, but more sirens surrounded her. Just when she thought they were going to stop her, a firm, authoritative voice flooded her mind.

"Let her go."

The sirens obeyed, backing away to give her a path. The voice was familiar. It was the same one she had heard at Imerta. Georgette's heart jolted. Her mother was Isis?

Suddenly, she did not care for answers. All she needed was to be with the Captain. After all, he had never lied to her. From the very beginning, he told her the truth. Even the ugly parts of it.

Georgette swam faster and faster, soaring through the sea, bubbles flowing past her like stars. When she strained her ears, she could hear Captain Stone's heartbeat. She did not know how she recognized it, but it guided her to him. She zoned in on it, taking deep gulps of water to fuel her energy. When she finally reached the waters near the island, she swam past the pirate's sunken ship and aimed skyward.

When her face broke the water's surface, the beaming sunshine heated her cheeks. She looked at the beach in the far distance and could just make out the shape of a man knelt by the water.

Grinning, she headed for him.

34

CAPTAIN STONE

C aptain Stone sank to his knees on the beach and watched with devastation as the pirate ship was torn apart by scores of sirens. The men screamed and wailed before everything fell eerily silent, except for the splashes. The sirens sang the most charming melody, sweetly. It was as though they were lulling the pirates to their endless sleep as the ship sank to Davy Jones' locker.

It was not the pirates Captain Stone's heart was breaking for.

Georgette was aboard that ship, and now she was gone. His heart ripped in two as he watched, helpless. Hot tears prickled, and even though he could not bear to look away, watching the attack caused him insurmountable pain. He wasn't sure whether to take his knife and drive it into his eyes, blinding him from the horrific sight, or plunge it into his heart to stop the pain once and for all.

He knelt on the beach and cried. Tribal men and women eyed him warily as they tended to their dead and wounded.

Waves crashed against the shore and seagulls warbled overhead.

Being the man that he was, he could not remain this way for long. He was devastated, but the business of finding safety on this strange island tugged at his mind. He had just wiped at his face and was about to rise when a new siren song flooded his ears. The song filled his ears and his mind as though it were just for him. There were no sirens in sight. They had all left the scene of their destruction. He tore his eyes from the sinking ship and scanned the water for the siren singing such a sweet melody. The words were of a language he did not recognize, but the voice was familiar. It soothed him, and his body relaxed, like he had been dipped in a warm bath of milk. He exhaled slowly and looked out carefully, certain the creature could not be far off. His eyes narrowed on a small figure in the water, heading for the shoreline.

Captain Stone wondered if the siren had come to take him to the bottom of the ocean. He thought that if that was the case, there were worse ways to die. Perhaps this siren was taking him to join Georgette in Davy Jones' locker. Perhaps he could persuade Hades to allow them to linger in the waters together.

The figure grew larger as it approached, and Captain Stone's thoughts scattered.

A long silver tail flicked up, sending a fountain of water over the siren. Water droplets fell like diamonds around her. She stopped singing to laugh, and even that sounded harmonious.

Her long, blonde hair floated about her in the water as if it had a mind of its own, and when the siren reached the sand, the large fin transformed into a pair of legs. Georgette walked out.

Captain Stone remained still, his heart hammering in his chest as he watched her approach him. Her long, blonde curls shifted over her bare breasts. She was entirely naked. But it was her ice-blue eyes that held him captive.

Captain Stone removed his jacket and staggered to his feet as she reached him. "You're a…" he whispered, staring at her eyes in disbelief.

"A siren," Georgette replied, her voice more tranquil than he'd ever heard it before. Captain Stone shook himself as though to break out of a daze. Then he picked up his jacket quickly and wrapped it around her with a grin. "I dare say, I had my suspicions," he said.

Georgette chuckled. "You did not! Your face is as white as a ghost."

Captain Stone stopped smiling and picked her up in his arms. "I thought I had lost you," he said, his voice growing hoarse. The memory flooded him with fresh dread.

Georgette reached up and placed a cool hand on his cheek, calming his senses once more. "You'll never lose me. I'm yours."

Captain Stone's heart soared as he carried Georgette back to the treehouse. The tribal men and women watched in revered silence, too stunned to speak. Many of them had been on the beach and seen Georgette's exit. Perhaps they were quiet out of respect, Captain Stone did not know. Nor did he care to.

They went up into the treehouse, and when he kicked the door shut behind them, he wasted no time in throwing Georgette on the bed.

The next three days and nights passed by in a whirlwind of rampant lovemaking. They would have sex until Georgette began to whimper. Then they would pause to just hold each other. Before long, Georgette would be kissing him again, prompting another round of it.

She gripped his shoulders as he buried himself in her, and her nails pierced his skin as she clawed his back. He sucked on her sensitive skin and rubbed her until she arched her back and begged him to take her again.

Captain Stone growled, devouring every part of her milky skin. She tasted like the sea, and he felt like a sailor discovering new lands.

He took great delight in exploring every inch of her.

It became impossible for Captain Stone to know where he ended and she began. They had become one soul.

On the third night, they collapsed in each other's arms, panting and utterly spent. But it did not stop Captain Stone from touching Georgette, pinching and caressing her body to check that she was real. He worried that she was an oasis and might vanish at any moment.

They whispered secrets to each other, talking about everything and anything that entered their minds. Georgette laughed when Captain Stone told her about the adventures he and his brother got up to when they were kids. They intertwined their fingers as she told him about the long, lonely nights she had spent wishing her mother was alive.

"All this time, you were telling me the truth," she said, looking downcast. Captain Stone grazed his thumb over her cheek. "I wish I had been lying," he murmured, before he planted a kiss on her temple.

She met his eyes with a sad look. "There are so many

secrets my father kept from me. If my mother is Isis, what does that make me?"

Captain Stone smothered her face in kisses until she was smiling again. "You are fierce and brave," he said, picking up her arm. "Clever, kind..." he said between kisses down to her elbow. He cupped her breast, and she rolled her head back as he sucked on her earlobe. "You are a true force of nature. I am both aroused by you and terrified of you."

Georgette giggled, rolled over and climbed onto him. She sat on his hips, her long, luscious hair flowing down her naked body. He gripped her hands as she began to roll her waist, sending ripples of pleasure through his body.

"You *should* be afraid, Captain Stone," she said with a chuckle.

Captain Stone sat up and stroked her hair with tenderness before he gave her a thoughtful smile. "You can call me by my name, you know," he said.

Georgette cocked her head to the side and seemed to think on it. Then she scrunched up her face. "No. You will always be Captain Stone to me."

Her smile faded, and she turned pensive. Captain Stone watched her.

She reached over, picked her things from the pile of

forgotten clothes and began to dress. Captain Stone watched her, frowning. "What is wrong, my love?"

Georgette finished getting dressed and started to braid her hair. "More pirates will come. And they will keep coming until…"

"Until what?" Captain Stone said, reaching for her waist. "I am immortal, and you are a siren. Let them come. We'll destroy every ship that comes our way."

"Until what?" Georgette asked, her eyes flashing dangerously. "Until all the pirates in the world are dead?"

Captain Stone shrugged. "If necessary. Yes."

"And what about Isis and her sirens? Innocent men are dying, not just pirates."

Captain Stone sighed and pulled on a pair of pants. "I see that beautiful head of yours has already concocted a plan. So, what is it?" he asked, fastening his belt.

Georgette took his hand and rubbed her fingers over his ring. "We have to give it back to Isis." She gave him a hard look, daring him to argue. Captain Stone knew it would be fruitless to try. He sighed.

Besides, he was completely spent after the past three days. She could have asked for anything and he could not say no.

"You're forgetting the fact we are stuck on this island," he pointed out. Georgette's face brightened and she gestured to the window. "Not for long."

Captain Stone followed her line of sight and noticed the large merchant ship approaching the shipwreck. He met Georgette's hopeful stare. He would have gladly stayed in the treehouse forever, but she was resolute. He sighed again.

"All right, my love. Lead the way."

35

GEORGETTE

Georgette and Captain Stone were both relieved to discover the merchant vessel was full of fisherman and sailors. When Georgette looked at their charter maps, she saw that the maelstrom had sent them far off course. It was going to take weeks to get to Imerta. Luckily, they were headed for Spain, and they would sail near Imerta on the way.

She was keen to get the plan over with, but Captain Stone seemed uninterested in being in any kind of rush.

He wanted to make love every chance he could get. Georgette had no complaints; now that she had a taste of him, she couldn't get enough.

They had a small room in the belly of the ship which offered very little privacy. But neither of them cared for privacy. Captain Stone picked her up and thrust her on the wall with a thump. Georgette wrapped her legs around his waist and they kissed with as much passion as two lost lovers after years apart. Captain Stone was always ready, and whenever his calloused fingertips grazed her bare skin, she rolled her head back and moaned without restraint.

He worked on her body like an expert, knowing the exact places to caress to make her cry out with pleasure. Each time he claimed her, it felt new and exciting. His hands roamed freely under her clothes, even when they were on the deck. Georgette stifled a giggle at the furtive glances of the other sailors.

"Are they on their honeymoon?" one of them muttered to another.

After a fortnight at sea, they calmed down.

Georgette took up playing cards with the sailors under the moonlight. When she won three games in a row, they stopped playing with her. Captain Stone smirked. "You play much better than your father," he remarked. His smile faded as soon the words left his mouth.

Georgette frowned and hugged herself as she looked out at the dark sea.

She had tried hard not to think about her father. A swirl of conflicting emotions took over whenever she did.

She remembered the last thing he said to her, just before the engagement ball.

"Everything I've ever done has been for your benefit."

She wondered how it benefitted her to be kept from the truth. And why he had lied about her mother. Perhaps the most dreadful part of it all was the knowledge that he had sold his own daughter to a pirate. What kind of loving father could do that?

She turned to Captain Stone and planted her hands on his chest. "Tell me, did he show any remorse at all?"

Captain Stone cupped her face and grazed her lips with his thumb. Georgette stared into his eyes, searching for the truth. "He did," Captain Stone said. "I am afraid I am responsible. I put him in a very difficult position, after all."

Georgette shut her eyes with a sigh. "He should never have gambled in the first place."

"If he hadn't, I would never have known you," Captain Stone said. He bent to her ear. "And I confess that I am very happy to know you. I plan to keep knowing you for the rest of my life."

Georgette giggled as his voice rumbled against her eardrums. When Captain Stone tried to coax her back to bed, she placed a hand on his arm. "You go, I am feeling a little seasick. I'm going to stay here and take in the fresh air for a while longer."

He gave her a brief look of concern, but consented and walked below deck alone, leaving Georgette to her thoughts.

She hugged herself as the sea breeze slapped at her cheeks and arms. When she closed her eyes, she could sense the sirens in the water. Now that she was attuned, she could send them messages. They allowed the merchant ship safe passage.

But knowing that they would come to no harm did nothing to soothe Georgette's nausea. She placed a hand over her stomach and lost herself in her thoughts.

When she heard shuffling footsteps, she jumped and gripped the side of the ship.

"Georgette."

She turned at the whisper and squinted in the silvery moonlight.

A sailor looked around carefully before he approached her, then he took off his hat and stepped into the light.

A pair of piercing blue eyes made her gasp.

The man was dirty, his face covered in a dark, wiry hair. But those eyes were unmistakable.

"Edward?" she whispered back, clutching his arms.

The man looked around them again to check they were not being spied on, then nodded.

Georgette blinked several times, trying to process the news. "How did you survive the storm?" she whispered, thinking back to the horrific maelstrom.

Edward guided her to a dark part of the ship, far away from the night guards. "I floated on a piece of drift-wood for three days before this ship picked me up. I have sent a message to the rest of the Navy, with co-ordinates for Imerta."

Georgette swallowed nervously as Edward started to unwind the rope from one of the rescue boats. "Now is our chance, Georgette."

When he finished releasing the boat, he lowered it quietly to the water. "I've stocked the boat with enough provisions to get us to Imerta, where the Navy will be waiting for us."

He made to help Georgette over the side of the ship, but she shook her head. "I can't go with you, Edward," she said. It was her turn to cast her eyes about nervously. She half-expected to see Captain Stone emerging from the lower deck at any moment.

Prince Edward followed her line of sight. "He's asleep. He won't know you're gone until morning," he said. "Don't be afraid. I'm going to—"

"He's your brother," Georgette said, studying his face.

To her surprise, Prince Edward did not even flinch at her words. She frowned. "You already knew?"

When he did not reply, Georgette placed her hands on her hips. "You would kill your own flesh and blood?"

Prince Edward grimaced. "I want to end piracy and force him to return to the palace. That is where he belongs."

Georgette dragged her hands through her hair with a dark laugh. "He will never go back to palace life. He values freedom too much."

Prince Edward sighed, shoulders slumping as he looked down. "You don't think I know that? He's made his choice. I can't control what happens next."

Georgette touched his arm. "And what happens to him at Imerta? You know he's going to return the ring."

Prince Edward met her stare for a long moment. "The plan. *Your* plan is all in hand."

Georgette shook her head. "I did not plan to have him killed." Then she began to pace. "I merely wanted to stop the siren attacks and go home."

Prince Edward took her hand. "We don't need him. Let him ruin his own life. Come with me and I'll take you back to your father."

Georgette pulled her hand away with a scowl. "I cannot just leave him here. I will not."

There was a beat of silence, then the Prince gasped.

"How is it that a smart, astute young woman such as you are, has fallen in love with her captor?"

"He is my husband," she corrected. But she could not argue that she had fallen for Captain Stone. Her heart squeezed at the thought.

Prince Edward was about to argue, but his face darkened at the sight of something behind her. She turned to see Captain Stone towering with his knife pointed in the direction of the Prince.

"I thought I could smell a rat," he said.

Prince Edward spat at his feet. "How dare you," he growled. The two men squared up to each other, knives drawn, and began to circle each other like cats. Georgette protested, but her voice landed on deaf ears. The brothers glared at each other.

"You're not taking her from me," Captain Stone growled.

"You think you're good for her? Think you will provide the stability she deserves?" Prince Edward hissed.

Georgette shoved them both and balled her hands into fists. "I'm right here. How dare you talk as if I'm not even in your presence. Don't I have a mind of my own?"

Captain Stone gave a smug smile and gestured to her. "See? The lady has spoken."

That riled Georgette even more. She gave him

another shove. "Both of you, stop it! We're going to Imerta, giving back the ring, and—"

"And then I'm taking you home," Prince Edward finished for her.

Captain Stone lifted his knife to his brother's chest. "She's already home. With me."

"*Stop* it!" Georgette hissed, placing one hand on Captain Stone's chest and the other on Prince Edward's. "I am not going anywhere. We're all going to Imerta, *together*." She glared at them both. "The pirate lords will have their treasure, Isis will have her ring, and…"

"And what?" Edward and Captain Stone asked in unison, looking at her expectantly. Georgette chewed her lip as she looked between the two of them. "And then we all move on with our lives," she said with a note of finality. Captain Stone sheathed his knife, satisfied, but Prince Edward continued to scowl. "Fine," he said, meeting Georgette's hard stare. Then he climbed over the edge of the ship. "Imerta is a day from here, but the ship is moving north. So, we need to leave. Now."

Georgette and Captain Stone exchanged looks for a moment. She shrugged and followed Prince Edward into the small boat. Captain Stone groaned and joined them.

Georgette's heart raced as they bobbed in the little boat.

For a moment, she thought about getting in the

water. She could push the boat and they'd be there a lot faster. But something held her back. She was not ready for the Prince to find out what she was yet.

She had not given much thought to what it meant. After all, sirens were the enemy. She could not be one of them.

Instead, she kept quiet and still while Captain Stone and Prince Edward took turns rowing the boat. The two were like cat and mouse, exchanging snide remarks. As she listened to them bicker, she grumbled to herself, glaring up at the starry night sky. Then she heard the soft chuckle of sirens.

"I told you," one said, her voice entering Georgette's mind. "Men are bad."

Georgette wrapped her jacket around her and sighed, thinking it was going to be a long night.

36

CAPTAIN STONE

T he soft silhouette of Imerta loomed over the tiny rowboat as they approached. The sun was high in the sky and its ray scattered across the surface of the sea like glitter.

Captain Stone rowed in silence, and Prince Edward looked about them with raised brows. "Look at all those sirens. They seem so harmless. Unmoving," he said, in awe. Sirens had surfaced around them, head and shoulders bobbing in the water as their boat went past.

Georgette fidgeted in her seat with a pained expression. He guessed she was fighting the urge to jump into the water and join them. Captain Stone watched her close her eyes and take deep breaths, and he wondered if their voices entered her mind. What secrets were they telling her?

"No sign of any pirate lords," he muttered, looking around.

"They're waiting on the other side of the island," Georgette blurted, confirming his suspicions. The sirens *were* talking to her. Prince Edward frowned. "How do you know that?" he asked her.

Captain Stone cleared his throat to distract him. For whatever reason, it seemed that Georgette did not want the Prince knowing she was a siren. He was more than happy to keep that information from his brother. The fact that she did not want Edward in on the secret told him she did not fully trust the Prince. That knowledge brought Captain Stone much delight.

"They are your men, I believe," he said, nodding to the west. Georgette and Prince Edward looked and saw a vast line of ships approaching with crisp, ivory sails. Edward's face broke into a grin, then he stuck a hand in the water and splashed his face.

Georgette shuffled away as he proceeded to wash and smooth out his hair. Meanwhile, Captain Stone laughed to himself as he continued to row the boat. He thought it typical that his brother's first thought upon seeing the Navy was to clean up his appearance. The man was usually so well kept. It must have pained him to hide under the guise of a humble fisherman these past weeks.

Finally, they reached the shore. Prince Edward was still tying back his hair as they climbed out.

"Freshening up for your comrades?" Captain Stone said, giving him a wink. Prince Edward gave him a nasty look, but dropped his hands. He must have realized how futile his efforts were. No amount of smoothing could tame his now-tangled beard and hair. He glanced at his disheveled reflection in the water and looked defeated.

Georgette gave Captain Stone a reproachful look and tucked a stray strand of hair behind Prince Edward's ear. "You look fine, Edward," she said, her voice soft. "Your men will respect you with or without your uniform."

Captain Stone chuckled. "I, however, will always see you as my awkward baby brother," he said, nudging the Prince in the ribs.

A flash of annoyance crossed Prince Edward's face before he broke into a grim smile. It stirred something in Captain Stone's chest—a feeling that was not entirely bad. For a moment, it was as though they were both back at home, bantering with each other. He was not a prince. Captain Stone was not a pirate. They were two brothers. Equals.

He took Georgette's hand as they walked across the sandy beach and his chest flooded with warmth. *Not equals*, he decided, as the Prince glanced at their linked hands.

After all, the woman was *his*.

They followed a narrow path through the tall palm trees in silence. The tide rolled in and out like the ocean was a sleeping dragon taking long, deep breaths. Leaves rustled and fragrant blooms flooded Captain Stone's nostrils. He glanced at Georgette. She looked about them in wonderment.

"I've never seen anything like it," she whispered to him. "It's so beautiful here."

Captain Stone squeezed her hand and his heart panged. "Yes, it is beautiful. But keep your guard up. One wrong step and you could end up taking your last breath."

It was true. The oversized flowers looked appealing to the eye and had an alluring scent, but many of them were toxic. Just like the sirens could lure you to your death with their timeless beauty.

He tried not to think about the fact that Georgette was one of them. He wondered if she too would turn on him someday.

He made a mental note to stay on her good side from now on.

The winding path ended at a set of polished stone steps leading out of the tree growth. They climbed them out of the forest and found a golden palace looming over them.

Isis's palace looked more like a tower. Inside was another set of steep steps leading up.

Georgette hesitated, and Prince Edward stuffed his hands in his pockets. "This is where I leave you," he said. "I shall wait for my men and meet you on the other side."

Captain Stone lifted a brow. "And what will you and your men do?" he asked with an inquiring look. The corner of Prince Edward's mouth lifted into a wry smile. "What we do best. Kill pirates."

Captain Stone thought about the pirate lords waiting and gave a grim smile of approval. But then his chest grew heavy.

The pirate lords were formidable enemies, and Prince Edward did not possess an immortality ring. They had their disagreements, but Prince Edward was his baby brother. Would this be the last time he saw him?

He rested a hand on his shoulder. "Try not to get yourself killed," he murmured.

Prince Edward's expression softened for a moment, and he gave a curt nod. Then he turned to Georgette and planted a kiss on her cheek.

"You know where I'll be," he said in a low voice.

Captain Stone stiffened at the exchange, but Georgette gave his hand a reassuring squeeze. "Stay safe," she said to Prince Edward. Then she walked inside the tower.

Captain Stone rested his hands on Georgette's waist, supporting her as they climbed the spiral staircase. Their footsteps echoed and the sounds of the sea were muted by the walls. Deep dread spread in Captain Stone's chest as they climbed in silence. He could not think of a logical reason to be wary, other than the knowledge that Isis was a goddess—an unpredictable one.

The evidence suggested she was Georgette's birth mother. Surely, she would not harm her own daughter.

The steps led them to an oval-shaped throne room at the very top of the tower. The small throne room held a golden throne with long, ornate legs. Captain Stone held his breath when he saw the tall woman on the throne. Her golden locks reached her toes and fell in soft waves over her red lace gown.

She was the picture of Georgette, only taller and in bigger proportions. Isis's ice-blue eyes rested on his and her voice entered his mind with such intensity, it nearly brought him to his knees.

"My daughters have granted you safe passage because I am told you have something for me," she said.

Georgette turned to look pointedly at him, her eyes misty. Captain Stone took the stone ring from his finger and swallowed.

He had worn the ring for so long, it felt odd to be getting rid of it.

Isis's mouth lifted into a knowing smile as she stretched out a hand and waited. She seemed to sense his hesitation. "Such magic should never have been in the hands of a man," she said in his mind. Her gaze drifted to Georgette, and she looked forlorn for the briefest moment.

"My sweet Georgette," she said aloud. "How cruel of your father to have kept you from me."

Captain Stone dropped the ring in Isis's hand and the goddess turned to Georgette. Georgette ran into her open arms.

"So, it is true?" she asked, tears flowing freely down her cheeks. "You are my mother." She pulled out a golden locket from under her shirt and opened it for Isis to see. Isis smiled and gave a slow, regal nod.

"Now, you never have to leave me again," she said, smoothing her daughter's hair.

Captain Stone tensed. The exchange was tender and sweet, but something was off. He could not work out what it was, but there was a flash of anger in Isis's eyes when she looked at him. The flash disappeared as quickly as it came.

"We can't stay," Georgette said, sniffing as they broke apart. "I only came to ensure the ring was returned. You will release the treasure to the pirates, now. Will you not?" she asked.

Isis blinked steadily before she gave another nod. Then she rose to a stand and towered over Georgette. "Come. Let us walk."

Isis led the way out of the tower, and the three walked through the trees for a long time. When they reached the other side of the island, Captain Stone could see that the pirate lords had congregated by the beach and already had lines of men filling up their ships with treasure chests.

He wondered why the Navy had not yet made an appearance, but he supposed Prince Edward was waiting for the pirates to finish loading up the treasure. It would be convenient for the British Crown to seize everything and declare the end of piracy.

They continued to walk until they reached a small clearing—a crescent of white stones surrounding a white altar. Markings on the stone were worn down, but the stone sparkled under the sunlight. Isis stopped and reached out for Georgette's hands.

"I have watched you from afar, my sweet Georgette," she said, blinking slowly. "I have seen you overcome seemingly unsurmountable challenges. All on your own." She gave Captain Stone a quick glare before she settled on Georgette again. "And that was before you awoke the siren in you," she added.

Georgette chuckled but stopped when Isis turned

serious and lifted her chin with a fingernail. "You possess more powers than you can possibly comprehend."

Georgette glanced at Captain Stone for a moment, and he could see that she was conflicted. He clasped his hands. "If you wish to stay, I will support that decision," he said. But to his surprise, Isis flashed him a look of annoyance again. It seemed he was not to speak unless invited.

Georgette looked out at the boats in the distance, then she touched her stomach in thought. "I have so many questions," she said, turning back to Isis. "Why did you leave me and my father? How could you allow me to think…" She stopped and looked down, tears rolling down her cheeks.

Isis lifted her chin again. "I will tell you everything. Stay, my child. You have no need to worry," she said. But Georgette pulled away and started to shake her head. "I need to speak to my father first. He doesn't know you're alive. And there are questions only he can give me answers to."

Isis's delicate lips turned downward for a moment, and when she spoke again, her tone was hard. "There is nothing but heartbreak waiting for you off this island."

Georgette took Captain Stone's hand and stepped back. "No," she said, fire in her voice. They began to walk, and Isis hissed, moving quick as a flash to block their path. Her face paled and her mouth turned into one thin line. "You are walking into death and decay," she whispered, her eyes darkening. Captain Stone tensed, but Georgette led him calmly around her mother. Isis remained immobile.

Georgette shook her head. "I need to go back to my father. At least, one last time."

The two of them hurried down the path toward the beach. To Captain Stone's relief, Isis did not follow them. Now he was certain she could not force Georgette to stay.

The pirates stopped and turned to look as they approached through the trees. "Look who it is," one of them shouted. "Captain Stone. The pirate with nine lives."

A chorus of laughter followed, and the men continued to move the treasure. "You are lucky, mate. Our lords have named you a hero," someone said.

Captain Stone took in a deep breath and waved. "I am glad to hear it," he said. "All is forgiven, then? No more bounty on my head?" he asked. The men chuckled again.

"Yes, yes. Now get over here and give us a hand," they shouted back.

Captain Stone turned to Georgette and gripped her arms with a broad grin. "Are you sure about this?" he asked her. "Running off with a scoundrel like me? It does look rather nice here."

Georgette smirked and rested her hand on his cheek. "Not a scoundrel. A pirate." She rose on tiptoes to kiss him. "*My* pirate."

Captain Stone took her up in his arms and kissed her with every fiber of his being. She smiled against his mouth and clutched his back.

An ear-shattering bang shook them apart.

Captain Stone looked about wildly and saw that the Navy had arrived. He frowned. "Come on," he said, grabbing Georgette's hand and walking forward. "We need to take one of those ships before Edward sends all of them down to Davy Jones."

Georgette laughed as she followed, but a sound stopped Captain Stone in his tracks. The screech flooded his soul with such terror that he only stood and stared wide-eyed as Isis flashed into view. Her open mouth revealed long, spiked teeth and her eyes were twice their former size; now entirely black. She was yards away one minute and right before him the next. A claw like hand lashed out and ripped into his chest.

Captain Stone sank to his knees, numb, while Georgette's shriek rang faintly in his ears. The whole world had slowed and Georgette was clutching his body, screaming. He fell into her lap and time came to its normal pace again as she scrambled to apply pressure to his chest.

Within moments, her hands were soaked in blood.

"No, no, no. Don't leave me. Don't leave me!" she yelled. Captain Stone touched her cheek and smiled. "I told you the day would come that you would beg me. Though I confess, I never imagined it would be like this."

Georgette's hot tears fell like rain on his face. "What did you do?" she screamed at her mother. "Fix him right now!" She broke down crying.

Captain Stone could not see Isis anymore. In fact, his vision was turning white. As the last of his life left him, he only saw Georgette's blonde curls shining in the sunlight.

The last words he heard were hers. "I love you," she sobbed.

Then his hand dropped, and the immortal Captain Mannington Stone died.

37

GEORGETTE

A tsunami of emotions erupted from Georgette's chest and an earth-trembling scream ripped from the very depths of her soul. Her vision was flooded with tears, but she could just make out Isis standing afar off, watching in silence.

Captain Stone lay white-faced and limp in her arms. She was drowning in blood, and the sound of cannon fire filled the air. Georgette's tears flowed freely, and she began to hyperventilate.

"I told you, my child. Death and decay are all that waits for you now," Isis's voice entered her mind.

"Get out of my head, you evil witch!" Georgette screeched. "Bring him back! I love him. Bring him back!" Her screeches turned into pleas, but to her utter dismay, Isis had turned and was walking calmly away. "He was going to die anyway," the goddess said, flippant. "I merely accelerated the process."

Georgette sobbed as she rocked back and forth, clinging to Captain Stone's lifeless body. Her soul ached with longing. If only she had the power to craft an immortality ring for her love. But she did not know how, and her mind was too splintered to focus.

She prayed to all the gods, hoping that maybe just one might hear her prayer and bring Captain Stone back to her.

She cried and prayed and stared down at Captain Stone's body until his corpse had gone stiff in her hands. A shout finally broke through her grief, and she looked up to see Prince Edward running toward her. His face paled when he caught sight of his brother's body.

"You must come with me now," he said, breathless. Georgette howled in grief when he tried to pick her up and she wrestled away from his clutches. "I can't leave him. I won't leave him," she said between sobs.

Prince Edward tore her away and wrapped her up in his arms. "He's gone, Georgette. You must come with me now." He said into her hair as she sobbed into his chest.

Georgette went limp. When she did not protest, he picked her up in his arms and carried her toward the beach.

It took the Royal Navy two long weeks on the raging seas to return to England. The clouds rolled in thick, and the winds tossed the ship back and forth for so long, many hard-boiled sailors were sick to their stomachs.

Georgette stayed in the captain's quarters, curled up on the bed facing the wall. Prince Edward offered her food and water, but she rejected the food and refused to have more than a few sips.

Every time she closed her eyes, she saw Captain taking his last breath. Cruel memories invaded her dreams. She could still feel the imprint of his hands on her thighs… The graze of his stubble on her skin… The pressure of his lips on hers.

The part that hurt most was knowing that he had just been delivered from his enemies when her own mother brought him to his demise.

Georgette hugged herself as more tears leaked out of her eyes. Her mother was a monster. A vengeful, wicked monster. And her father was a liar.

What does that make me? she wondered.

When Port Harbor came into view, Georgette felt nothing inside. She had imagined that there would, at least, be a glimmer of relief to be back home. Leaving the sea was like leaving Captain Stone all over again. Yet, now that he was gone, she had no desire to return to the water.

Sirens cried for her pain. Through the mystical telepathy that linked all of them, her suffering became theirs. They pleaded with her to return to Isis, to turn back from the disappointments of men.

They were her sisters, and now that she had been transformed, she recognized the bond, but she couldn't bring herself to agree. *Men are not all disappointments*, she'd snap back. *Captain Stone loved me.*

Prince Edward helped her onto the deck and wrapped an arm around her waist to stop her from falling. She had grown weak in her time on the ship. She stumbled as he led her through the busy English port.

Seagulls honked overhead and the gray skies parted to let in a weak ray of sunshine. None of it did anything to lift Georgette's mood.

"You shall stay at the palace where I will take care of you," Prince Edward insisted. Georgette shook her head and rested a hand on his soft cheek. He was clean-shaven once more, and she had to remind herself that her hand was no longer soaked in his brother's blood.

"I need to go home," she said.

Prince Edward's jaw jutted out, but he gave her a curt nod. She knew he did not want her out of his sight again. "I will come and see you in the morn," he said with a note of finality. His eyes bore into her, daring her to argue, but Georgette was grateful for his concern.

She forced a smile. "I would like that."

THE CARRIAGE ROLLED UP TO THE IRON GATES OF Harrington Manor and Georgette stepped out, looking around at the quiet grounds. In her mind, she had played out all the scenarios of talking to her father. Some scenarios were of her throwing her arms around his neck and sobbing into his chest. In other scenarios, she slapped him hard across both cheeks. In all of them, she demanded answers.

How had he met Isis? Why did he gamble away the stone ring? What possessed him to keep her away from her mother? Did he know that Isis was cruel and wicked? Or was it his own foolishness that had made her that way?

The biggest question of all was, why on the god's green Earth did he sell her to a pirate?

Georgette pushed at the gates and they opened with a squeal. She swallowed hard as she walked up the path to the heavy oak doors.

There had never been much noise at the Harrington

Manor, but the grounds and castle seemed unusually still. When she knocked on the door, she did not hear any footsteps on the other side.

It was a Sunday. She reasoned that her father would most likely be in his office. Perhaps he had not heard her knock because she was so weak. She made a fist and rapped her knuckles against the wood as hard as she could. After several minutes rolled by, she hummed in thought.

"Where is the doorman?" she wondered aloud.

She tried the handle. To her surprise, the door clicked and swung open.

"Father?" she called into the dusty entrance hall. As she stepped inside, she coughed, waving dust away from her face. The floors and furniture were covered in a layer of dirt. It appeared nobody had lived in the manor for some time.

She walked through the house looking in all the rooms and found no one. Not even a note.

What became of the Governess? Had she moved back to live with her great-uncle and his family in Scotland? Knowing that her father had gambled away his entire fortune, Georgette wondered if he had sold the manor and gone to live in the city.

But then she saw a gold light under the door to her

father's room. Georgette halted outside the door with her hand on the brass knob, her heart beating wildly.

Then she pushed the door open and her eyes scanned the room.

Books and papers were littered all over the bed. In the corner, she saw a pair of feet dangling in the air.

Overcome with nausea, Georgette lifted a hand to her mouth, flew out of the room and collapsed in a heap on the floor.

Angry tears flooded her vision as she hugged herself.

The selfish fool could not even offer her any answers, she thought in despair. Isis was right. All that waited for her back home was death and decay.

Georgette thought about laying on the floor and letting nature take her body. It would only take a few more days, she reasoned. Then she would be reunited with her love.

But as she lay there grappling with her grief, she realized her survival instinct was too strong. She couldn't die. Not here. Not like this.

She rolled over on to her back and rested a hand on her bloated stomach. It had been over a month since her last bleed. With no Governess to ask, she could not be sure, but when she shut her eyes and listened, she was sure she could hear another heartbeat. She did not know if it was her imagination or another siren ability, but something told her she was carrying a baby.

She had to live. If not for herself, then for the innocent life she was carrying. A life that was a part of Captain Stone.

She wiped her eyes and sniffed as she sat up. Looking around the desolate hall, she knew there was no future for her at Harrington Manor. She had nothing. A woman with a child out of wedlock was unwelcome in 18th century England.

Her mind returned to Prince Edward. Even after everything that happened, he still looked at her with such care and devotion.

He was a good man. A man of honor and duty. She could not begin to love him as much as she loved Captain Stone, but he would offer the security she needed. And to the best of her ability, she would offer the same to him.

Later that night, Georgette returned to the palace and Prince Edward dashed out to her, taking her hands in his. When she told him about her father, he shut his eyes for a moment, then looked at her with so much tenderness. "Georgette. I am so sorry," he said, pulling her in for a tight hug.

Georgette nipped her bottom lip and gave him a brave smile.

"If your offer is still open..." she said weakly. Prince

Edward nodded quickly as he held her by the arms. He looked down at her with kind sincerity. "My feelings remain unchanged for you, Georgette. If you will have me, I will give you everything."

Georgette sniffed and gave him a smile. "Then let us not wait. I cannot bear to suffer a moment longer."

Prince Edward kissed her forehead. "Of course, my love. Come inside."

IT TOOK TWO WEEKS FOR THE PALACE TO MAKE THE preparations for a royal wedding. Despite Georgette's protests, the King and Queen of England were adamant that the wedding be grand and open to all their esteemed guests. The lords and ladies of every county were present, and every royal on the western hemisphere was in attendance.

Georgette sucked in a breath as the maids fastened her corset. Then they helped her into the heavy silk gown. It was long and white as snow, with real white roses sewn into the skirt. She looked at her reflection as one of the maids finished pinning the last curl at the crown of her head.

The day had finally come. She was marrying Prince

Edward, just as it had been planned since she was a child.

Still, she could not bring herself to smile. Even as one of her maids handed her a large bouquet of red roses.

Soon, she would be married to a prince. One who had no idea she was carrying his brother's baby. None of the maids had uttered a word upon sight of her little bump, but Georgette could see the disapproval on their faces. They were not so discreet either that she did not notice them exchanging looks.

Truth be told, she could not care less. This was a matter of survival, and even though she did not love Prince Edward the same, she would do her best to be a good princess. For him and for the kingdom.

The string quartet announced her arrival and her heart sank as she stood alone with no one to give her away. The guests whispered to each other and rose to a stand while she carefully walked toward the altar.

Prince Edward stood by the archbishop, dressed in his Naval uniform. His face glowed with joy as he watched her walk down the aisle, and a tiny glimmer of something lit up inside of her. It was not quite happiness, but she thought it might be hope. Hope for a better future; one that did not bring more heartache.

When she reached him, Prince Edward took her

hand and his eyes sparkled at her while the archbishop instructed everyone to be seated.

Georgette took a deep breath and stared into Prince Edward's eyes as the archbishop talked. Their surroundings blurred, and she tried to think of all the reasons why she was doing the right thing.

The more she thought about it, the harder it was for her to swallow. She gripped his hands for comfort and heard him say, "I do." Her heart began to beat wildly. The archbishop picked up again. This time, she knew he was asking if she took him to be her lawful husband. The priest went silent, and Georgette swallowed. Then she opened her mouth to say she did too.

A door banged with such ferocity; the flagstone floors trembled.

"I object!" a deep voice bellowed, echoing around the chapel.

Voices flooded the air as the guests looked around to see who would dare interrupt a royal wedding.

Georgette frowned, trying to see through the sea of faces and heads. The archbishop looked affronted. "On what grounds?" he asked no one in particular. He too was trying to see who intended to put asunder.

Steady boots thudded on the stone floors, and Georgette dropped her bouquet as one face emerged from the crowd. "Because she is my wife," Captain Stone said, reaching them.

Georgette stood still, too stunned to move as she took in the man standing in the aisle. His shirt hung open, showing a long scar down his chest. His hair was neatly combed, and when he grinned at her, one of his teeth sparkled.

"How?" Prince Edward asked.

People in the congregation were asking themselves who Captain Stone was.

"Manny?" the King asked, rising to a stand. He peered at Captain Stone like he was staring at a ghost.

Captain Stone walked forward, but Prince Edward withdrew his sword. "You cannot waltz in here on my wedding day and—"

"And you cannot marry my wife," Captain Stone cut in, lifting a hand.

Then he looked at Georgette again, but she couldn't feel her feet. She wondered numbly if this was a dream.

Prince Edward looked from Captain Stone to Georgette and made a sound of frustration before he swiped his sword through the air. "Very well! I challenge you to the death," he said. Horrified cries greeted his words.

Captain Stone withdrew his own sword and winked at Georgette. "It will take more than killing me to keep me away from my love," he said.

The two men began a sword fight right there within the church. People scattered. Their blades clashed while guests fled from the chapel. The King's guard coaxed a bewildered King and Queen away, and soon the chapel was empty but for the brothers in battle and Georgette.

"You died!" Prince Edward cried, as though this new development was most inconvenient. Georgette frowned. Feeling was coming back to her toes.

Captain Stone touched his scar. "Did you know a siren's tears have healing powers?" he asked, winking at Georgette again.

Prince Edward's face screwed up in confusion as he blocked several of Captain Stone's advances. "Why would a siren cry over you?"

But understanding struck him mid-stroke, and he lowered his sword to look at Georgette, as though he was only seeing her for the first time. Georgette bit her lip under his stare.

He turned back to Captain Stone with fury. "You can't be alive. You can't come back and ruin everything. I'm to marry Georgette. I love her!"

He kicked Captain Stone's shin and brought the hilt of his sword down on his head. Captain Stone staggered back, but then tossed his sword aside and opened his arms. "I refuse to fight you, baby brother. If you want to marry my wife, you will have to slaughter me."

Prince Edward looked conflicted for a moment, then he looked at Georgette. That seemed to help him find his resolve. He turned back to his brother and raised his sword above his head.

Georgette cried out and ran into his path, shielding Captain Stone with her body.

"Please Edward," she begged. "I am with child."

Prince Edward blinked several times and lowered the sword. "But we didn't... We haven't..." he sputtered.

Then his face paled, and he looked at Captain Stone behind Georgette. A look of disgust flooded the Prince's face. He flung his sword away, and his expression turned neutral. "You are both dead to me," he said in a cold voice.

Georgette reached for his hand, "Edward, I'm so sorry," she said. Prince Edward shrugged her off. He turned his back to her and walked out of the chapel without another word.

Georgette could not bring herself to stay upset for long, though. Captain Stone's broad hands soon found her waist. "Is it true?" he asked, looking down at her stomach. "You're having our baby?"

Georgette looked at him and caressed his cheek, hardly believing him to be more than an apparition. "Are you really here?" she whispered. She had imagined him coming back to her for so long, he did not seem real now that he was here.

Captain Stone scooped her up in his arms and kissed her with gusto. She gripped his shoulders and kissed him back, reveling in the familiar rush of tingles flowing through her.

When they broke apart, he cradled her face and rubbed his thumb along her jaw. "I will always come back to you," he said. "No one will ever stop me."

Georgette traced the scar over his chest. "But you died," she whispered. "I saw you die."

Captain Stone's smile faded, and he looked serious. "I did. But somehow, your tears restored me."

Georgette hugged him, resting her head on his chest to listen to his heartbeat. "My father is dead," she whispered into his chest. Hot tears prickled her eyes. "He hanged himself before I could even get a chance to see him. And you were gone. With the baby... I..."

"You did what you thought you had to do," Captain Stone said, kissing the top of her head. "I do not blame you."

Georgette took in a deep breath. "Now what? Have you come back to reclaim your place at the palace?" she asked, breaking away to look at him. Captain Stone's mouth lifted into a lopsided smirk. "Not exactly."

He guided her out of the chapel and nodded to the

docks. Georgette looked out and recognized the Duchess bobbing in the water. She turned to Captain Stone. "Are the pirate lords…?"

"Well, they're not happy about the fact that the Royal Navy was at Imerta. Many of them hold me responsible." He sighed. "And Isis is more furious. I can certainly say we are in more danger now than ever before."

Georgette clung to his shirt with a grin. "Freedom has a price," she said, rising on tip toes to hover close to his mouth. Captain Stone squeezed her waist. "Aye, my lady. So, what do you say? Can you suffer a perilous life at sea with a pirate for the rest of your days?"

Georgette took Captain Stone's hand and placed it over her small bump. "We both will," she whispered.

They sealed the promise with a kiss.

THE END

EPILOGUE
PRINCE EDWARD

Prince Edward stood still and silent as his father surveyed the room of Naval officers waiting for instructions. After listening to his report of the siren attacks, King George looked grim. There was not a sign of compassion on his features for the way things turned out with Georgette.

Nor did he bother to ask about Prince Mannington and whether he would return. He supposed that though Mannington was firm and commanding like their father, Prince Edward possessed his ability to shut away emotions altogether.

Since Georgette and Captain Stone had chosen to sail away on the Duchess to whatever ungodly danger lay ahead, the King and Queen had not uttered a single word on the matter.

A formal announcement was made that Prince Edward and Georgette's nuptials would not take place due to a conflict of interest, but nothing stopped the whispers around the palace. The staff looked upon Prince Edward with pity, and he hated it.

His father's cold stare was a welcome change.

King George's lips formed a thin line as he hummed deeply for several long moments.

Prince Edward knew what orders were coming. He had numbed his emotions after losing Georgette, but his stomach tightened all the same when his father finally uttered the instructions.

"I, King George, command the British Royal Navy to hunt down and kill every siren in the Pacific Ocean. Edward, you shall work with the blacksmiths to create weapons made of steel—as I understand it is their weakness."

Prince Edward curled his fingers to make a tight fist. He did not want the sirens to attack innocent sailors, but he could not condone hunting them like prey and slaughtering them in cold blood.

There had to be a better way.

Arguing with his father, however, was a one-way ticket to the Tower of London, so he held his tongue and gave a curt nod.

When they were excused, his heart weighed heavily

as he walked out of the palace with his men. He walked in silence, listening to the soft murmurs of the men around him and ignoring the stares from the city folk on the streets.

When he reached the docks, he took a left away from his men and found the water's edge. He walked along the sandy shores for what seemed like several miles until he found himself on a private beach surrounded by rocks. The sun had already begun to set.

He shut his eyes and uttered the one name on his mind. "Serena."

When he opened his eyes, a head of red hair was emerging from the waters.

To his surprise, the sight of the siren brought him comfort. He found himself smiling despite his low mood.

"Hello, my prince," she said, her voice laced with sympathy. She tilted her head and seemed to look right into his soul. He was certain she could see past his regal mask and feel the pain he was forced to endure.

"What happened with your lady Georgette?" she asked, her voice soft and musical.

Prince Edward's chest tightened at the name of his lost love. When he spoke, he tried to keep his voice steady. "She is a siren."

Serena's lips curved upward in a lopsided smirk.

Prince Edward inhaled deep and slow. "But you knew that already, didn't you?"

When Serena did not argue, he dragged a hand over his stubbed chin with frustration. "All this time you knew, and you did not tell me?" he asked.

Serena swam closer and raised her torso out of the water, her fin peeking several feet behind her. The burnt orange sunlight danced across the shimmering scales of her fin in the most unearthly way. It was oddly soothing to watch.

"It is not my truth to share," she said simply. "But that is not the reason she is not with you." Her eyes bore into his.

Prince Edward scratched the back of his neck, unsettled under the strength of her discerning gaze. "She fell in love with the pirate," he muttered under his breath. Serena nodded, and he knew she heard his words. Then he frowned. "But you knew that too, didn't you?"

Serena swayed and began to play with her damp hair. It dazzled in the amber light like a waterfall of fire. "Then tell me something I do not know," she said. "Why did you call me?"

Prince Edward sat on the sandy beach to meet her eyes. "There is a war brewing between men and sirens. The King has ordered my men to hunt and kill any that cross Pacific waters."

Serena's shoulders stiffened, but she kept her expression neutral. "You underestimate our powers if you think we are frightened by the whims of a few men."

"This is not a few men," he insisted. "The entire British Navy and its allies from abroad will be on the hunt." He clenched his fists. "I cannot stop it. Nor will I be a part of it," he said, removing his Naval jacket with a noise of frustration.

Serena blinked at him slowly. She seemed to remain unfazed by his words, so Prince Edward gave her a piercing stare. "They're making weapons of steel."

Those words hit Serena hard, and she jumped back as though he had thrown a dagger in her direction. Her pretty eyes widened with alarm. "Why are you telling me this?" she asked.

Prince Edward shrugged and started to trace lines in the sand with his finger. "You went above and beyond to help me in my endeavor. It is time I repay the favor." He finally met Serena's gaze again as a cool ocean breeze rippled through his hair. The wind picked up a sweet scent, and he wondered if it was hers. "I cannot bear the thought of you being hunted," he confessed.

Serena's face brimmed with happiness as though he had recited the most romantic poem for her benefit.

He interlocked his fingers and sighed as he crossed his legs. "Can you get me a meeting with Isis? Perhaps I can talk to her and we can arrange an alliance of sorts?" he thought aloud. Serena scoffed.

"That is entirely impossible," she said, giving him a frank look. "Isis is vengeful, and she is done talking with men. You want your heart ripped out? That is all that waits for you if you approach Isis."

Prince Edward chewed the inside of his cheek as he recalled the sight of his brother's lifeless body on Imerta. As friendly as she appeared, he did not think Serena would offer up a single tear for his benefit should the negotiations go wrong.

He thought again. "What about Poseidon? He is your father, no? Can you get me an audience with him?"

Serena hummed lightly and swayed from side to side in thought. "The god of the sea does not deal with land folk. Especially men."

She twirled her hair and her gaze trailed down the Prince's body before meeting his eyes again. "Except..."

"What?" Prince Edward asked, leaning forward with rapt attention now. "If you think of a way I can speak with him, then whatever the price, I shall gladly pay it."

Serena's teeth glittered in a dazzling beam. "He will grant audience to a man who wishes to ask for the hand of one of his daughters," she explained, shimmying her shoulders now. "And you are right, Lord Poseidon is my father."